ANNA QUON

Invisible Publishing

Halifax & Toronto

Library and Archives Canada Cataloguing in Publication

Quon, Anna L., 1968-, author
Low / Anna Quon.

ISBN 978-1-926743-32-5 (pbk.)

I. Title.

PS8633.U65L69 2013   C813'.6   C2013-902943-5

Edited by Michelle MacAleese

Cover & Interior designed by Megan Fildes

Typeset in Laurentian and Slate by Megan Fildes
With thanks to type designer Rod McDonald

Printed and bound in Canada

Invisible Publishing
Halifax & Toronto
www.invisiblepublishing.com

We acknowledge the support of the Canada Council for the Arts,
which last year invested $157 million to bring the arts to Canadians
throughout the country.

Invisible Publishing recognizes the support of the Province of Nova
Scotia through the Department of Communities, Culture & Heritage.
We are pleased to work in partnership with the Culture Division to
develop and promote our cultural resources for all Nova Scotians.

NOVA SCOTIA
Communities, Culture and Heritage

Canada Council   Conseil des Arts
for the Arts   du Canada

For my father and mother, Dr. Charles
Quon and Patricia Joan Wagstaff Quon
who have been my there for me through
all the crazy darkness and in the light.

Darkness within darkness.
The gateway to all understanding.
—Lao Tzu (Tao Te Ching)

In the darkness all cows are black.
—Slovak proverb

CHAPTER 1

Adriana. Adriaannaaa. The sound of her name echoed through the stark corridors, empty of nurses, doctors and patients. There were no visible intercoms or speakers either, just her name repeating over and over, with no instructions to report anywhere. Still, she felt queasy not knowing what was wanted of her.

"Adriana. Adriana, wake up." She opened her eyes slowly to see her father standing at the foot of her bed, grasping her big toe. This was the way he had always awoken her. She had done the same to him one, many years ago, as a round-faced toddler. Even then, she had known better than to cry or giggle, lest she rouse her mother.

Adriana felt some relief, that it was her father and not some nameless authority that she had to answer to. And not her mother, eight years dead, floating down the halls in a fluttering white shift.

"What time is it?" she asked, raspy with sleep and rubbing her hands over her face. She was sure her father had already visited her earlier that day.

The room where Adriana lay was desolate and unorna-mented. Despite the hundreds of people who must have passed through as patients, there was no shadow of any of them. Not a single personal mark, not an initial carved in the furniture or even a scrap of tape was left of them. It would be the same when she left this place, Adriana thought, but that was fine with her. She wouldn't want to leave anything of herself behind.

Mr. Song sat on the plastic hospital chair and leaned forward, his elbows on his bony knees. He looked haggard, his hair uncombed and wisping everywhere. He looked, in fact, like a patient, Adriana thought.

"Penny had a stroke this afternoon," he said. There was a downward swoop of crows in Adriana's stomach. "She's unconscious, she's not going to last long."

Aunt Penny in Toronto had become the adoptive mother to Adriana's much younger sister, Beth, who had only been a few months old when their mother was diagnosed with breast cancer. After Viera died, their father, heart wrung with grief, had decided to send Beth to live with his favourite sister. Penny's sour mouth melted into a heart shape when she held Beth, so Mr. Song knew he had done the right thing.

Adriana pushed herself up to sitting with her back against the headboard. She knew her father was in agony. Mr. Song pulled his hands down his face, as though he were washing it with a face cloth. From his red-rimmed eyes, Adriana thought he must have been crying. Where does an engineer go to cry? She imagined him at work, sitting in a storage closet or locking himself in the washroom.

"I want to bring Beth home," her father said, squinting at his hands. Adriana's insides tumbled again. Beth, here? She felt her face get hot. Her dislike of her younger sister was unfair and selfish but she couldn't help it. It had just been her and her dad for so many years.

Mr. Song looked up at her, his eyes brimming with sadness. Adriana realized, in that moment, that it hurt him that she didn't like Beth, that she had never expressed interest in her sister. Somehow he had managed to hide his feelings for years, but now he didn't bother.

"Adriana, please...she's your sister." There was anger in his voice. Usually that tone would make her sit up and take notice, but this time, she gave in weakly, lying back on her pillows.

Mr. Song stood to leave, his eyes soft and troubled. "You rest," he said. Adriana nodded. She felt she'd been awake for a century. Mr. Song hugged her head to his chest. It had been a long time since Adriana was small enough to do that, and he could only do it now because she was sitting down. "You get well," he said gruffly. Adriana knew he was holding back a flood of tears, that as soon as he got on the elevator, he'd be fighting to contain them, alone and without a tourniquet.

A feeling of guilt overwhelmed her, and she lay looking up at the ceiling, wishing it would come down and crush her.

Adriana thought she should have been a starfish or some other supine creature, without arms and legs. She wished her limbs would disappear, that she would cease to be recognizably human. Then no one would expect her to act like one, to live her life every day like a normal person.

She opened her eyes. There was the chair with the plastic orange seat, where her father had sat, telling her the news of Penny's death, and the fake veneer locker, narrow as a coffin, in the corner. The side table with a bunch of wilting flowers from her dad's garden, in a plastic jar. Nothing else, except her sneakers looking forlorn and abandoned near the door. They made her want to weep. But she had no tears. Her mind was corroded, a grey, metallic mass, full of little holes and eaten away by acid. It left a stain, like blood, when she tried to think. Adriana closed her eyes again, in the faint hope she'd go back to sleep; but her thoughts clacked against one another like dominos, beneath an industrial, almost deafening, hum.

CHAPTER 2

Adriana was spending more and more time in her room the summer before she was hospitalized. At first, her father seemed cheerfully oblivious. It was Jazz, Adriana's best friend, with her antennae for trouble, who noticed something was amiss.

"Come on," she said, pulling Adriana by the arm out of bed, one morning after a sleepover and ostensible study buddy session, at the beginning of the university's fall term. She pushed Adriana, always a reluctant waker, into the bathroom, closing and locking the door so Mr. Song wouldn't barge in on them brushing their teeth.

There's never enough morning, a weary Adriana thought. Or maybe it was too much morning. She always felt like a refugee—homeless and futureless—when she woke these days. It was enough to make her wish that, instead of this scratching every day on the door of life, like a stray animal, there was somewhere else to go. Adriana realized she was being dramatic. She tugged at her thoughts, and stood up straight.

Jazz pulled at her pony tail and stuck her tongue out at the bathroom mirror. Running her tongue around her gums, Jazz grinned at herself, then frowns. Yup, clean. Eyebrows up, eyebrows down, like a *plié* in ballet, Adriana thought. She cleared her throat, and Jazz wiggled her eyebrows at her.

Adriana splashed water on her face one more time. She liked a wet face, it woke her up, made her feel fresh. Made her feel half-way human. She picked up a women's magazine from the stack her father kept on the back of the toilet tank. As a single parent, he felt it was his responsibility to keep up with the latest parenting trends. Adriana squinted and frowned, then smiled mechanically, and repeated. It was good to have a relaxed face. Gospel according to Jazz.

"Do you know what your child is thinking?" popped out at Adriana from the cover of Chatelaine. It was an article about keeping the lines of communication with your teenager open. Adriana's forehead crinkled, until Jazz tapped on her cheek. How embarrassing, Adriana thought to herself, keeping her face entirely smooth. Parents and their teens were supposed to have one-word conversations. That was just normal.

Adriana understood that she was no longer a child, that she was barely even a teenager anymore. But she wished she could hang onto the fringes of childhood for forever. She thought about the only adult close to her, her father—awkward, sentimental, always on the verge of an emotional outburst. It was exhausting just to avoid adding any pain to his burden—something she felt she had the responsibility for, now that she was legally an adult. Is this what life is like? Adriana's mouth hung open at the thought. She closed her lips and then opened them again. This can't be what life is supposed to be like.

What is it supposed to be like, Adriana's mother asked,

arms crossed, in the very back of Adriana's head. Dead eight years from breast cancer, Viera always appeared to her daughter in a housedress, apron, and strangely, pointe shoes like a ballet dancer, ready to leap into action. Adriana shook her head, as if trying to clear water out of her ear. Her mother appeared to her in self-pitying moments, to chastise her, and in times of guilt and misery. Frown, smile, frown.

Jazz, mouth full of foam, put a hand on Adriana's shoulder. "You look so serious," Jazz said, spitting a gob of froth into the sink.

Adriana realized she never knew what her face looked like, and she didn't check the mirror that often, because it gave her a headache. Jazz was always the one to tell her. Jazz had the china-smooth skin and classical features that verged on the beautiful when she smiled. When she didn't her face was plain as dirt. Adriana felt à dribble of spit running down her chin and wiped it with a towel. "I *am* serious," was all she could muster as a comeback. "Now you look like a goat," Jazz giggled.

One of her father's magazines said that it was possible to begin to change our mood just by forcing ourselves to smile, and Adriana had been experimenting. Her forced smiles didn't fit very well with Jazz's agenda to ban all wrinkle-producing expressions, but to Adriana, it was worth it if it lifted her mood. Her aim, though, was more to distract herself than any real change of affect. She preferred to keep her feelings locked up in a box, in the hope that they would just disappear. I haven't had a good wallow since my mother died, Adriana thought.

Her father had, though. He watched their old home videos with a bottle of wine in front of him, tears running down his face. Adriana, embarrassed, slumped beside him, her eyes on the flickering television screen. Her mother's long curly hair swung from side to side as she held Adriana's baby's hands and walked her toward the camera. Viera laughed and talked to her in Slovak, a language Adriana had long since forgotten. The video was blurry and yellowing, turning everything a golden colour including Adriana's skin. Her mother walked her right up to the camera, so close that she disappeared, and only Adriana's serious baby face—shiny slanted eyes and puckered lips—filled the lens.

If it weren't for the home videos, Adriana could have allowed herself to doubt her mother had ever existed. Among the Song family photos, there were barely any of Viera because she was always the one who took them, while Adriana's dad was in charge of the video camera. That was the way things were in their house, the labour neatly divided. Her dad cooked, Adriana did the supper dishes and her mother did the laundry, smoked the cigars with a tumbler of brandy, and cut the family's hair. Adriana and her father always had the same bowl-shaped hairstyle when her mother was done with them. You could tell they were father and daughter, with their straight dark hair in what her Dad would call the Song family haircut, and their slanted eyes. Her mother was the odd one out in the family. Her people were from the old Czechoslovakia, an ocean and a continent away.

Adriana wondered if her mother's heart was hard because she lived so far from her home and family. What she remembered most about her mother was the time she grabbed Adriana's arm and yanked her into the bedroom to make her bed. Adriana had been having a quiet afternoon, making a tent of her sheets and blankets for her Barbie dolls, and had gone to the bathroom for a glass of water, so as not to cross paths with her mother in the kitchen. When she returned to the door of her bedroom, Viera was there, and grabbed her arm, screaming, "You worthless girl. Look at this mess. You're no better than a gypsy!" The headscarf slipped off Viera's head, and Adriana was horrified to see the patches of baldness between soft clumps of short hair. Viera covered her eyes with her hands and collapsed on the floor. Sobbing, she tried to gather Adriana in her arms, but she shrank to the far corner of her bed, away from her mother. The weakness in Adriana's stomach was linked to this memory, as though they were handcuffed together.

Mr. Song, who had emigrated to Canada as a teenager and still thought of himself as Chinese, was gripped with grief when his wife was diagnosed. This country had given him an education, a career and a family, but now, according to life's unfathomable arithmetic, it was time for subtraction.

Jazz patted her mouth with a hand towel and handed it to Adriana. Somehow Adriana thought there should be some kind of face cream involved at this point but Jazz never touched the stuff. "I swear to God, face exercises and fish oil capsules are all you need," she always said. Adriana thought of her mother, hair wrapped up in a towel and cream slathered on her face every morning. "Come on, we're going to be late for class!" Jazz was always rushing.

"I'm not going," Adriana said. Jazz turned toward her. She had a look on her face that Adriana found disturbing. It was curiosity.

"Why not?" Jazz asked, attentive.

"Well, I don't feel well," Adriana said, averting her eyes. It was true. The weak feeling in her stomach paralyzed her .

Jazz had put her mascara on and fluttered her eyelashes

experimentally. She put an arm around Adriana's shoulders. "Peter again?" she asked, eyes shining with sympathy. Adriana hated that, she didn't want Jazz's pity. Yes, Peter again. She could barely stand to say his name.

Jazz touched her hand, lightly. "Sorry," she said. "Give me a call later, eh?" Jazz's backpack was right outside the bathroom door. She never ate breakfast at Adriana's house, and liked to be gone before Mr. Song got up, with his plaid slippers and awkward handshakes.

Even Jazz didn't know that Adriana skipped a good number of classes last year. She remembered the first one. Sitting in a café, stirring her milky tea around and around with a spoon, she looked up at the clock and realized her stats class had started five minutes before. Her hand went limp. She'd never missed a class before except when she was ill. The next couple of days she was diligent about getting to her classes on time, sitting near the front and ignoring everything around her except the professor—but she could feel her resolve crumbling. The weakness had tentacles that spread through her chest, as though something were growing inside her. The next week, she went to only one of her classes, first year English. It was held in a cavernous room with two hundred students crammed into little wooden seats. The sound of students talking and laughing echoed around her. The professor shuffled his papers and cleared his throat. She didn't know why she was there.

Despite her absences, Adriana passed the year—a year in which she gradually came apart at the seams, after breaking up with her boyfriend, Peter, who never even called her anymore. After their fight he phoned her maybe once every couple weeks, seemingly to test the waters. But one day, tired of waiting for his call, she phoned him and left a teary message. He never called again, and a month later she saw him walking across campus, with a girl she didn't recognize beside him.

It was stunning, how hurt she was. The same night, she lay in bed, trying to remember what the girl looked like. From far away, it seemed she had auburn hair and a pale face. Adriana couldn't get more of a fix on her than that. She wondered if it were someone she knew, if Peter had known her when he was still going out with Adriana. It sent knives through her to think that he might have liked this girl before he'd broken up with her. What if they were in the same class together? Had he smiled at her first?

Over the summer, Adriana had been working at a fabric store with a flock of motherly, middle-aged women - and taking a course in Russian history, which was full of unhealthy young men and women, with fingers stained by tobacco and serious obsessions with Dostoyevsky and Nabokov. Among them, she had felt stifled by melancholy and torpor. At home, she had had crying jags which seemed to come out of nowhere, and passed as quickly as a thunder shower. There were moments of frantic energy and hysterical laughter over nearly nothing, then the inevitable crash. Jazz put Adriana's head in her lap and caressed her hair. "He's gone, buttercup," was all she said.

Despite everything, Adriana had quietly decided that in September she would continue working part time at the fabric store as a cashier, and take just two courses, during the mornings, to get them over with. She told Jazz but not her father, because she feared he would have too many questions. She could see his face, pained and concerned, as she tried to explain her motives. "I just need a break, Dad," was all she could think of, and that answer would simply raise other questions in her father's mind. A break from what? Wasn't the summer enough?

And even this, this compromise with herself, she hadn't been able to live up to. She had gone to the very first day of classes and no more, and the fabric store had let her go at summer's end, her supervisor telling her firmly and politely that she needed to "take care of herself" and that the store could not afford to let her do that on its dime. Adriana came home from that meeting and sat at the kitchen table, the future yawning before her like a wasteland, grey and terrible. She fingered the paring knife that her father had left that morning on a plate with a spiral of orange peel. She felt like that, like something has been stripped from her.

Mr. Song was an engineer, and expected his daughters to be educated, and productive. Adriana had tried. But it was as if her head was locked in a deep sea diving helmet, which nothing could penetrate.

CHAPTER 3

After Jazz left, Adriana went back to bed. She gazed up at the wallpaper. There were big, dusty roses on it. Her mother's choice, no doubt, though she never asked her father about it. On a small desk by the window, the same one she'd had since childhood, there was a large textbook, open to two black and white photos of the human brain—one whole and perfect, the other partially dissected with black lines spiking from it like a sea urchin, neatly labelled.

The brain was such an armoured thing, solid and impenetrable—but in the end, just as vulnerable to human curiosity and exploitation as the moon or the ocean. Adriana was used to staring at this picture, trying to differentiate the hippocampus from the surrounding tissue. It amazed her that brain scientists had been able to pinpoint that it was the hippocampus, which lay curled in the brain in the shape of a sea horse, that was the seat of memory. Without it, Adriana thought, life would cease to have meaning.

Adriana wondered if there was something wrong with her hippocampus. Lately she remembered the past with agonizing clarity but had a difficult time recalling whether she had eaten breakfast or had a shower. The days seemed to blur into one as though they'd all been spun in a blender.

Adriana was 11 years old, when her mother, Viera, wrathful as a hurricane, died and left the Song family in her wake. Adriana remembered sitting at her desk staring at the roses on her wallpaper, clutching her ears so she wouldn't hear Beth's insistent cries, and Aunt Penny's hushed but urgent tones as she tried to comfort the baby and her grieving brother at the same time. Then one day Penny and the baby were gone and it was just Adriana and her father in a house so quiet it could have been a tomb.

Not long after, back in Toronto, Penny met a Chinese widower whose own children were grown and who could appreciate Penny's well-aged, motherly beauty. He died two years ago, leaving Penny the house in downtown Toronto; still, for much of her childhood, Beth had a ready-made surrogate family. Mr. Song, who had agonized over letting Beth go, was thankful but grief-stricken all over again when he heard Beth had called Penny's husband "baba." Adriana heard him get up in the middle of the night to sit at the kitchen table, and the muffled thump of a bottle against the tabletop. This went on for a week and a half and then one night her father slept through the night, the sound of his snores from the next room as reassuring to Adriana's ears as the blanket she slept under.

Closing her eyes, Adriana willed herself to get up, folding the bedcovers aside neatly as she always had, the way her mother taught her. She'd slip her feet into her mother's old slippers, stand and stretch, and cough on the swirling dust motes disturbed when she raised the blind. She'd look out the window at the dry, late summer grass in the backyard, punctuated by a dead maple tree whose upswept crown was leafless and brittle. Her father had said several times, absently, that he must get someone to cut it down for firewood, but Adriana knew he had forgotten, and the maple would stand there all winter. That was as far as she got. Something about that tree stopped her in her tracks, and she never got beyond it to imagine what came next.

Adriana wanted to hang on to sleep for just a little longer, since she had once again failed to find her way out of bed. And because she knew that when she opened her eyes, her mother would be standing in the doorway, glaring at her.

It was a long time before Adriana woke up again and went to the kitchen. Her father must have left for work when she'd still been fast asleep. What had he thought about her skipping class? He'd been too meek to force her awake.

She ate breakfast the way she liked it, by herself with the radio on, a huge mug of coffee in her hand. She imagined her mother seated across from her, a cigarette between two languid fingers, blowing smoke in Adriana's face. Adriana wondered what she'd tell her father. That she couldn't see the path ahead of her? That it frightened her that she didn't know what tomorrow looked like, what came next? Then there was her mother, arms crossed, smiling wickedly. *What does come next?*

Adriana's mother turned blurry at the edges, her face stern, matter of fact. Adriana felt weak. There she was, having followed Adriana around all these years, commenting on her messy handwriting, her unorthodox haircuts, and her penchant for chaos. Adriana had always looked hurriedly away, corrected her mistakes and made her bed the way her mother taught her. She had never asked her mother a pointed question, like, *Why did you leave me? Why did you die when I still needed you?*

Adriana was afraid to ask. She was afraid to chase the last of her mother away, when that was all she had of her. Suddenly, she felt quite empty, as though a valve had been opened, and all the things that filled her up had drained away. Adriana had felt this way before, like a yawning cavern had opened inside her. She went back to bed, curled in on herself, hugging a pillow to her chest. The phone rang several times but she ignored it. She was asleep when it rang again at lunchtime and in the mid-afternoon.

Later, Adriana awakened to hear the soft sizzle of onions in the wok. Her father was cooking supper. She stood for a moment in the kitchen door, watching him, and feeling hollow as a reed. There was something wrong with her but talk wouldn't help.

Mr. Song didn't hear her standing in the doorway. He was humming something under his breath, at home in the kitchen, with her mother's old apron on. Adriana couldn't believe her father had survived this world, as fragile and goofy as he was. She sat down at the table, soundlessly. Somehow her father knew she was there. Without turning around, he said, "We're having steak, hon. I got a tip today." Adriana's mind let that turn over. Did engineers get tips? "It's a bonus, really," he said apologetically. "But it's a small bonus. More like a tip."

Adriana didn't realize that her father was joking—she barely acknowledged that he had a sense of humour, especially now that her own was so ragged. Her stomach was delicate as a butterfly. "I'm not hungry Dad," she said, and it was true. She felt weak, but heavy, as though lined by cement. Adriana stood up, dragging her blanket around her, and trailed out of the kitchen. Mr. Song raised his hand with the metal spatula, as though he was about to strike a fly, and watched her go. Then he turned back to the stove, where a pot of rice was bubbling. Out of all the things in his life that had changed, he thought, the bubbling of the rice pot remained the same.

CHAPTER 4

Mr. Song realized eventually that Adriana had stopped going to class and called in sick to the fabric store one too many times. He'd given up trying to coax her out with things she liked, such as coffee milkshakes, games of Boggle and home movies. At least, he thought she liked those things. She used to. Mr. Song was full of fear, his face shiny with it. She was such a bright little girl, always bursting with something—enthusiasm, a secret, hot dogs. Round-bellied, bubbling with laughter, her short legs carrying her twice as fast as her father wherever she wanted to go. Now she was pale, drawn and melodramatic. He felt something was eating her from inside, and that one day he'd wake up and there would be nothing but a pile of sawdust.

Mr. Song thought about trying to talk to Jazz about Adriana, but he felt too awkward with her to actually have a conversation. Something about the way Jazz looked at him with those cool eyes of hers bothered him. He felt like he never quite measured up, as though Jazz were the parent, and he were the one under scrutiny. He and Jazz never had anything to say to one another, but he was grateful for her friendship with Adriana.

Instead of talking to Jazz, Mr. Song called the helpline one day and had a heart-to-heart with one of the volunteers. Adriana was depressed, he figured. The helpline volunteer told him there were options—the mental health crisis unit, for example—if things got too bad. "You've got to get her to talk to someone," the woman said. Mr. Song pictured the volunteer as a middle-aged woman, dyed blonde hair, a wad of chewing gum stuck to its wrapper in front of her.

Can you get her to see someone, was where they left it. And no, he couldn't get her to see someone. They barely talked. When he got up the courage to knock on the door of her room, she didn't answer, and when he opened the door, she was sleeping, her face to the wall. She seemed to sleep all the time he was in the house, even when he lay in bed at night, waiting to hear the fridge door open or some other sign that she was alive.

That day, when her father came home from work, he sat on the edge of her bed, his briefcase between his feet. He didn't look at her. "Addy, I need you to talk to someone." His voice was tremulous. He knew she was asleep, that he was only practicing, but nevertheless his stomach jumped around nervously.

It was the same feeling he used to get when her mother was alive and he had something to say that he knew she wouldn't like. She would look at him with heavy-lidded eyes and laugh a low, throaty laugh that thrilled and terrified him. "Dahling, you're full of shit," she would say in her Slovak accent. He felt reassured that she didn't disown him, that she allowed him to say his piece, even though he was wrong and she of course was right. Often a day or so later he would discover that she had in fact come around to his point of view. She showed him as much in discreet ways, such as by folding his socks together instead of tubing them, as he had asked, or by changing the bathroom scale to one that measured kilograms instead of just pounds. "I like kilograms," she said, smiling slyly. "They make me feel slimmer."

The day Mr. Song ate steak alone at the kitchen table, was the first time he noticed Adriana's face. Pale, with dark circles under her eyes. She looked haunted. And what cut to his heart, she looked distant. Disdainful of him and his open-arm policy. As if she would have respected him more if he'd taken a more firm and forceful approach. That just wasn't his style—in fact it was so foreign to him that he couldn't even imagine what it would look like. Would he yank her from her bed and cart her off to the doctor? Mr. Song ran his hand through his hair, thinking. He couldn't do that. He had no other choice—it was time to talk to Jazz.

"I don't know what to do," was all he could think of to say when he called Jazz to meet him at a coffee shop. Jazz sat, spine as straight as a book, in the chair opposite, while he poured her tea.

She gazed at him impassively. He took another stab. "Could you—is there something you could do to help her?" He had never asked anything of Jazz before, and it seemed like a momentous occasion that he was doing so now.

Jazz pulled out her wallet. "I think Adriana needs a night on the town," was what she said. "I'd like to take her to see Bartholomew Banks at the Westin, but it will cost twenty dollars." Mr. Song, thinking Bartholomew Banks must be some kind of teen heartthrob, handed her twenty dollars no questions asked, and felt something like relief, to know that Jazz had a plan of some kind.

The barometric pressure of Adriana's life was about to

change. She didn't know it at the time, but it was as though an inexorable plough were pushing the trash of her life up against the landfill fence.

CHAPTER 5

When Adriana woke up in the late morning, there was a red light blinking on her phone. It would be Jazz. They hadn't talked in a couple days because Adriana knew if she called Jazz, it would be the end of the silence that contained what she wasn't yet ready to give up. Depression, with its familiar blue fingers encircling her throat, and a bottle of sleeping pills that she'd bought at the pharmacy, the day she was let go from the fabric store.

Adriana felt like a candle burning down, its singed wick drooping in a cave of wax. If only she could pull the pieces of herself together into a pile, it would be less obvious that she had fallen completely apart. Jazz was still possessed with the notion that Adriana could pull herself out of this funk, with affirmations and will power. Adriana didn't bother to contradict her. It took too much energy, even to entertain the idea.

Adriana's mother watched her, stern as a drill sergeant. A dutiful daughter, Adriana had tried. But weakness had overtaken her. *You are so like your father*, her mother said with scorn.

There was a ceiling fan in Adriana's bedroom. She liked

to keep it on, even on cool days, because she liked the feel of air moving on her face. But today her teeth chattered and the sound of the fan's whirring blades terrified her, as she imagined they were an instrument of torture which would descend from the ceiling and drill right through her as she slept. It took a minute for Adriana to remember she could turn the fan off with the flick of a switch. She wobbled out of bed, seasick, ducking under the fan on her way to the wall switch. The whirring blades gently slowed to a stop, and Adriana, exhausted and relieved, fell back into bed.

She pulled a blanket up to her chin and tried to fall asleep. This is what a corpse feels like, she thought. The Egyptian mummies, Tut and his kin, had their arms folded across their chests. Adriana tried it too. She felt as though she'd been laid on a ceremonial slab in order that her brains could be extracted through her nose. The thought made her giggle, a high unnatural sound that frightened her. She was afraid that her father would come home and find her like this, laughing like a mad person.

Adriana dozed, never quite sleeping; then, resigned to the fact that she was awake, folded the bed covers aside neatly, as though turning the pages of a book. The red light on her phone, still blinking, was a beacon of a sort; an urgent pulsing, like the light on a police car. She called Jazz, without listening to the message. The phone rang a few times before Adriana, nonplussed by the thought of the incessant ringing in an empty room, hung up.

Adriana pulled the blanket at the end of her bed around her shoulders. She tried not to think about the bottle of sleeping pills she'd bought at the drugstore and hid in her bedside table, but it was as if they were magnetic and her thoughts were iron filings. To escape them she made her way to the kitchen. It seemed like days since she'd eaten, but her stomach felt iffy so all she had was a cup of tea. She sat at the kitchen table, hunched under her blanket, hollow inside.

There was a sound at the door and Adriana looked up, startled. Jazz had her face mashed against the screen, and was making strangled noises. "Let me in!" she rumbled. Adriana, stomach drawn, got up and unlocked the screen door.

Jazz went straight to the fridge. "I'm hungry, what do you have in here?" Adriana shrugged helplessly. Adriana looked to her like one of those starving children on Oxfam commercials, not just because she was thin, but because of how limp she seemed in the face of life. Jazz wanted to shake her, but there was the chance she'd break.

Instead, Jazz sat down opposite Adriana and thrust an apple at her. "Here," she said, "I have news I want to share with you," Jazz said, as grandly as she could with a mouth full of apple. "We've got tickets to a fun evening with Dr. Bartholomew Banks." Adriana didn't react. Jazz leaned toward her, cupping her hand to her ear. "Who is this Dr. Banks, you ask?" Jazz leaned toward her then and in a confidential tone, said "He's a celebrated spiritualist and psychic who can..." Jazz then put her hand on Adriana's forehead and proclaimed loudly, "HEEEAAAAL the sick. HEEAAALLL, I say."

Adriana looked down at her hands. A spiritualist? She wasn't even sure what that was. Did Jazz think she was sick?

Jazz put her hands on Adriana's cheeks. "Come on," she said quietly, "it can't hurt worse than it already does." She took two tickets from her pocket and waved them at her. "Huh? Huh?" Jazz coaxed. Adriana took a ticket and examined it. "Bartholomew Banks, celebrated spiritualist, psychic, and healer." Adriana's nose wrinkled, until Jazz punched her in the arm.

Adriana looked at her blankly and handed the ticket back. "No, thank you," she whispered.

Jazz lost patience. "Listen, Miss Snot Nose, these tickets cost me two hours housecleaning money," she said. Adriana looked at her, stricken. Jazz had spent her hard-earned money on crap because she thought it would help? A tear trickled down Adriana's nose. Jazz softened. "You really do have a snotty nose," she said, as Adriana began to bawl. "Come on, bubble gum," Jazz said quietly, pulling Adriana's head to her cheek.

The night of the spiritualist's performance, Jazz came by for Adriana around 6 p.m. They were planning to take Mr. Song's car, Jazz driving and Adriana sitting slumped in the passenger seat. But at the last minute, Mr. Song decided he would prefer to drive them himself. Jazz fixed him with a cool stare. Looking sheepish, Mr. Song said "I'll run a few errands while you're at the... spiritualist," he said, glancing at his daughter. Adriana sat with her head down, stringy hair hanging.

Adriana had wearily explained to him that Bartholomew Banks was no one she knew, but that he was a spiritualist, and Jazz had tickets. He had nodded sagely, and offered the car, but secretly felt bewildered and perturbed. From the dictionary definition, he gathered that a spiritualist was something like a fortune teller in China, someone who could converse with the souls of the dead. Although he had long since given up his belief in such superstitions, he found himself frequently wishing he could talk to his wife. She had grown pale in his mind, faded to a wisp, especially since the recent troubles with Adriana. But if anyone knew what to do about their daughter, it would be her.

Jazz sat in the passenger seat with Mr. Song on the drive to the hotel where Bartholomew Banks was to perform. Their conversation was stilted. Usually Mr. Song tried harder with Jazz but he didn't want to be distracted while driving. Adriana was no help at all, slumped in the back seat. Her mind was grey and empty, the sounds of her father and Jazz speaking echoing around inside her like the buzzing of a bee.

"Uh, how is your mother doing these days?" Mr. Song asked Jazz, looking straight ahead, as they sat briefly at a four way stop. It was a bit of a throw away question, and he regretted it as soon as he asked. Jazz's mother was a tall, semi-attractive middle-aged woman whom he couldn't have picked out of a crowd. She always looked prim and dour, even when she smiled.

Jazz peered out the window at a homeless guy, bumming change. Sometimes she fantasized that her father was one of these street people. She would look into their face and see her own blue eyes staring back at her. "My mum's just dandy," she replied, "Just dandy."

Mr. Song didn't know whether Jazz was being sarcastic or not but suspected she was. He realized with shame that he didn't even remember Jazz's mother's name. She wasn't someone he ever thought about, and he was sure Jazz knew that. Jazz knew a remarkable number of things. It was difficult to keep anything from her.

At the hotel, Jazz told Mr. Song, "We'll be done at 9:30" The ticket actually said 9 p.m. but Jazz didn't want to risk him arriving early. She opened Adriana's car door and pulled her by the hand. "Upsy daisy, butterfly," Jazz said.

Adriana hadn't been outside the house in days and felt entirely miserable to be arriving at the hotel in what Jazz called her "Depression Era clothes." In the haze of talk about the spiritualist, she had not registered that everything would take place at the hotel. Somehow she had imagined it being at the Forum, where there was lots of room in the cavernous rink. A thrumming anxiety overcame her and she panicked, eyes wide.

Jazz took her by the elbow. "It's okay, honeycomb. Come with me." Adriana clung to Jazz's arm as they passed the doorman, who opened the door for them but, it seemed to her, gave them a wide berth. Adriana felt the sting of contagion, as though her depression were spreading, like a cold does, from her mouth and nose.

Jazz was chatting away to Adriana, to distract her from the glances of hotel staff and guests. They got on the elevator to the second floor, and when the door opened, they were facing a woman in a pink skirt and blazer standing beside the doorway of a darkened room. She smiled as Jazz handed her their tickets, and ushered them into the darkened conference room, whose only illumination was thanks to a spotlight on the podium in front of a bank of chairs.

Adriana wanted to sit near the back of the room, but had no energy to put up a fight. Jazz steered her toward the front where a few people were already sitting. Wide-eyed and excited, Jazz hung on to Adriana's arm as she shrunk into her seat. "We're going to talk to the dead!" Jazz thrilled. Adriana felt the blood rush to her face. Jazz whispered loudly, "I've been waiting forever to talk to the dead!"

Adriana turned her head away. So this is what a spiritualist was, someone who talks to dead people? Adriana thought of her conversations with her mother. The last thing she wanted was to talk to her in front of all these people. She turned to Jazz. "I'm leaving," Adriana said. Jazz looked up at her in disbelief. "Let me get by," Adriana pleaded weakly.

Jazz held her hand. "Adriana, wait. Do you know why I brought you here?" Adriana couldn't guess, except that perhaps Jazz thought it would help her. "Number one, because it will be a fun time and Lord knows, you could use a little fun. But number two is because I want to talk to my father." Jazz gulped. Adriana stood beside Jazz, her hands open to the empty air. She felt ashamed. "It's not all about you, you know?" echoed in her head. She'd heard those words many times from Jazz.

Adriana sat down. Jazz was still clutching her arm, her face full of anguish. Adriana figured she was thinking about her Dad, who had gone missing when she was only a toddler. At first, it was presumed he had drowned in a New Brunswick lake where he had gone fishing with a friend. But then he'd been found hanging in a fishing shed from his own belt.

Adriana had rarely heard Jazz talk about her father. He was an absence in her life that cast no shadow, Adriana had thought, partly thanks to Jazz's mother, who was of the opinion that the less her daughter knew about the man who had brought shame to her family, the better. Adriana blinked. Jazz was always so cool, matter of fact, but it occurred to Adriana that maybe her aplomb was an act, protective gear only.

Jazz wiped her eyes with a handkerchief. Adriana felt miles away from her pain, as though she were looking down the wrong end of a telescope. But she sat and waited for Jazz to stop sniffling. Jazz smiled at her, gratefully. "Thanks Addy, for staying. There was no one else I wanted to bring except you."

Adriana looked down at her hands, which lay lifeless in her lap. The darkness inside her head was impenetrably bleak, as though her skull were lined with lead. For the first time she realized that she was alone inside this darkness, that not even Jazz was able to enter. Only her mother, cold and relentless as a glacier, had found a foothold there.

A short, chubby man wandered into the spotlight. He cleared his throat, waited until a hush settled over the room, and began to read. "There are not many men who have done what Bartholomew Banks, tonight's illustrious guest speaker, has done. He has crossed through the shadows of the Valley of Death to reach out to those who linger at the edges of this Life, waiting for their time to pass into the Great Beyond." Jazz clutched Adriana's hand, riveted.

"Bartholomew Banks not only speaks to the Dead, he helps them find their way to the Light. I will not take your time to list all of Bartholomew Banks's accomplishments, but would simply like to introduce him as a man gifted beyond our understanding, and courageous and compassionate enough to use this gift for good."

Jazz clutched a handkerchief to her mouth. Adriana thought of her mother who, hands on hips, would no doubt poo-poo a man like Bartholomew Banks. Adriana doubted she was waiting in the shadows to speak with her—more likely, she was waiting off stage to castigate Adriana for being weak enough to attend an evening with an obvious charlatan.

Bartholomew Banks entered the spotlight and thanked the chubby man, who graciously disappeared into the shadows. Dressed in a buckskin jacket he gripped the podium with both hands, squinting into the darkness for almost a minute, while the audience held its breath—rapt, bedazzled by his solemnity. His gaze seemed to settle on someone behind Adriana and Jazz at the back of the room. Adriana was glad that they'd decided to sit closer to the front, where they were safe from his penetrating stare.

Banks cleared his throat, a sound that managed to express dignity and sobriety, and which, along with the eyebrows (shaggy beyond belief) made Adriana think of Abraham Lincoln. Banks nodded to Jazz, who sat stock still, clutching Adriana's arm.

"I see a man behind you," he said, clearing his throat. It was a perfectly ordinary voice, neither deep nor sonorous, not what Adriana was expecting. "What is your name, young lady?"

Jazz was speechless.

"Yes, you," Banks said, nodding in her direction.

"Jasmine O'Connell" said Jazz. Adriana had never heard her call herself by her full name before.

Banks gazed at her for a moment. "This man says that he is related to you." Banks frowned slightly. "He died many years ago. Do you know him?" Jazz nodded and sobbed. Banks softened. "He says he is sorry for leaving you alone." At this point Jazz's tears were uncontrollable.

"He says that he has been watching over you, even though you have grown up without him." Jazz nodded silently. Adriana gaped. "He wants to give you his blessing, before he goes into the Light," he continued. Jazz bowed her head and Banks waved his hand over her. "And he needs your blessing before he can depart." Jazz looked up, eyes wide. "Yes," Banks said, "He requires you to release him." Jazz's lips parted.

"I release you," she whispered.

Bartholomew Banks waved his arms with a flourish. "Go to the Light," he commanded. And soundlessly a door closed, a light withered and a wound in the air healed itself.

Adriana held onto Jazz, who was shaking. "Are you okay?" she whispered. Jazz nodded. Her face was radiant, peaceful, joyful even. Adriana wasn't sure why she felt anxious. Bartholomew Banks was smiling now.

"And you," he said pointing to Adriana. She sat motionless, as Jazz dabbed her eyes with a tissue. Bank's eyebrows drew together. "You have a wraith following you." Adriana looked blank. "It's a woman." Bartholomew Banks said, his brow furrowed. "She's saying... she's upset... it's hard to make out the words." He listened to the air once more. Adriana felt her heart beating in her ears. "She says that... you have everything... that there's nothing you need."

Adriana felt like she'd been struck. Could this really be her mother? She tried to picture Viera saying those words. The mother she imagined looked exasperated, throwing her hands in the air and turning on her heel to storm out of Adriana's bedroom. Adriana watched her go, in the gathering darkness. In her imagination, the bottle of sleeping pills fell over as her mother slammed the door.

The audience was stirring a little, restlessly awaiting their turn. Bartholomew Banks raised his arms in the air and brought his hands down slowly, like a conductor quieting an orchestra. He smiled for the first time, his blue eyes sparkling under the hood of his eyebrows. "The Dead only talk when you invite them to. Otherwise they are rather quiet." Banks said, smiling apologetically.

"Jazz," Adriana whispered. Jazz, still beaming, looked at Adriana "Do you feel better?" Jazz nodded blissfully. Adriana looked down at her hands. She wished she could say the same.

For the remainder of the evening, Bartholomew Banks was able to connect each person in the audience to the Dead, or to heal them of some minor or imagined misfortune. One woman felt her carpal tunnel syndrome had disappeared.

There were tears and someone even fell to her knees. Banks seemed aloof, otherworldly, almost unaffected by the commotion he was causing in the lives of the living. It was as though he wasn't quite here, but had one foot in the Light himself and was only marking time on this earth.

After the final applause, Adriana and Jazz waited in the hotel lobby for Mr. Song to pick them up. Jazz was radiant, Adriana, sunk in gloom. She didn't know why, but the fact that the mother who kept her company in her head was not the woman that Bartholomew Banks had summoned set up an almost intolerable anxiety in her.

Mr. Song arrived at 9:25, and they went out to meet him. "How was it?" he asked, handing each of them a takeout cup of tea. Adriana glanced at Jazz, who rested her forehead against the car window, smiling dreamily at the winking street lights. "It was fine," Adriana said, trying to sound bored. "Mom told me I have everything I need." Her father's eyes were shiny with worry. Adriana turned her head away.

When they arrived at Jazz's house, Adriana turned to Jazz. "Thanks," she said. Jazz, glowing, hugged her shoulders.

As she lay in bed that night, Adriana pondered why the spirit Bartholomew Banks conjured up had told her she had everything she needed. It wasn't as if she had been asking for something. In fact, quite the opposite, unless longing for complete oblivion counted as asking.

Adriana couldn't escape the question any longer. Was the version of her mother that Bartholomew Banks had conjured the fiction, or was the mother she had known for so many years, the mother who accompanied her thoughts every day as judge and jury? She didn't believe Bartholomew

Banks, but she couldn't afford not to. The thought of that mother opened up in her a longing, so keen and unfamiliar and irresistible that it was almost unbearable. She felt at the same time, like her life to that point had been an empty parking lot. Adriana pictured a tub of ice cream someone had come along and taken a big scoop out of, and then someone else had showed up and scooped some more. What was left was used up and hollow, something to be discarded. But it was all she had.

The day after the spiritualist meeting, Adriana got up and swept the kitchen floor. She had no more energy for anything else. Sitting at the kitchen table, drained, she drank some tea that her father had made for breakfast. It was lukewarm and bitter, which was how Adriana felt. She returned to bed, in a room which was about the same as the day her mother died, except for the Cure poster on the opposite wall.

CHAPTER 6

"You can call me Dr. Bob," said the psychologist as she seated herself opposite him in his office overlooking the campus.

Her father, who'd come home at lunch with cartons of Chinese takeout the day after Bartholomew Banks, had given her an ultimatum. "You'll see a therapist, or I'll drive you to the doctor myself." She barely cared, at this point. Adriana, who felt she'd reached the bottom of the well, was almost relieved to surrender.

"Tell me a little about yourself... what brings you here today?" Dr. Bob asked. The psychologist looked at her kindly, pityingly, she thought, pen poised in his chubby hand to take notes. Adriana hadn't been banking on that. She looked at him as though from far away, and tried to think.

"My dad thinks I'm depressed," she said. That was about all she could muster. Dr. Bob looked at her closely, taking note, she thought, of her unkempt hair and worn sweatshirt.

"And are you?" was all he said.

Adriana felt surprised. Of course she was. She nodded.

"On a scale of one to ten, how would you rate how depressed you are?" Dr. Bob asked. "One is severely depressed and ten is 'I feel great'."

Adriana attempted to think it over but got bogged down in the numbers. "Two?" she ventured.

His brow furrowed. "It sounds like you are feeling quite depressed. How long have you been feeling this way?"

Was it several months, or a year? Adriana could barely think. She squinted at him and shrugged her shoulders.

"Have you had any thoughts of... harming yourself?" he asked.

Adriana realized she had such thoughts, and that the bottle of sleeping pills was more than a thought—but there was also a recurring vision of her mother standing over her with fiery wings, and the stern face of Archangel Michael. That was her mother's favourite Biblical figure—she swooned over Archangel Michael as though he were a movie star, even though she never went to church except at Easter and Christmas. Adriana wasn't likely to harm herself with her archangel mother to answer to; but the Viera Bartholomew Banks had introduced her to seemed to drift like a veil of snow between them, and everything was less clear to her than it had been before.

Dr. Bob was squinting at her. Adriana looked at his hands, his short, stubby fingers. He looked like a bear cub. She smiled slightly and Dr. Bob frowned back and repeated, "Have you... had any thoughts about dying?" Adriana shook her head but the dishonesty reddened her cheeks. She had wished for death, but was too afraid to attempt it. She was fearful of her mother's wrath, if indeed there was another world after this one; and if there wasn't, of the possibility of her mind winking out forever, like a candle on a birthday cake.

Dr. Bob sat back in his chair. "Adriana," he said. "I don't know you very well since we have just met, but it seems

to me you might need more help than I can give you."
Adriana looked up at Dr. Bob. The distance between them
seemed enormous—a Great Lake or an ocean. Dr. Bob
tried to get her to look him in the eye, but she wouldn't
meet his gaze. He spoke loudly to try to get her attention.
"Adriana?" he said. "I think you should see Dr. Stoneaway...
She's a psychiatrist who has a private practice upstairs in
this building. She's very competent and works with a lot
of young women with depression. Will you allow me to
refer you to her?"

A psychiatrist? Adriana shrank from the thought. She
wasn't crazy, was she? A psychiatrist would give her pills.
She didn't need pills the way she didn't need a bucket full
of garbage dumped on her head. Dr. Bob leaned forward.
Adriana shook her head.

Clearly Dr. Bob was accustomed to that reaction. He
smiled and sat back in his chair. "Well," he said, "What do
you think you need to feel better?" Adriana looked at her
knees. She didn't know.

"A hot bath?" she said weakly.

Dr. Bob leaned toward her, intense and earnest. "Adriana,
I think you and I both know that you've gone way beyond
the hot bath stage. I think you need to see someone who
can prescribe medications. They can be an amazing help to
people who are severely depressed, which I think you are.
You'll still need therapy and Dr. Stoneaway is very skilled in
that area. I can give her a call right now, if you like."

Adriana felt like running, but where would she run to?
And wouldn't it be proof of her alleged madness if she just
took off out the door? Even in her state, she realized that it
was advisable that she stay calm (or at least, that her face
stay smooth and expressionless) and politely refuse. "No,

thank you," she heard herself say in a voice which seemed small and prim and slightly shaky.

Dr. Bob tried one more time. "Adriana, your father is very worried about you. He says this down phase of yours has gone on for much longer than usual and that he doesn't know how to help you. I am also concerned that at this point, talk therapy isn't going to get you very far. In my professional opinion you need to speak to someone about medication."

Inside herself, Adriana threw up her hands, weakly. She had refused pills out of a certain pride, but part of her just wanted to lie down and take whatever the doctor would give her. It was a kind of giving up. But at the last minute, to her own dreary dismay, she felt an unreasoning stubbornness take hold of her. "No," she said, in a child's voice. Dr. Bob frowned slightly, then sat back in his chair and stroked his chin. It looked to Adriana like he was pulling ice cream cones out of a dispenser, and she giggled, a sound high pitched and slightly unhinged.

Dr. Bob let out a breath which could have been exasperated, but was definitely worried. "Alright Adriana, I can't force you. I don't think there's much need for you to make another appointment with me. I hope you'll decide on your own to see someone who can consider starting you on meds."

Adriana felt as though she were holding her breath and turning blue. Inside, she jangled, appalled at her own recklessness. She stood up shakily and nodded her head to Dr. Bob, who nodded back, smiling, but with brow furrowed. As she walked out into the street, she thought she felt his eyes on her, and it was all she could do not to turn around in surrender.

Mr. Song was cooking supper when she got home. He turned as she came in the back door, and his sweet, expectant look made Adriana hate herself. "How did it go with Dr. Bob?" he asked, moving a spatula around the wok to stir-fry a handful of shrimp. Adriana watched them turn red, and wondered listlessly what genetic secret made a shrimp change to such a cheerful colour. What good was such a display when the shrimp was already dead?

Mr. Song bent toward her and looked into her face. "Adriana, are you okay?" he asked. She knew he wanted the real answer.

"No," was all she said. She felt as though she were wandering in a treeless slough.

Her father sat down at the kitchen table and pulled her by the hand into the chair next to him. "Adriana, honey, this can't go on," was all he said. He stroked her hair and she dropped her head as tears leaked silently down her cheeks.

That night she slept fitfully, her dreams a monotone grey. In the morning she woke exhausted and lay in bed, hoping that the sun would never rise. But it did, its piercing rays reaching under her blinds like sharp swords. She wanted to sleep, no, she wanted to forget, to forget herself most of all. If only she were a chameleon. If only her conscious mind could morph into something; static on the radio, the pattern of the wallpaper, anything other than the medium of her thoughts.

Her mother, grey faced and swathed in white, stared at her reproachfully. Adriana wondered why her mother watched her, after all these years. Surely there was something better to do, in the afterlife. She wondered if her mother would graduate to the next phase, whatever that was. Or retire.

The mother that she knew was not the one the spiritualist

had contacted. Her mother was not one to tell her that she had everything she needed. She was more likely to cast a withering eye upon her for not making her bed or for dropping out of school. Yelling didn't seem to be possible in the afterlife, at least, not for Adriana's mother. Maybe that was why it has such a reputation for quiet.

Adriana lay back in her bed, aching. She felt so weak, so helpless—so damaged. Was it possible she was mentally ill, that she needed a psychiatrist and drugs, simply in order to limp from one day to the next? And she had refused them. It was the end, then, she thought. She couldn't muster the strength to get up, to wash or eat. Her mother's stony silence beat in her ears like a pulse, accusing her of something—she didn't know what, but she felt guilty all the same.

CHAPTER 7

Adriana's father called the ambulance. She'd swallowed the bottle of sleeping pills that she'd been keeping inside the drawer of her bedside table. Weakly, Adriana had sat up in the dark of the early morning, after a dream in which she'd watched her mother fall down a long flight of stairs, while she stood at the top and watched. Just before she woke up, she had gazed out of her mother's eyes at the young Adriana above her on the landing, a wave of pain and regret washing through her.

Adriana woke in the dark, shivering from the cold. There were birds outside in the dead maple, beginning to sing the songs of late summer. Things were coming to an end, and the crickets which she loved, had found their voice. That's the sound of angels, her mother had told her when she was very young. As her mother braided her hair before she went to school for the first time, Adriana felt the tug of her mother's hands, the too-tight pull of the braids, and the chirping of the angels, which sounded plaintive and mournful to her young ears.

Adriana swallowed each tablet separately with a gulp from a glass of water. Then she lay back, listening to the creaking of the crickets, and reading from a Bible that she remembered her mother stealing from a hotel. Adriana felt her mind darkening, and the text falling apart, as though the words were written with ink on water. Then she was opening her eyes as a tube was pushed through her nose into her stomach to pump it. She saw the light above her and masked faces bending over her, and it seemed to her she might be in a coffin in the ground, her parents, Jazz, and her sister Beth hovering above her. She wanted to reach out for them but her arms wouldn't move.

Adriana woke up again in the emergency room. Her father was sitting in the chair next to her, pale and dishevelled, having fallen asleep while reading a book. Adriana looked at his hands which were long-fingered and brown. They looked tired. She didn't move but tears trickled down her cheeks.

A nurse came by and pushed back the curtain surrounding the bed. Mr. Song jerked awake and Adriana closed her eyes, not wanting to look at his worried face. The nurse, in a loud business-like voice said, "Adriana, open your eyes." Adriana refused. "She's awake," said the nurse with irritation. Mr. Song took one of Adriana's hands in his and squeezed it. "Adriana, we have to give you some charcoal to drink now," the nurse said in a loud voice. "It's to coat your stomach."

Adriana stared up at the light. If only she could disappear into one of the little holes in the ceiling tiles. Mr. Song was squeezing her hand too tightly. Adriana put on a shaky, terrible smile and looked at no one.

The nurse raised the head of Adriana's bed so that she was in a sitting position. Adriana felt totally exposed. "Here," the nurse said, more gently this time. "You're not going to like this but you need to drink it. All of it." She thrust a plastic bottle with a straw sticking out of it into Adriana's hand.

Adriana took a sip. It was sweet, with the texture of ice crystals, and the flavour of charcoal. Horrible. She turned her head away. Mr. Song took the bottle from her and mixed the charcoal around with the straw. "Here," he said in a voice she had never heard before, as though he were so angry he had trouble forming the words. "You are going to drink this, Adriana." His hand was shaking. "You are lucky I found you. Now drink this."

Adriana looked at her father. "Drink," he said.

Adriana drank the whole bottle of charcoal, and near the end, she threw up on the floor. Black vomit splattered everywhere. The nurse sighed irritably on her way past and soon returned with an orderly with a mop. "Can you get up?" she asked Adriana, who nodded. "Then maybe you can go to the washroom to clean yourself up." Mr. Song held her by the arm as she put her legs over the side of the bed. She was wearing a johnny shirt, and the nurse thrust another clean one into her hands. She felt weak and hollow, her stomach aching from the retching. Her father's eyes were on her. She closed the bathroom door and caught sight of herself in the mirror. Her mouth was a ragged, blackened "O", her johnny shirt spattered with black. She looked pale as a ghoul.

Adriana cried as she wiped the charcoal from her mouth and chin. She took off the johnny shirt and bundled it up. There was charcoal at the ends of her hair and on her fingers. She cleaned herself up as best she could, averting her eyes. When she glanced in the mirror, she imagined a horrified audience behind her. Head down, she made her way back to where her father sat.

Ms. Song helped her back into bed. She turned on her side, away from her father's eyes, and felt her own eyes burn, as another nurse quietly addressed him. "Dr. H is on his way," she said and tapped Adriana's arm lightly. "You'll be alright, sweetie," she said.

Adriana knew this to be a lie designed to pacify her and her father. In fact, nothing would ever be alright again. She closed her eyes against the harsh fluorescents, the colourless floor tiles, the green curtains between her bed and the next, where someone's laboured breathing rattled into an oxygen mask. She had never had a nightmare as hellish as this.

After a minute, Adriana heard the curtain being pulled aside. It was a man in hospital greens and a hair net. "Mr. Song? And this must be Adriana," he said. Dr. H had a British accent and looked soft in the middle with a slight stoop. "Can you turn over, Adriana?" he asked rather loudly. "I'm going to need to talk to you as well as your father." Adriana hesitated for a split second. What if she simply refused to acknowledge the doctor's request? But she was meek and despite the terrible darkness that grew like a tree inside her, her desire to please was stronger. She turned over slowly.

The doctor smiled briskly and sat down in the chair next to Mr. Song. "Adriana, you gave your father a scare. I hope you'll think twice before you do something like that again." Mr. Song gently rubbed her arm. The doctor continued, "Your father tells me he has been concerned about you for several months. Do you know how long you've felt depressed?" Adriana had no idea—it seemed like forever. "Can you tell how long you've felt suicidal?" Adriana remembered the first time she thought about taking pills. Could it have been just a week ago?

Dr. H gazed down at her. She squinted, wishing he couldn't see her. "Are you still feeling like harming yourself or someone else?" he asked. Harming someone else? The thought made her panic. Did they really think she wanted to harm anyone besides herself?

Dr. H waited a moment, but Adriana didn't know how to answer. Mr. Song's face was agonized. Adriana could see he was trying not to display any particular emotion and was struggling not to cry. Such a terrible thing she had put her father through. She covered her face with her hands.

Dr. H adjusted himself in his seat, sighed in a slightly exasperated tone, and turned to her father. "Well, Mr. Song, it is my opinion that Adriana would be safest in the hospital. If you are willing, Adriana, I will refer you to the Nova Scotia Hospital where you will be assessed and hopefully admitted.

Mr. Song was incredulous. "The mental hospital?" he asked. Dr. H nodded. "As I said, it is probably the safest place for her at the moment. If Adriana will agree to go, there will be no need for her to be admitted involuntarily. That would be preferable for all concerned."

Adriana looked up at Dr. H. He nodded at her and said in a loud, falsely jovial tone, "What do you think Adriana?" She looked at her father. If she didn't go, he would have to worry about her, when he went to work, or when he fell asleep. Adriana knew it was right for him to worry, but she could save him from the worst of it if she agreed to go to hospital. There was nowhere else for her to go, anyway.

A vision of a wall with a window covered in wire mesh rose before her.

CHAPTER 8

Mr. Song drove Adriana from the ER to the mental hospital. Her head against the window, she stared at the rain puddles, at cars rushing by on the wet asphalt and a few people dressed in T-shirts, enjoying the late summer shower. It was the most precious sight she had ever seen. In a moment she would go from being one of those people, free and unfettered, to a mental patient.

At the gates to the Nova Scotia Hospital, there were a few people hanging around smoking. Adriana tried not to look at them as the car passed between them. There was nothing more depressing than watching mental patients smoke. Adriana thought the gates of Hell must look like this—the stark stone face of the hospital in the distance, the wretched looking souls loitering at the edges. As her father drove around the loop in front of the hospital, looking for a parking spot, Adriana felt the familiar tug of dread, like an undertow.

She had felt it at her mother's funeral, so many years ago. Adriana's father steered her past the audience of mourners, to the front of the room where her mother lay in a casket, under a spotlight that lit her up like a window display. Adriana didn't want to look at her, but her father, pushed her gently forward to lay a single flower at her side. Adriana was not so much afraid of death as she was afraid of her mother's unpredictability. What if she opened her eyes, and snatched the flower from Adriana's hands? Then everyone would stare at her, her mother's parents, weeping quietly in the front row, and Aunt Penny, with Beth squirming in her arms. Adriana quickly dropped the flower on her mother's shoulder, where the wig of long curls, so like her mother's own hair before the chemo, fanned out around her like the Lady of Shalott. And when she turned to look for her place in the front row, it was like a dark wave had flooded the room and was receding, pulling with it all the people who had formed the stuff of her mother's life. Only her father and herself remained, in a pool of light, with her mother's corpse.

On their second trip around the loop, a car pulled out of a parking spot very near the front of the hospital. Mr. Song whistled, perhaps forgetting for a moment the bleakness of his mission. It occurred to Adriana, huddled under the blanket, that her father was protected from the worst of life by a kind of cheerful resilience that she had not inherited. As far as she knew, neither had her sister Beth.

When Mr. Song got out of the car, Adriana felt terrified. He opened her car door and took her hand. "Adriana honey, come on," he said. He gently pulled her from the car. She felt like a heap of broken shells.

Mr. Song seemed strangely upbeat, and Adriana couldn't help but think how quickly his mood had changed. Maybe he was doing his best to put on a brave face, or more likely, he was simply relieved. Adriana looked at the pavement as they walked toward the hospital. At the front door, there was a rainbow of oil on the pavement, left by a car that must have sat there idling some time ago. It fanned out like the feathers of a peacock. For Adriana it was a portent of some kind, as a rainbow always is, even such a rainbow as appeared in the oil leaked in a mental hospital parking lot. She would be admitted and stay there, with the promise that something would resolve out of the oily blackness. She held on to that thought as her father pushed open the hospital doors.

Coming toward her down the hall was a middle-aged woman dressed in a red parka and men's boots, heading outside to smoke, Adriana thought. "Hi, dearie!" the woman said in a loud, shrill voice that sounded like a caricature of herself. Mr. Song smiled at her, but she didn't acknowledge him, continuing toward the doors with a strange, ambling gait. Adriana put her head down and held her father's arm.

After checking in with the assessment unit's nurse, Adriana and her father sat in the waiting room for two hours, waiting for a doctor to see them. Adriana felt the darkness inside her spreading like a swarm of ants, creeping from her body into her head. She held her head with both hands, and covered her eyes. She didn't want to see her father's sad smile, or his tears, if there were any.

Adriana thought about Jazz, and how she would hate Adriana for trying to kill herself. Jazz had just learned to let go of her father's suicide and wasn't likely ready to cope with Adriana's feelings of utter despair. She didn't want to see Jazz at all. She couldn't bear to see her eyes.

After half an hour Adriana gave into exhaustion, and leaning her head against her father's shoulder as he sat reading a magazine. She did what she had always done when faced with overwhelming dread—she slept.

She dreamed of Peter and the pale girl with auburn hair. His face was painted white with black circles around his eyes, and he gripped the girl's wrist with his white hand. She seemed terrified of him. Adriana looked at her face and saw it was her sister Beth's, and that she was fading, blending into her surroundings. Adriana jerked awake, and blinked up at the ceiling. Her heart beat fast inside her chest and ears.

Beth. In the dream, she looked as her mother had, in photos from many years ago, when she was a girl sun bathing on the beach in Croatia. At 14 or 15, she wore a striped bathing suit and showed off her long legs for the camera. Beth would not be so bold—she was still a little girl in Adriana's books—but she had the same angular face that her mother had, the same long curls. Where her mother had been given to anger and screeching, Beth was timid and hysterical.

Adriana didn't know why Beth would appear in her dream, since she barely spent any time thinking about her younger sister. Beth was simply someone who reminded her of her mother, and of her mother's absence.

But Peter... Adriana tried to remember Peter's face but couldn't. Had he been lustful, violent or crazed? She didn't think so. Menacing, perhaps, and clouded—but in the light of day, it was hard to remember why he appeared so threatening.

Peter had never hurt her physically and his emotional clumsiness wasn't his fault, Adriana thought, as she drifted painfully toward sleep. They had got together one night after a party during which they both drank too much and fell asleep next to each other in a sea of bodies Adriana awoke to see him still groggy with sleep, squinting at her and trying to place her. She felt exposed and her reaction was to giggle uncontrollably, although her stomach was drawn and sensitive to the light, and her head felt luminous and balloon-like.

He blinked at her and smiled, and suggested breakfast.

Peter was a talker and Adriana was a listener. She knew he would never understand her timidity and sensitivity, but she wasn't looking for understanding—she was dazzled by the idea of having a boyfriend. Peter asked for her number or her email and she gave him both. From that afternoon she was waiting for his call, and over the next few days she lost a little hope. She concluded that his interest in her was casual, friendly, without malice but without depth. Disappointing, appalling and humiliating. And yet, when he finally called, to ask if she wanted to get together, she couldn't help but leap at the chance to begin that long, un-ravelling, journey into the fog, punctuated here and there with bright mountain peaks that looked like happiness.

CHAPTER 9

"What do you want on the pizza?" Adriana woke with a start. Healthy voices, normal everyday voices. A tall, beefy-looking orderly asked his smaller female colleague. "Do you want Hawaiian again?" as they pushed a stretcher toward the glassed in corner room. Only then did Adriana notice someone sleeping there, on a tall bed with white sheets and blankets.

"I'm good with whatever, except anchovies," the female orderly said. The man pretended to shudder.

"Ugh, anchovies" he said. They didn't glance Adriana's way.

Her father stirred, opening his eyes reluctantly. The orderlies moved the woman in the bed onto the stretcher. At least Adriana thought it was a woman. She had lipstick on, though her face had strong, almost masculine features. Her hair was grey and sprayed into a neat helmet, and when she opened her eyes a little, she smiled weakly. "She's going to Mayflower?" the male orderly asked.

"Yup," said his counterpart briskly. "Same as always." Mr. Song looked disturbed. Adriana watched them wheel the woman out the door, thinking how strange it was that there was nobody with her, no one to comfort her.

A nurse appeared in the doorway to the waiting room. Adriana shrank from her cheerful smile as though from a snake. "You can come with me, Adriana," she said in a loud voice. "The doctor will see you now." Adriana stood up, clutching her empty stomach. Her father helped her by pushing up on her elbow and she felt his hand on the small of her back. He wants me to go, she thought to herself.

The doctor was a brown-skinned man with an English accent, wearing a white lab coat over a shirt and tie. The nurse's expression had turned businesslike, as she helped Adriana sit up on the examination table. "Hello," he said, diffidently. "I am Dr. K, the general practitioner. I need to give you a physical check-up before you see the psychiatrist." Adriana looked at his shoes. They were worn and scuffed, comfortable shoes that reassured her somewhat.

"Any physical complaints?" he asked, as he looked in her ears and mouth with an otoscope. Adriana shook her head. She was surprised to remember the name of the instrument, a word that Jazz had used in a game of Scrabble. "What medications are you taking?" he asked. Adriana thought a moment. She wasn't taking anything. She shook her head. The doctor gave her a severe look. "Can't you talk?" he asked in a loud voice.

Adriana felt her face redden. "No," she whispered.

"Why are you whispering?" he demanded. The nurse turned around, with a suppressed smile on her face. Adriana, swimming in misery, said nothing.

The doctor frowned. "I'm going to test your reflexes," he said. He got out the hammer. "Just relax," he said, brandishing the instrument, "It's not going to hurt." Adriana felt anxiety grip her. He struck her knee with a dull blow and

Adriana's leg bounced in response. She started to giggle nervously at what seemed like a cartoon version of a trip to the doctor, acutely aware that she had forfeited control of something essential to her.

"You think that's funny, do you?" the doctor asked, clearly displeased. Adriana was crying now, silently. The GP softened slightly. "The psychiatrist will see you shortly, Adriana." he said "For now you can sit in the waiting room"

Adriana returned to where her father sat, asleep, his head tipped back, and snoring. What had just happened? Everything was jumbled together—her bottomless sadness and humiliation and mortification, all of it tangled together like string inside her. Adriana was glad her father couldn't see her cry. It didn't seem natural, the number of tears in her. Outlandish was the word that came to her.

She wished her father weren't there. She didn't want him there and she didn't want to have to try to act as though nothing were wrong, though it was already a bit late for that. She felt hollow, her heart thrumming in her chest like grasshoppers in an ice cream bucket. Her arms felt weak and useless, as though, like her gall bladder, they once had a purpose but were now hopelessly outmoded.

The places in her that had been strong and firm were dissolving, and inside her head, her illness glittered like black beads. She couldn't stop the beads from clacking like an abacus.

Mr. Song, awake now, gripped her by the shoulders. "Adriana," he said. Her mind had telescoped to focus on the black beads, their noisy calculations. Wild-eyed, she pulled her mind away from them, like a dog on a leash

A man had appeared in the doorway—the psychiatrist, Adriana thought, her skin suddenly clammy. Wearing a blue-striped shirt that seemed somehow ridiculous, he shook Mr. Song's hand and then offered it to Adriana. "I'm Dr. W. You must be Miss. Song. I'd like to interview you in the next room," he said—dry, cool and impersonal, much like his handshake. Mr. Song stood up. The doctor shook his head. "I'm afraid I need to interview your daughter alone though a nurse will be present of course."

Adriana stood up as her father sat down, deflated. She walked into the hallway, following the striped shirt. It turned into a doorway off the long hallway and into a small examination room. A different nurse was there, ripping a long sheet of paper to place on the examination table. She smiled and sat in a chair in the corner near the door while the doctor settled opposite Adriana.

"Now Adriana, I understand you tried to hurt yourself by overdosing on sleeping pills." Adriana peered up at him as though from the bottom of a pit. His face was boyish, clean shaven and his eyes were sharp and shrew-like. "Is that right?" he said loudly. "Can you tell me why you took the pills?"

Adriana looked up, bewildered. Wasn't it obvious? "I wanted to die," she whispered.

The doctor frowned. "Was there something in particular that made you want to die?" Adriana remembered the darkness engulfing her mind after taking the pills. What had happened just before? She couldn't think.

"Come now, this is serious. Something must have happened to trigger you to take those pills."

Adriana remembered feeling like she had reached the end of a road, when Dr. Bob told her she needed to see a psychiatrist and take medication. But before that...the revelation that the mother in her head—familiar, dependable and severe as a winter storm—had been turned upside down by Bartholomew Banks.

Dr. W. watched her from a comfortable swivel chair. He leaned back, flexing his fingers. Adriana cleared her throat. She sensed this doctor was getting tired of her, that he wanted to go on to someone more interesting. "I... I think I was... I don't know," she said, lamely. How could she describe her intolerable anxiety about her mother, who had taken up residence in the dusty back corner of her imagination like a spider? She felt guilty and bereft, traitorous and like one betrayed—a dilemma that she neither wanted to expose, nor thought anyone else would understand.

Dr. W. had moved on. "Have you been feeling sad lately?" Adriana nodded. "Have you been sleeping more than usual?" Adriana looked down and nodded again. "What about your appetite?" She shook her head. "Does that mean you don't have much of an appetite?" Nod. "On a scale of one to ten, with one being terrible and ten being great, how would you rate your mood?"

Adriana tried to think. "Five?" she offered.

Dr. W. raised an eyebrow. "Five is in the "okay" range. Are you really at five?" Adriana reconsidered "Three?" she ventured. The psychiatrist frowned and scribbled something down on his notepad. He raised his head to look at her "Do you feel like you might harm yourself or someone else?" Adriana held her head and began to sob, a slow, anguished, looping sound.

"I think perhaps for your own safety, you should consider staying in hospital for a little while." The doctor shifted the notepad on his knee. "Would you agree to being admitted to the Short Stay unit?" Adriana gripped her head in her hands. Her hair was damp and her skull felt fragile. "Adriana," the psychiatrist said kindly. "Look at me." Adriana looked at his shoes, embarrassed, her nose running. "There are some very good medications that will help you feel better, I promise you that." Adriana nodded, unconvinced. Her mother's eyes were on her, cold and grey.

The doctor opened the door for Adriana. She walked out shakily, into the hallway. Her father was on the phone in the waiting area, his eyes squinting, fiercely concentrated on his conversation, but when he saw Adriana, he said a quick goodbye and hung up. Adriana figured it must have been Aunt Penny he was talking to. Now the Toronto relatives would know. A crushing blow to her spirit.

Dr. W. addressed Mr. Song as though he were a customer. "Adriana has decided to stay in hospital for now," he said. "Given her mood and mental state, I support her decision wholeheartedly. We'll admit her to Short Stay for observation."

Mr. Song looked stricken. Through her tears, Adriana squinted at his shoes. He rubbed her back awkwardly, as she let her hair fall in front of her face, unable to look at him.

"Alright," said Mr. Song gruffly. "Alright." He wiped his face.

The door to the Short Stay unit at the end of the hall opened and a middle-aged man came out, dressed in a coat that looked too small for him, and what looked like a Russian fur hat with ear flaps. He wore tinted sun glasses, and his pot belly overflowed his trousers. As the doctor led the way toward the Short Stay unit, Mr. Song walking forlornly behind them, the man stopped in the middle of the hall, clicked his heels and gave a salute. "Long live Chairman Mao," he said in a slightly garbled voice. "Are you Chinese?" he asked Adriana's father.

Mr. Song tried to smile. "Don't bother these nice people,

Redgie," said the doctor, shooing the man away.

Redgie looked offended. "I'm not trying to bother them, doc," he muttered and kicked his foot in the air as he continued erratically down the hall. The psychiatrist took no notice.

Adriana stood on the threshold of Short Stay. If she crossed it she would become a mental patient. The nursing station directly across from the unit entrance was cheery, with a stencilled border of ivy leaves and a couple stuffed animals perched on the counter. Behind it, a heavy set middle-aged woman with a blonde perm smiled at Adriana. "You must be Miss Song," she said in a hearty voice. "I'm Joanne. And is this your Dad?" she gestured toward Mr. Song. He nodded. "We'll get you settled in," she said, "and give your Dad some information." Mr. Song, his eyes pained, let go of Adriana's arm. She had a feeling of slipping away in a current, while her father stood on dry land, watching her go.

CHAPTER 10

Her father left, giving her a rough kiss on the cheek to try to hide his distress. Adriana stood in the middle of the hall on Short Stay, swaying a little. It was quiet, except for the television in the corner of the common room, which no one was watching.

A woman came out of the bathroom wearing a johnny shirt, a purse on her arm. Her eyes were teary and her straight, thin brown hair wisped as she walked. She smiled weakly at Adriana and, as though in slow motion, walked toward one of the bedrooms. Joanne spoke to her as though to a child. "You going to lie down sweetie?" she asked in a loud voice. The woman nodded.

Joanne opened the door to a small single room with a view of the harbour. Adriana gazed at the rectangle of light. She couldn't see the water from the doorway, just the bleak light from the cloud-filled sky. The bed was smooth and cold looking, covered with a tawny bed spread, the white sheet beneath it turned over neatly.

Joanne opened a closet door next to the room. "Here's a couple johnny shirts and a pair of slippers," she said briskly, bustling to put them at the bottom of the bed. Adriana looked around drearily. There was a chair, a bedside table with a drawer, and a locker. The tiled floor was waxed to a dull shine.

"Your dad is going to bring you some clothes and things. If you need anything, just give me a shout," Joanne said, slightly out of breath. "I'll be your nurse till 7 this evening." She departed, leaving the door to the room open halfway.

Adriana sat on the bed looking at the door. She didn't know whether she was allowed to close it or not. But just then, a man with dark skin and black sunglasses shut the door with a loud bang. Adriana startled, but did not get up. She heard other doors further down the hall bang shut, and Joanne's angry voice yelling" Melvin, keep that up and you're headed for *TQ*."

Adriana wondered wearily what TQ was. She sat on the bed, looking at her hands which were white and cold and useless. She got under the covers and curled in on herself. Her eyes were wide open, the clicking of the abacus of her thoughts, deafening. She lay that way for ten minutes until her eyes closed and the muffled sounds from the hallway blended into one another.

CHAPTER 11

Adriana woke the next morning, hollow. On the chair next to her bed was a bag with a few things in it. Some T-shirts and underthings, a pair of jeans, a tooth brush. Also a bag of chocolate covered peanuts, but the thought of eating made her nauseous.

She looked at her watch. It was 10 a.m. and she'd slept since yesterday afternoon. Even though she'd just woken, the day seemed old and stale as a crust of bread. Maybe that was how things were here—dry and endless.

Adriana doubted that the nurses would let her stay in bed all day. As if on cue, there was a knock at the door and Adriana expected to see Joanne's blonde perm. But instead, it was a younger woman, a strikingly attractive one, who stuck her head in. "Feeling like getting up?" She asked, kindly from the foot of Adriana's mattress, her honey-streaked hair still neatly pinned behind her head. Adriana felt a sudden pang. Her mother had never taught her how to take care of her hair. She looked away toward the dark scuff mark on the wall.

"Someone's been moving furniture," the nurse said leaning forward to try to catch Adriana's eye. "I'm Fiona. I'll be your main nurse," she said, smiling and twinkling. "We'll get to know each other a lot better soon," she said. "In fact I'm going to have to be completely impolite and get your weight and your blood pressure, my dear, before we've even been properly introduced. The doctor wants to see you this afternoon, so we need to get them before lunch."

Adriana closed her eyes and didn't bother to answer. It didn't matter to her whether they drained every last drop of blood from her body, really. Fiona was quiet for a moment then patted the bed. "You rest for now," she said. "I'll be back later."

Adriana lay there, but couldn't close her eyes. She stared up at the ceiling tiles, which were full of little air holes, and she imagined snakes falling from them. If only she could sleep. The sunlight glittered on the surface of the harbour. To Adriana it was like a man cheerfully leering at her; the sun was so unreachable from the cave she inhabited, that its very existence seemed questionable. She closed her eyes and let the darkness of her own mind, a familiar darkness, shelter her.

She woke to the sound of a telephone ringing in an empty room. Fiona stood at the foot of her bed. "I bet you'd sleep through an earthquake, what?" she said, smiling. Adriana blinked. The fire alarm was ringing. "It's just a drill," she said, "but we have to go outside."

Adriana got up and made sure her johnny shirt was tied in back. Fiona handed her another one to wear as a bathrobe, covering the gap in the back and took Adriana's coat and boots, from the locker. "You're going to need these," she said. Adriana put them on. They were about all she had, until her father brought her things from home.

The hallway was full of people. They gathered at the

end of the hall near the fire exit. A nurse with a clipboard hurriedly checked to make sure all were present. "Okay, everybody, follow the dude with the red hat." A male nurse wearing a red toque put his hand up and waved.

Redgie, silent and stoned-looking, walked past Adriana without saying a word. The woman in the red parka clutching her purse, muttered something about the stupidity of the drill, and how she couldn't even have a smoke, which was the only reason she'd even go outside. They were a motley bunch, Adriana thought, watching their strange, shuffling gaits in boots too big or two small, jackets open over their johnny shirts.

They made their way downstairs and outside onto the back lawn. There were other groups of patients and nurses. Adriana could tell who the nurses were, sticking together in little groups, talking animatedly and laughing. The patients were the ones that seemed adrift, barely hanging on to the group. At the far end of the lawn was a swing set, where patients sat on the swings without swinging, their feet dangling on the ground.

Redgie kicked at a tuft of grass. "Whatcha doing, Redgie," a tall male nurse asked, his voice tinged with accusation. Redgie muttered something and walked away. "Stick with the group Redgie," the nurse called, then started walking after him. Redgie broke into an awkward run, tripping and sliding down the grassy hill. At the bottom he stumbled, and ran again, as the nurse called for help. A couple security guards joined the chase and tackled Redgie when he got to the sewage pond.

Adriana could hear the male nurse asking Redgie why he ran, and Redgie, sputtering with angry tears, shouting, "I hate it here. Why won't you let me go?" A nurse nearby chuckled and said something in a low voice to Fiona, whose smile tightened. She didn't say anything but moved away from the nurse to talk to the woman in the red parka.

"Marlene," she said. "Are you going to bake some more of those yummy oatcakes you made last week in Occupational Therapy?"

Marlene thought about it for a moment. "Well, I was thinking of making brownies," she said seriously, then smiled. "You liked my oatcakes, huh?" She puffed out her chest.

Fiona nodded, her eyes big. "But I'd take a brownie!" she said and gave Marlene's arm a squeeze.

Adriana felt mildly uncomfortable. Something about the way Fiona gazed at her, as if to make her complicit in this exchange. Adriana was alert to condescension even in its most seemingly benign forms.

Someone shouted "All clear!" and people began to filter back inside. Adriana noticed her little group was much smaller than the two other units' crowds of patients. Redgie went straight to stand in front of the med room door, but the nurses ignored him. Marlene sagged into the rocker in front of the television. Adriana stood in front of the nursing station, looking around her. The patients all seemed tired, while the nurses were energetic and chatty. Even Fiona, wisps of hair coming loose from her bun, was laughing as she worked.

Adriana stood in front of the nursing station, looking around her. She felt like she wanted to talk to someone— well, Fiona actually—but she was almost embarrassed to admit it. Fiona was rushing around as usual. With an armful of bed linens, she called, "Upstairs, downstairs," over her shoulder to another nurse who gave her an exaggerated grin and a wink. Adriana wondered who the upstairs people were. Not the patients surely? But who else's bed linens would Fiona be dealing with?

Adriana went to her room and got into bed, pulling the blankets up around her chin. The room reminded her of a shoe box, with the lid on tight. She was gripped by a wild fear that she'd never get out. But she continued to lie there, her heart beating against the ceiling, as though it would burst the lid off the place. Eventually she closed her eyes and after awhile, she fell asleep, as if it were the only solace and protection available to her in that place.

Late in the afternoon, Adriana awoke to a knock at her door. It was Fiona. "It's time to get up my, pretty," she said cheerily. "Dr. Chen would like to speak to you, and I have to get your vitals first."

Adriana was mildly surprised to hear the doctor had a Chinese name. She folded the blankets aside and stood up shakily, then trailed Fiona to a room down the hall. Melvin was coming toward them but gave them a wide berth, crossing the hall to close Adriana's door, firmly and quietly.

Fiona patted the examination table. "Right up here, my love," she said. She took the blood pressure cuff from the cart and Adriana gave her her arm with the sleeve rolled up. As Fiona pumped up the cuff, Adriana felt her heart beating on her ears.

"Blood pressure's up," said Fiona. "Are you nervous about talking to the doctor?" she asked, confidential and friendly. Adriana shook her head slowly. "No need," said Fiona, smiling as she peeled the cuff from Adriana's arm. "She's just a little bit of a thing, wouldn't hurt a fly."

Fiona left Adriana in a long narrow interview room while she went to find Dr. Chen. Adriana looked around her at the vinyl covered chairs—institutional, like everything else about the place. She didn't understand how someone thought it could be healing, to be surrounded by impersonal ugliness. Instead it left her with a stark hungover feeling, made worse by the florescent lights. And Fiona, she was like a cheerleader for this place. She was sunny and warm but Adriana would bet anything she had a golden life—a well-off husband, beautiful children—and that she shook the dust of this place off her shoes at the end of the day without a second thought.

There was a knock on the door, and Fiona entered, followed by a petite Chinese woman with a polite and fleeting smile. Dr. Chen shook her hand and sat in the chair closest to the door, which Adriana thought she likely chose in order to be close to an escape route. When Dr. Chen smiled again, her face wrinkled in an alarming way, as though it was not accustomed to the expression. She scratched something at the top of a yellow legal pad. Adriana slumped over her hollow stomach. "So?" Dr. Chen asked. "What brought you here to hospital?"

Adriana gaped slightly. Surely it was on her chart that she had taken an overdose. "I swallowed sleeping pills," she said, her voice quavery and hoarse. Fiona smiled, sympathetic and encouraging.

Dr. Chen nodded. "And... what was your intention when you swallowed those pills?" she asked, in a conversational tone. Adriana felt confused. "I wanted to die," she said. It seemed to be the expected answer. Dr. Chen nodded and scratched something on her legal pad. "And why did you want to die?" she asked. Adriana gaped.

"Surely there must have been something that made you want to end your life," Dr. Chen asked, with a small tight smile. Her pen, in her small brown hand, was poised to write. Adriana tried to think. She'd quit going to classes and it had felt like a wall had crumbled from beneath her. And then there was nothing, days and days filled with nothing, her mother's eyes always on her, reproachful and accusatory. Adriana had tried to escape Viera's gaze—but then when Bartholomew Banks conjured her mother from the dead, it was as though she was a different person than the one Adriana had clung to for all these years. She didn't think the doctor would understand, how this discrepancy had swept the earth from under her.

Dr. Chen shifted in her seat, leaning toward Adriana. "Was there a trigger? Did something happen that pushed you over the edge?" Adriana shook her head, giving up. Then said weakly, "My mother."

Fiona looked concerned. Dr. Chen looked at her notes. "Your chart says your mother died when you were 11 years old," she said. Adriana nodded. Dr. Chen pushed on. "So what was it about your mother that made you feel like killing yourself?"

The words seemed too harsh, to Adriana. She let her hair fall in front of her face, and refused to speak. Fiona cleared her throat, a small, apologetic sound. Adriana looked up at her, saw her eyes shining with concern.

Dr. Chen sat back and waited, but Adriana was not prepared to offer her anything. Dr. Chen made a point of sighing. "Okay Adriana, I understand that you have been depressed for some time."

Adriana nodded, but didn't look up. She closed her eyes, and tried to hear the sound of the waves breaking against the shore, down the hill below the railway track. Dr. Chen seemed to soften. "How would you feel about my asking your father for some information about you? It would help me understand you and your situation better." Adriana nodded. "Alright?" said Dr. Chen. "I think we're done for today." She stood up and bowed slightly, ushering Fiona and Adriana out of the room.

When Adriana finally emerged from her room again, in the same rumpled johnny shirt they'd given her to wear at the ER, Fiona ran Adriana a bath and gave her some shampoo to wash the charcoal out of her hair. "It's good you're getting cleaned up now, my duck" Fiona had said in her warm Newfoundlandese, handing her a towel and a couple fresh johnny shirts.

Adriana lay in the bathtub in the little room off the women's washroom. Like the toilet stalls, the door had no lock, but a little knob to turn the sign under the handle from "vacant" to "occupied." Adriana was miserable enough that it barely mattered. Her middle, sunken below the level of her jutting hip bones, allowed water to pool between them. Having her stomach pumped had given her a raw throat and a feeling of being scoured internally. Then she'd thrown up the charcoal drink they'd insisted she finish to coat her stomach, leaving her as empty as she'd ever been. Adriana covered her face with her hands and sank lower into the water. She had stopped doing her face exercises , and every other routine that had given form to her days, to concentrate on the wound that had opened inside her, like a split seam.

CHAPTER 12

Someone rapped on the tub room door and Adriana sat up slowly, hugging herself with her arms. The bathwater had grown tepid around her. She could almost pretend she wasn't a patient in the mental hospital, except for the smell—a flat, industrial-chemical scent. "Ma'am?" the person at the door said in a loud, but garbled voice. "You almost done? I wanna shower."

Adriana, her voice croaky from disuse, said "I'll be out soon." Whoever was at the door mumbled something and turned on the tap at the sink and began brushing her teeth.

Adriana had no idea how long she'd been sitting there. Her fingers had wrinkled and there were goose bumps all over her arms. She felt weak enough that she turned to face the side of the bathtub and used her arms to push herself up to standing.

After putting on the fresh johnny shirt Fiona had given her, and another one to cover her back, Adriana opened the door. The woman in the red parka was standing at the row of sinks, her mouth full of foam. She made room for Adriana to get past her, but Adriana indicated she was headed for the toilet stalls. "Good lunch today, hon." The woman

in red said. "Shepherd's pie. The Lord is my shepherd."
Adriana nodded, awkwardly. "Everyone wants to know
why I wear this coat. It's my coat and I don't want anyone
to steal it. God damn thieves," she said with vehemence. "I
don't mean you, hon. Don't worry, I don't mean you. I can
tell you're honest. I'm Marlene by the way. You have a good
pee," she said, spitting the last of the toothpaste in the sink
and disappearing into tub room.

Adriana sat in the stall and let her bladder relax. She
was mortified, but somehow her eyes were dry. What was
she doing here, in the mental hospital, with people like
Marlene in the red parka? Bizarre people, people who were
stragglers on the edges of humanity. She was afraid of them,
and most of all, she didn't want to be one of them.

Someone came into the washroom, weeping. Adriana
could see fluctuations in the light on the bathroom floor,
indicating the woman outside was moving around. Adriana
waited for a few moments, wondering whether she could
stay in the bathroom stall unnoticed. But the woman began
to sing, in a tearful voice, "We Shall Overcome" and Adriana felt she couldn't just sit there. She opened the door of
the stall and walked to the sink beside the weeping woman,
who was combing her wispy brown hair as she sang. The
woman took no notice of her. Adriana looked at her own
face in the mirror—it was pale with dark rings under her
eyes, like a drowned woman.

She opened the bathroom door to the hallway, not sure
what she'd find. In the common room, the television was
blaring an ad for some medication or other. Redgie was sitting in a rocker, rocking away. He was wearing a Russian fur
hat, a johnny shirt, faded track pants and army boots. Adriana stood in the middle of the hall, unsure of what to do. The

man pointed at the TV without looking at her. "You see that? That's the drug the CIA gave me when they were trying to get me to talk about what I knew about 9/11." He shook his fist in the air and began to rock with fierce purpose.

The man glanced over at her during the next commercial. "Hey you're the Chinese girl," he said, smiling. "I like the Chinese. You're going to take over the world." He continued rocking and nodded toward the television, as though to acknowledge he was still listening. Suddenly, he stood up, his face expressionless and walked out of the common room. Adriana heard him tell Joanne, the middle aged nurse with the blonde perm who had first greeted her in short stay, "I need a dose."

Joanne clucked her tongue sympathetically, and unlocked the door to the med room. "TV getting to you, Redgie?" she asked. He nodded, his face pale and sweating. "Why don't you go lie down for awhile and let this Ativan get to work? In the meantime," she said winking an exaggerated wink in the direction of the nursing station, "We'll change the channel." Redgie swallowed the small white pill and with the strange slow motion gait of a drugged man he walked toward his room.

Adriana felt suddenly, drastically alone. The TV blared on, but the common room was empty except for her. She got up, clutching her johnny shirt around her. Her stomach was empty but the thought of eating made her feel sick. She went back to her room to lie down, under the white blanket that made her think of a shroud.

Adriana was asleep when her father came to visit that evening. It was her first full day on Short Stay, he noted. Thankfully, he'd had his own doctor's appointment and had been able to take the time off work, which seemed to him, at this particular time in his life, an irrelevance. He'd told his GP of 20 years that Adriana was in hospital and that he felt a kind of vertigo, as though he stood on the edge of a cliff. The doctor nodded his head and asked him about his sleep. Mr. Song realized he'd spent half the night awake, thinking, but the last thing he wanted was a prescription for sleeping pills. He didn't want them anywhere in his house.

Mr. Song sat quietly in a chair at the end of her bed, reading the paper. He always folded the paper up to show only the article he was reading, never spread out the pages like Jazz liked to do, which is part of what drove them crazy about each other.

When Adriana awoke, her father was immersed in the news of the world. He shook his head, squinted, and whistled under his breath. Adriana blinked at him and shifted to a sitting position. She felt angular, every bone aching.

Her father looked up, and his face was strange to Adriana. She noticed the wrinkles around his mouth, the pain in his eyes. She turned her face away. Mr. Song tried to erase his sad expression. "Hi, honey," he said. Adriana raised her fingers and let them fall back on the bed. Mr. Song took her hand, noticing how cold it was.

"Last night I brought you some clothes and things from the bathroom at home," he said helplessly. Adriana looked away from her father at the locker in the corner of the room, as there was no where else to put her eyes. The locker was brown, with a fake wood grain pattern, and a latch for a lock. It was, she noted, for a very thin person, big enough for a coffin.

Mr. Song looked at his hands and cleared his throat. "Have you talked to the doctor today?" he asked.

Adriana responded hoarsely, "Yes." She let her chin fall to

her chest and closed her eyes. She hadn't called him to let him know, Mr. Song thought, a small hurt, but a significant one. She didn't want to talk to him about what was happening to her.

Mr. Song stood up, saying, in a trembling voice, "I just have to go to the bathroom." Adriana did not acknowledge him. As he left the room she lay down again, hugging one of the pillows to her chest.

When he returned to her room, after splashing water in his face in an attempt to dissolve his worry, there was no one around, only the television blaring in the common room. He opened Adriana's door slightly, saw she was asleep and stood looking at her. Her lips relaxed and slightly parted, her face finally smoothed of the ravages of her depression. She looked much like she had as a child, on an early summer evening, when his wife made her go to bed, despite the fact that neighbourhood children were still playing outdoors in the sunshine. He would check on her 15 minutes later and find her with her eyes closed, breathing quietly and rhythmically, her face golden in the setting sun. His wife had been right that she was tired, right that is was time for bed. It always reassured him that she knew what was best, that there was safety in this world after all.

As Mr. Song turned to leave, Fiona stopped by with her clipboard. She cocked her head to one side. "Still sleeping?" she asked in a low voice. Mr. Song nodded. "Would you have time to talk to the doctor?" He eagerly agreed.

Fiona led him to an interview room, and Mr. Song was surprised to see an Asian-looking woman sitting in one of chairs. She smiled primly and nodded, out of a sense of kinship, Mr. Song thought. "Sit down please," she said.

The chat with the doctor lasted 20 minutes, at the end

of which Mr. Song exited the interview room, looking anguished. The doctor had quizzed him on Adriana's early life, her relationship to both her parents and her sister, her school years and his own role in her upbringing. It was painful to remember his wife's death, her sometimes stormy relationship with Adriana and harsh approach to raising her. Many a time he had stood between them, shielding Adriana from the wooden spoon that her mother brandished over her for some perceived misdeed. She never mocked his gentleness, but she also never paid attention to his soft remonstrations, though he stood in front of his daughter and received the blows meant for her.

He had never thought his wife abusive—merely volatile and overly passionate—but it seemed that was not the conclusion the doctor had drawn from talking to him. "Does Adriana have any scars?" Dr. Chen asked. Mr. Song was taken aback. He didn't know. It hadn't occurred to him that she might. The thought that his wife would have damaged Adriana in a physical way horrified him. Somehow it seemed more real than the depression, easier to point to as evidence that something really was wrong with his wife's behaviour.

"Adriana needs medication," the doctor said, "but she also needs psychotherapy. We don't do much of that here but I will refer her to a psychiatrist with a private practice before discharge."

Mr. Song nodded, miserably. "That could be in a couple weeks, depending on how she does." Mr. Song wondered what that meant, but the doctor had already put away the file and was standing up to leave. She shook Mr. Song's hand and held the door open for him. Mr. Song had the distinct feeling that he was peripheral to all that happened to Adriana in this place, that he wasn't needed or wanted except for the information he could provide.

Mr. Song walked out to his car, out of the depressing dimness of the hospital. He wondered if mental illness was contagious after all, because he felt shaken, oppressed, and weary. It could just be the barometric pressure, he thought. He drove past the gates where Redgie and the woman in the red parka stood smoking. Both of them waved at him, with the friendliness of those with nothing more to lose. These were Adriana's compatriots, he realized, with a strange mingling of hope and hopelessness. Mr. Song raised his hand to acknowledge them and Redgie, standing tall, saluted him.

CHAPTER 13

The next day, Adriana got out of bed long after lunch hour to go to the washroom. The sound of regular, muffled banging came through the wall. But when she stepped into the hall-way, she no longer heard it. There was no one around, either at the nursing station or the common room. She could see the backs of a couple nurses as they worked on their computers, oblivious to the absence of people on the unit. The TV blared as usual, like a mad person talking to itself, Adriana thought anxiously, her hands curled in tight fists. She escaped into the washroom which was empty, splashed water on her face and felt some semblance of normalcy,

On her way back to her room, she swayed slightly, her stomach drawn and empty. When she reached her door, she heard an urgent tapping coming from the door next to hers. She hadn't noticed before but there was a window in the door, covered with a small curtain, and the door was bolted on the outside.

Adriana hesitated for a moment, knowing she was about to break some kind of rule. She opened the curtain and, startled, jerked away from the face pressed against the Plexiglass.

"Hey," he said through the door "Don't worry, I won't tell. Can you just open the door for me?"

Adriana stood still. "Please," he said. "I need to get out of TQ."

So this was TQ. Adriana froze. The man's face contorted. "I need a cigarette. I need to pee." He started to cry. "Get me outta here." He said to no one in particular, turning away from the door. Adriana heard him unzip his pants and she turned away from his sobbing as he emptied his bladder into the corner of the room.

A surge of anxiety engulfed Adriana. She went to knock on the door of the nursing station. Joanne was talking on the phone and seeing it was Adriana said, "Just a minute." She turned her back to Adriana and continued speaking in a low voice, doodling on a message pad.

Fiona was walking down the hall toward her. "What can I do for you, love?" she asked Adriana. It was hard to get the words out, for some reason.

"The guy in TQ," she said. "He needs to get out. He...he peed himself," Adriana said, bitterly. The whole world was narrow and dark.

Fiona looked concerned. "Adriana, it's kind of you to worry about Jeff, but he can take care of himself. He needs to be in Therapeutic Quiet right now, but don't you worry about him. You just concentrate on what you can do for yourself." Adriana covered her face with her hands. She had the urge to collapse on the floor and just let whatever happened, happen, but instead she walked back to her room. There was no sound from TQ and Adriana didn't look through the Plexiglass window to make sure Jeff was still there. She lay down on the bed and thought about Jeff lying face down on the mattress, with the stench of piss rising from the corner. An image flitted through her mind of her bed at home, and how she'd left it unmade. She knew what her mother would think, but for some reason her mother was silent on the issue, glowering at her from the shadows of her mind.

Adriana was woken at supper time by the call, "Trays are up." She noticed the door to TQ was ajar. She didn't look to see whether Jeff was still there, but she doubted it

In the kitchen people were eating supper from grey plastic trays. The clock said it was a quarter to five, too early to eat, she thought. But she sat down at a table where Marlene was carefully pushing mashed turnip onto her fork with a plastic knife.

"Hello, dearie," she said, "Do you want your dessert or can I have it?" Adriana took the lid off her tray. There was a couple slices of grey roast beef, mashed potatoes and turnip, and a small dish of apple crumble, which she passed to Marlene. "Thanks love," Marlene said, patting her shoulder. "You're alright, dearie."

Adriana looked around. Redgie, the man with the Russian hat, now wore only his sunglasses and street clothes. He must be doing better, Adriana thought. At the same table was a thin young man with dishevelled hair and the shakes, shovelling mashed potatoes into his mouth. It was the guy from TQ, she was pretty sure. He was focussed on his food, as though he were tunnelling though a mountain.

Redgie pushed himself away from the table abruptly and stood up. "Can I buy a smoke off you, Jeff?" he asked the young man, who looked up briefly and shook his head.

"I don't have enough for myself," he said. "Sorry." Redgie mumbled something and went to the door of the unit. He pushed the buzzer.

"Hey can somebody let me out?" Adriana realized that she was now locked in, and it made her feel panicky.

She made her way back from the kitchen to her room. It felt like the dead end of something, a place from which there was no escape. She realized that hiding there away from the other patients was a bit like a self-imposed TQ. Only sleep gave her some respite, but even that was beginning to lose its sweetness. Her body was weary of it, she realized.

CHAPTER 14

"I want to bring Beth home."

In Adriana's other life—before hospital—she sometimes thought about Beth, wondered how she managed. Wondered whether, at the age of 11, when their mother was dying, she could have taken care of her younger sister. Beth had their mother's brown curls and blue eyes, and stood out from her adopted family like a peach in a basket of plums. She was only ten years old and spoke Chinese fluently, whereas Adriana knew not a word. When Adriana and her father went to visit, her sister had crying spells and shrank behind Aunt Penny, as though from a poisonous snake. Adriana thought she must be afraid that they would try to whisk her off to Nova Scotia.

And now her fear—and Adriana's—was coming true. Beth would parachute into her and her father's life, like an enemy soldier.

On their last visit to Toronto, Mr. Song had come away pale and shaky. He saw his wife's features in Beth's face and wanted nothing more than to embrace her and claim her as his daughter, but she would have none of it. She hid behind Aunt Penny, who did not push her forward, as Adriana would have done, but talked to her in whispers to convince her to greet her father. Beth became more and more hysterical the harder Aunt Penny tried, so in the end both she and Mr. Song gave up. Beth hid her face in Aunt Penny's shoulder and they left without saying goodbye.

On the plane ride home, Adriana put her hand on her father's hand, and sent him telepathic messages. Don't worry, she will come around. Don't worry, she's still young and there is plenty of time. Mr. Song kept his eyes closed, his forehead wrinkled with pain. Adriana wished she could smooth his brow, comfort him, but she knew she there was nothing she could do. Her father's pain made her feel like a new born baby, not yet oriented in time and space—helpless.

Adriana used to write Beth letters, in language an eleven-year-old could understand. "We were happy to see you in Toronto," she scrawled. "I hope you can visit us sometime." There were stickers, hearts and dogs and cats. Secretly, Adriana thought she might be terrifying her sister with these notes, and hoped that was the case. She didn't really want a spoiled pre-pubescent in her life. Beth never wrote back except at Christmas and on her birthday. Adriana could tell the dutiful notes that said "Thank you for the gift" and not much else must have been Aunt Penny's doing.

Mr. Song went to Toronto for a few days, during which time his sister Penny died and Beth had a kind of breakdown. At least that's how Adriana thought of it, when her father described what had happened over the phone. Adriana clutched the payphone receiver in the hallway on the day she was allowed to start wearing her street clothes again, while her father described how Beth sat next to Penny's bed, holding her hand, even after the machines stopped working and Penny's head fell sideways on her shoulder. Mr. Song had to pull Beth away when the gurney came to take Penny's body, and Beth walked all the way to the service elevator with her hand on Penny's arm, until one of the burly orderlies cleared his throat and told her kindly that she wouldn't be able to come with them. Beth fell into a clump on the floor and Mr. Song had to haul her up by the armpits, a dead weight.

CHAPTER 15

A few days later, Mr. Song arrived at the hospital with a bag full of White Rabbits and sesame candies from Toronto's Chinatown. He hugged Adriana and she could feel his relief, that he was home with both of his daughters nearby, as troubled as they were. "Beth is in a state of shock. I can't leave her alone or I'm afraid she'll do something drastic," he admitted. She was actually in the car with Madeleine, the neighbour woman with red hair, manicured nails, and a smoker's rasp, who had shown an interest in Mr. Song after Adriana's mother died. Mr. Song was friendly but did not return her affections—still, she made herself available any time he needed a favour, and he needed one now.

"Can I ask Beth to come up?" Mr. Song put the question to Adriana, meekly, but with his eyes narrowed and mouth tight. He was expecting her to refuse, but Adriana nodded her head weakly and watched her father soften. "Okay, darling, I'll go get her," he said with a relieved smile, brushing the hair from his face. He still had a full head of black hair, after all these years, Adriana noted dully.

Adriana was sitting up in bed, her eyelids squeezed shut as though she were in pain. When she heard the door open, she opened her eyes and saw Mr. Song standing behind Beth with his hands on her shoulders. Adriana raised one hand but did not smile.

"Adriana's ill, Beth," Mr. Song murmured. "We won't stay long." Adriana wanted to stretch one of Beth's curls and watch it sproing back to hit her in the head.

Beth's face was pale and fearful. Adriana put out her hand. "I'm sorry about Aunt Penny," she croaked. Beth put her hands over her face and turned to Mr. Song, who hugged her awkwardly.

"Beth, Adriana is only here temporarily. She'll be better soon, and then she'll come home and you'll both be able to keep each other company." Beth was sobbing into her hands, a sound that Adriana remembered well. Blubbering was what she'd call it, a graceless sound, heavy with grief. Adriana suddenly felt sorry for Beth, who thought she had no one and nothing, even though her family was right here around her. Beth looked up at her with red-rimmed eyes, and suddenly stopped, hiccupping loudly. She stared at Adriana, as though she were trying to place her.

Adriana put her hand out to Beth. "It's okay," she said, "I'm not contagious." Beth made no move to step toward her and Adriana let her hand fall on the bed.

Later that night, after her visitors had gone home, Adriana lay in her bed, wishing she could see the stars. There were a few visible through the wire mesh; their clean sparkle tantalizing and unreachable. Once when her parents had taken her on a road trip across the country to visit relatives, she had stood outside their motel in the dark, astounded by the spill of the Milky Way across the sky. She had never seen it before, and it made her feel small, but also like she belonged to creation, in a way she hadn't felt since.

Now she was part of a tiny constellation—herself and Beth and their father—pinned against the darkness. She *belonged* to something. Family was the gravitational bond that kept a person from being swept off, alone, in the ineluctable expansion of the universe.

There was a knock on the door. It was Jerry. "Adriana? You Adriana?" he said. Adriana squinted into the light of the hallway. It was the first time a patient had said her name. "Phone's for you," he said leaving her door open. Weakly, Adriana made her way into the hallway to the pay phone, which dangled by its cord.

It was her father. "How are you, darling?" he asked.

Adriana hesitated. How could she tell him? That Beth being here had altered the map of things, of everything. "I'm okay," she said, and it was a lie that was nevertheless tinged with truth. She felt somehow calmer, perhaps resigned, waiting for whatever came next. Her mother stood inside her, faintly mocking. What does come next? But somehow she looked paler, and her voice seemed to drift toward Adriana like a ghost.

"Guess what Beth said on the drive home from the hospital?" Mr. Song asked, happily. Adriana didn't really care that much. "What?" she asked listlessly. She could hear Mr. Song smiling on the other end. "She said you look like her mother." He laughed.

Adriana was confused for a moment. She didn't look anything like their mother, who had died eight years ago. But then it struck her—Beth was referring to Aunt Penny, whom she had called Mum all her young life. Just as when Adriana looked at Beth and saw Viera, Beth saw Penny's features mirrored in Adriana's black hair and slanted eyes. And

Adriana had the strange revelation that when she and her sister looked at one another, they were each seeing someone from beyond this world, someone who unexpectedly took leave of their lives to make the long journey beyond the star-filled universe.

Adriana woke up the next day and ate her way through her breakfast tray. The eggs, toast and cereal, all of them obstacles to her freedom. Fiona had told her yesterday that if she started eating, she could have passes to go outside on the hospital grounds. That, Adriana thought, was blackmail. As if sensing her hostility Fiona sat down on the edge of Adriana's bed. "We need to know you're not going to keel over from hunger," she said, a little bit of Newfoundland slipping into her voice.

After breakfast, Adriana headed back to her room, because really, what else was there to do? She needed something to occupy her, so her mind didn't grind like rusty gears. Adriana made a couple origami cranes out of an old newspaper she'd found in the common room and left them on her window sill. Something stirred in her brain, like a sluggish goldfish in a bowl of water. Something in there was trying to connect. She felt miserable, the darkness in her a permanent, tumescent bloom. Every fold of the paper was painful, cutting into her consciousness like a sharp-edged thing.

Someone knocked and Fiona stuck her head around the door. "Can we talk a minute, love?" she asked. Adriana felt relief. Something to do, that would relieve the pressure in her brain. Fiona stepped inside and sat down in the chair. "How was your visit with your sister yesterday?" she asked. Adriana's eyes widened. Was it possible Fiona knew how she felt about her sister? "Your father told Joanne on his way out last night about your family situation. I am sorry to hear your aunt passed on," Fiona said, eyes shiny with sympathy. Adriana felt guilty. She hadn't given Penny a second thought. It frightened her, that her telescope was so focussed on her tangled self that everything around her seemed peripheral. Her mother, arms folded, mocked her. *You are so self-centred, you can't see what is in front of you.*

Adriana rubbed her forehead. Fiona leaned toward her. "What is it?" she asked, her voice gentle with concern Adriana felt her resistance dissolve. Everything was too much for her. She shut her eyes and wept.

Fiona sat beside her on the bed and put an arm around her shoulder. Everything spilled out of Adriana in a flood. Between sobs, she talked about how she resented her sister, how her mother wouldn't leave her in peace, how she feared the future and didn't see her way out of this mental hospital. Fiona, cooing reassuringly, stroked her hair in sympathy. Adriana wailed and whimpered, but at the end of it, she felt—instead of emptied, instead of humiliated and broken— like something had been filled in. Adriana wiped her dripping nose on her sleeve.

"There, my duck. That's a bit better isn't it?" Fiona asked softly. Adriana hung her head, and nodded, her hair hiding her face, which she imagined was blotchy and red. Fiona pushed the hair out of her eyes, and patted her hand. "It's not surprising you're worried about how it will be now your sister is home," she said. "It sounds like your thoughts about your mother don't help matters." Adriana felt partly relieved but couldn't give up her wariness entirely. Didn't Fiona judge her? And even if she didn't, did that make Adriana any less worthy of censure?

"It takes a lot of energy to talk about this life stuff," said

Fiona. "You just rest now. The doctor might want to see you later." Adriana realized she *was* very tired. It was a real kind of tired, not the endless malaise she'd been feeling for months. She closed her eyes and imagined her mother, looking somehow smaller and less substantial, sitting at the kitchen table, smoking a cigarette.

Adriana was asleep when the doctor came to her room. She awoke to the sound of the door opening, "Sorry to disturb you," said Dr. Chen. "Can we have a talk in the interview room?"

Adriana put on a pair of foam slippers and a sweater. She was beginning to look the part of a mental patient, she thought, and tried to pat her tousled hair into place. The doctor sat in the chair near the door, next to Fiona while Adriana sat in the farthest seat by the window. The distance between them was awkward and cool, but none of them remarked on it.

Dr. Chen cut to the chase. "We're noticing you sleep a lot in the daytime Adriana," she said. Adriana looked down. "That's okay, but you're going to have to try to make an effort to spend more time awake. We'll get you to look at the schedule for Occupational Therapy with Fiona. There's also the gym and the pool. Do you swim?" Adriana looked up.

Adriana opened her mouth but no words came out. Fiona leaned toward her.

"Are you okay? Do you need some water?" she asked. Adriana nodded, and Fiona left the room, leaving the door ajar. "I'll be back in a jiffy," she said.

Dr. Chen cleared her throat. "How have you been sleeping at night?" she asked.

"Fine," she said.

"You've definitely been sleeping more than necessary for

someone of your age. In fact no one but a newborn needs as much sleep as you've been getting." Dr. Chen's nose crinkled when she smiled but her eyes remained distant and appraising.

"Fiona mentioned you talked to her about your mother, and how she criticizes you. Can you tell me more about that?" Adriana was stunned. Of course she should have known that what she said to Fiona would be shared with the doctor, but somehow she hadn't considered how she would feel about it.

Fiona was back with a small paper cup of water. Adriana took it and drank the water down. She hadn't realized how thirsty she was, and now that she did, her throat seemed to burn as though she'd emptied a shot glass.

Fiona reached out to Adriana's arm. "I was croaking for a drink too," she said winking.

Dr. Chen shifted in her seat and neatly tucked a stray skirt edge under her. Fiona leaned back in her chair, looking back and forth between them. "I was just asking Adriana about how her mother appears to her, in the back of her mind."

Fiona nodded slightly. "I mentioned to Dr. Chen about our talk the other day," she explained. Adriana nodded back, but refused to smile.

"I'd like to start you on an anti-depressant," Dr. Chen said. One that will hopefully give your energy levels a boost." She said the name of the drug but Adriana had never heard it before and forgot it almost immediately

"Are you willing to give it a try?" Adriana looked down at her hands. She felt like she was on the edge of a cliff. "Adriana?" Dr. Chen asked.

Adriana looked up. "Will I have to be on it for the rest of my life?" she asked.

Dr. Chen tittered, putting a small ringed hand over her mouth. "The rest of your life is a long time," she said, but didn't answer Adriana's question.

Adriana looked at her hands. They were useless things, she thought. If she didn't agree to take the pills, what would happen? Would she be able to go home? She was aware that her eyes were burning holes, that Dr. Chen was having trouble meeting her gaze. She was afraid of pulling people into her eyes, which she imagined had a strong gravitational pull, like black holes. Was it actually possible that were true?

Adriana covered her eyes with her hand. Dr. Chen tipped her head, curiously. "Is something hurting your eyes? Is the light too bright?" she asked. Adriana shook her head.

"Adriana, can you look at me?" Dr. Chen said. She couldn't. The doctor sounded slightly exasperated. "We would like you to agree to start on medication." Adriana nodded. Her whole body felt like it was being drained of colour and vibrancy, that she would soon become transparent and boneless. She opened her mouth to explain what was happening to her but nothing came out. "Do you agree?" Dr. Chen asked. Adriana felt that it would be pointless to refuse and perhaps whatever pill they wanted to give her would end the intolerable monotony of her thoughts, though she very much doubted it. Adriana nodded and gave Dr. Chen and Fiona a crooked smile.

"Don't worry," Fiona beamed with what seemed like gratitude. "You'll be right as rain, it will just take a little time." Adriana looked at her. Fiona's blonde streaks were pinned up on the back of her head and her perfect, oval nails, painted a pale rose colour. She smiled as though her life was untroubled as a cloud. Adriana could not understand her at all.

CHAPTER 16

In the common room, Melvin sat silently, still wearing his dark sunglasses. Adriana had noticed that something had changed in him—he still spent time pacing the halls, closing doors but, it almost seemed like a formality to him now. She had seen him passing an open door and forgetting to close it, then turning back to correct his "mistake". Could it be that his medications had started working, and whatever it was that compelled him to close doors was fading? Or perhaps it was because he had found a friend in Jeff, who at this moment sat next to Melvin on the couch, watching the Weather Channel.

Adriana plunked herself down into the rocker, noticing Jeff looked harried and his eyes, fearful. Adriana wanted to take his hand and tell him everything was okay, but of course she didn't know if it was true. People were in the hospital for all sorts of reasons. Some had had terrible lives, full of abuse and neglect and addiction. Some would be back again and again, and others would pass this way once and never return. Adriana hoped she was one of these. She didn't know what kind of patient Jeff was.

Jeff looked around him wildly. "I don't know what's

happening with the weather. Something's not right," he said. Adriana looked at the TV. It was hurricane season and the Gulf of Mexico was always full of storms brewing. Adriana pictured driving rain lashing the windows of the hospital, soaking the brickwork; and remembered a young girl from her neighbourhood that she'd babysat a few times, who was afraid of rain. She would begin to cry as the first drops fell and would curl up with a blanket and suck her thumb until it stopped.

Adriana rocked in her chair, watching Jeff shake. She thought he must be cold. "Do you want a blanket?" she asked. He looked at her, his unseeing eyes wide with terror. Jeff rocked back and forth, hard, as though it could take him somewhere. Adriana felt pity, which embarrassed her. What right did she have to feel pity for this man?

Jeff got up from his chair, soundlessly, heading for the bedroom which he shared with Melvin. They often paced the hall together these days, Jeff speaking in a low tone a steady stream of observations, suspicions and theories, and Melvin nodding sagely, quietly shutting doors along the way. But this time, Melvin watched Jeff get up and leave. When he was out of sight, he changed the TV to the shopping channel.

Adriana stood and went to the kitchen to make a cup of tea. She felt like her bones were sticking out everywhere, and her stomach was empty. There was bread to make toast and jam, peanut butter and Cheez Whiz in little packets. She didn't feel like eating but there was a small part of her, clamouring to stay alive. She could hear its voice coming from deep inside her, as she dragged herself back to the common room. The television was now showing a rerun of Star Trek. In his place, Melvin sat quietly, back straight as a ram rod, and his hands crossed on his knees.

Redgie and Marlene came back inside from their smoke. Redgie flopped down where Jeff had been sitting, next to Melvin. Marlene sniffed the air. "What's that, toast?" she asked. Adriana nodded and Marlene went to the kitchen to make some for herself. Redgie took off his sunglasses, rubbed his forehead and stared at Adriana, as though trying to place her. Adriana focussed her gaze on the television and kept chewing. Redgie rubbed his eyes and yawned. After another minute, he laughed loudly, as if in response to someone else's comment and slapped his knee "You know who you remind me of?" he asked Adriana, his eyebrows arching. Adriana shook her head. First Aunt Penny, and now, who? "You're like Yoko Ono!" Redgie slapped his knee. "Don't she look just like Yoko Ono?" he asked Marlene as she entered the room with her toast. Melvin grinned, the first time Adriana had seen him smile, and Marlene her mouth full, shrugged. A little put out, Redgie muttered. "Damn right. She looks just like her."

Peter had once said the same thing. When she wore her hair around her shoulders, he told her, "I'll be John, you be Yoko." She was mortified to be associated with a woman so notorious and forward, the only Asian woman most people could recognize, for the simple fact of her race and no other reason. Nobody would compare a white woman with another white woman simply because they were both white. Adriana had always felt like something of a curiosity, to Peter. She was acutely aware that he saw her as slightly exotic, and his interest in this aspect of her was superficial and easily discarded. And although she had tried her best to be something more than that to him, she realized there was a gap between them that was in some way unbridgeable.

Redgie could see he'd struck a nerve. "I don't mean no harm," he told Adriana. She nodded and hoped that would be the end of it. "I don't have no hard feelings about Yoko. As far as I can tell," he said leaning forward with effort to untie his boots. "She was a fine woman for John."

Adriana looked out the window of the common room. There was a seagull taking advantage of an updraft. It hung in the sky, doing a slow spiral upward. She felt like it had something to say to her, she didn't know what. Redgie was talking to Marlene. He had taken off his boots and had put his feet up on a stool, wiggling his toes in his woollen socks. "Did you get yer feet wet?" Marlene asked. Redgie nodded and leaned back in his chair. Head tipped back, Marlene laughed, a screeching sound. The sea gull drifted upward, out of view. Adriana felt strange, as though something had turned upside down. She clutched her stomach.

What Adriana wanted was to blend in, to disappear among the masses—and yet even here, in the mental hospital, she stood out. Not for her sanity, but because she looked Asian. And it made her sick to think how hurt her father would be if he'd known she didn't want that distinction—she wanted to be remarkable for her absolute ordinariness. This goal involved a certain amount of strategic individualism, in a star-studded North American society. Hence her lopsided haircuts and friendship with Jazz, both of which she knew her mother would disapprove.

Adriana's father understood the desirability of conformity, but for him, it meant being a dutiful son and a proud Chinese. Still, he was never quite comfortable among his Chinese peers. The men would smoke and drink together at Mr. Liu's house, slapping one another on the back as they egged each other on to gamble just a little more of their paycheques. Mr. Song, wearing a crooked smile, would sit quietly among them, sipping whiskey (which he hated) and sometimes injecting a misplaced comment here or there. Without even looking at him, the other men would wave their hands as if to erase his words from the air.

Mr. Song was, above all, a family man. One time when Adriana's mother was in the hospital for what must have been a chemo treatment, her father, with Beth bundled onto his back, took her for ice cream. They sat and ate it on a bench in the park, watching the people go by. Mr. Song pointed out a girl and boy whose white mother and black father were walking hand in hand. "Aren't they beautiful?" Mr. Song said quietly. Adriana looked at the children with their caramel coloured skin, hazel eyes, and dark curls, and she had to agree. But her father continued. "Just like you and Beth. Mixed race children are the most beautiful people in the world." Adriana had looked at him, eyes wide. He had never said such a thing before and she didn't know what to make of it.

A nurse came out of the office and frowned with irritation. "Redgie, were you out walking in the harbour again?" Redgie didn't answer. "You know you can't do that. It's too dangerous. What if you fall in?" Redgie hummed a song and tapped his fingers on the arm of his chair, pretending he didn't hear. The nurse turned back into the offices. Adriana could see her through the glass window, speaking to someone inside the nursing station. It was a young man, dressed smartly in a blue shirt and dress pants. He must be a student doctor, she thought, because he looked barely older than she was. He came out of the offices and sat down next to Redgie.

Redgie seemed to know him. "What's up doc?" Redgie

asked, good humouredly.

The young man put his hand on Redgie's shoulder. "Hey, Redgie."

Redgie wiggled his toes. "My socks are wet," he allowed.

The young man nodded. "Walking on water again?" he asked.

Redgie shrugged modestly. "Do you think you could do it in the pool, with your shoes off?"

Redgie looked like he was considering the idea, then he shook his head. "I need the waves," he said quietly "To spread my message." The doctor thought for a moment.

"Well, Jesus spread his message in other ways too. By talking to people. He didn't have to walk on water all the time."

Redgie looked a bit put out. "How about I give you a little pad of paper and a pencil?" the doctor asked. "You can carry it with you, and when you have a message you can write it on a piece of paper and let the waves carry it away." Redgie looked at him in disbelief. "That could work, couldn't it?" the young doctor asked. He looked like he genuinely wanted to know the answer.

"Well, I could try it," Redgie said gruffly. The young man slapped his knee and stood.

"Good. I'll ask the nurse to give you a pad of paper and pencil. Doctor's orders," he said, and with a brief smile to acknowledge Melvin and Adriana, whisked himself away into the nursing station.

Redgie took off his socks and wrung them onto the wet floor. The nurse who was coming with a pad and paper rolled her eyes but didn't say anything. She handed them to Redgie without a word. Redgie accepted them and smiled widely, "Thank you, ma'am" he said. When she'd left he whispered to Marlene and Adriana, "They hate it when you call them ma'am."

Melvin laughed soundlessly, and even Adriana smiled. It was the first time in awhile. She leaned back in her chair and smiled at the ceiling. Redgie stood up and did a little dance in his bare feet. "I'm free," he sang, waving his hands in the air. Marlene shrieked with laughter.

Adriana watched Jeff glide by in the corridor. He looked haunted, his face white with dark eye circles. She watched him slip out the door of short stay, his thin shoulders hunched, jeans bagging around the knees. She wondered whether the nurses knew he was hearing messages from the TV, and that he was afraid of the weather.

CHAPTER 17

It was an hour till lunch, but Adriana felt hungry for once. She wouldn't take her first dose of antidepressant medication until that night, but quite unexpectedly she had an appetite and she felt lighter than she had in months. Adriana's mind cogitated on this. Was it possible they were slipping drugs into her food? She felt a bubble of anxiety. What if they were giving her something that was making her artificially happy? She was seized with fear at the idea.

Adriana sat up in bed. She needed to do something—to knit or make something. Her fingers trembled. What was wrong with her? Were the drugs in her scrambled eggs making her nervous? She lay in bed, her muscles twitching. She took bunch of newspapers from the pile by her bed and began to fold cranes, but she was too anxious to fold them properly. She wished there were something else she could do, something useful. Adriana wrung her hands. What to do, what to do? She breathed in quick gasps.

There was a knock on the door and Fiona peeked her head in. When she saw Adriana, she opened the door wide. "You're hyperventilating. Slow your breathing down. Like this." She put an arm around Adriana's shoulders and breathed with her. Adriana did as she was told. When she managed to breath normally again, Fiona gave her a quick hug around the shoulders, saying "You let me know if you need something for anxiety. I'll leave you with your family now." And Adriana realized her father and Beth were standing just outside the doorway, Mr. Song with a very worried look and Beth, staring at her with horrified fascination.

Adriana had seen that look on her sister's face before, during one of many trips she and her father made to Aunt Penny's home in Toronto. Beth was only five years old, sitting cross-legged in front of the television, watching the Saturday morning cartoons. Adriana and her father sat behind her on the couch, as Penny had asked them to do while she made the usual weekend pancake breakfast. Mr. Song gazed tenderly at the back of Beth's head, not daring to hug or touch her, in case she got hysterical. Adriana, a bored 16-year-old, crossed her arms over her chest and pouted. She didn't understand why the adults of the house had to suffer a five-year-old's stupid cartoons. When her father left the room to help Aunt Penny, she decided a commentary on the antics of Sylvester and Tweety bird was in order. She leaned toward her sister. "Tweety bird thinks he's a smart little bird. Sylvester is just a big dumb cat for sure but just because Tweety is small and cute doesn't mean he's any smarter." Beth turned and stared at her. "In fact," Adriana said in a confidential tone, "Tweety gets eaten in the end. By a snake, in India. A cobra with big, poisonous fangs." Adriana bared her teeth and hissed. Beth gazed at her in horror, unable to move. "It's true," Adriana nodded. 'They don't let the little kids watch it, because it's too gory but that's reality. You'll see, when you're older" she said, with a sigh and a resigned shrug, settling back against the sofa as her father and Aunt Penny brought the pancakes in.

Adriana had suffered a lot of guilt for the words she's said to her sister that day. She figured that if someone made a cartoon of their lives, she would be the villain, the crazy cat to Beth's traumatized Tweety bird. It occurred to her what a sorry band of characters they made in real life—her father, agitated and bedraggled, as though he'd just got out of bed after a bad dream, and Beth, pale and shocked-looking. Then there was herself, a mental patient. The three of them, alone in the world.

Her father sat down on the edge of the bed and let Beth sit on the chair. She stayed as far away from Adriana as she could. Mr. Song decided not to comment on the hyperventilating—it was too much for him to broach the subject—and instead handed Adriana a note. "It's from Jazz," he said. Adriana fingered it tentatively, then put it down. "I'll read it later," she said. Meaning, she would read it in private, without the eyes of her family on her.

Mr. Song looked at Adriana's shoes by the locker. They were a worn pair of sneakers, no particular brand, that looked out of place on the dully waxed floor. Adriana cleared her throat. "The doctor is going to start me on medication," she said. Mr. Song looked up at the wall, his forehead wrinkled. "It's an antidepressant," she said. "I forget which." Mr. Song nodded. Beth tugged at a strand of hair, chewing the ends. She reminded Adriana of a terrier.

Mr. Song looked like he was trying to make a decision. "Your mother was depressed once," he finally said. "In fact, she was a patient in this hospital, once, many years ago. Adriana stared at him. Beth still had a glazed look. Mr. Song gazed down at his hands. "When you were born, Adriana. Your mother had postpartum depression and checked herself in here for a week. She was just—she just couldn't cope."

Adriana pictured her mother, long haired and almost as young as she was now, wandering the corridors of this hospital in a johnny shirt. Smoking distractedly, trembling with agitation, she didn't talk to the other patients, but paced the halls until she was exhausted. She didn't belong here, she wasn't like the rest of these people. Her father continued, "After a week she packed her bags and told the hospital she was going home. No one tried to stop her from calling a cab. When she came home she found me in the kitchen—I was testing the temperature of a bottle of milk on my wrist, with you in one arm, wriggling and red. I was so relieved to see her." Adriana nodded. She imagined her mother kissing her father hard on the cheek and taking the baby from him, the baby who looked up at her with dark, unseeing eyes. Humming a Slovak folk song, she sat down and looked at her husband. "Thank you," she said. Mr. Song nodded, eyes damp with relief.

Mr. Song was listening, as though Adriana had just told him the story. "Your mother was glad to come home. She was glad to hold you and take care of you," he said. Adriana didn't know how she knew, but she knew her father spoke the truth. At the bottom of her mother's anger there was something—a hurt of her own, a tender place protected by a thicket of thorns.

Mr. Song looked sad. "Your mother never took medication . When she left the hospital, she was done with all that." He shook his head. Adriana didn't know whether he was shaking his head to say "No, don't take medication" or "No, don't do as your mother did." Mr. Song continued. "She struggled, Adriana. She didn't have an easy life." Adriana looked down. In her head, Adriana's mother stared at her,

her eyes grey as stone.

Beth looked like she was going to fall asleep in her chair. Adriana didn't know how that was possible, after the revelation about their mother, but she realized that for Beth, who had just lost Aunt Penny, it was merely a story about someone she didn't know. Mr. Song rubbed a hand over his face. "I think, if the medication works, take it," he said. Adriana nodded. It had never occurred to her that her mother had been depressed. The thought was like a lead weight.

Beth began to whimper. Adriana felt a pang of sadness for her sister, lost as a bird in a church. Adriana held out an origami crane to her, its wings slightly crumpled. Beth took it but continued sobbing quietly, knees curled up to her chin on the chair. Mr. Song looked sad too. He shook his head at Adriana, as if to say, I don't know what to do. Adriana went to Beth and put her arms around her, awkwardly. She didn't feel she had the strength to do more than that.

Mr. Song stroked his chin as he always did when he was nervous or sad, as if the goatee he'd worn when he was younger still sprouted there. Adriana could hear him thinking, this is my family, this is all that is left of my family—one sobbing girl and the other mentally ill. He shook his head again then stood up. "I... I'll be back soon," he said.

Adriana, at a loss for what to do, began patting Beth on the back, like she was burping a baby. Beth eventually stopped crying and lay in the chair, legs stretched out, snot running from her nose. Adriana got the sense that she didn't care, that she'd given up, exhausted. "I hate it here," Beth said, in a calm, almost matter-of-fact voice. Adriana didn't know if she meant she hated the hospital, the town of Dartmouth or life on earth.

Adriana handed her sister a Kleenex. Beth sat up in the

chair and wiped her nose. She had cried as much as she could, Adriana thought, and now she was sick of crying. Adriana was sick too, sick of being sick. She sat back down on the bed, exhausted.

Beth was staring at her. Adriana smiled, weak and apologetic. "I know, I look like Aunt Penny, don't I?" she offered. Beth nodded. "And you look like my—like our mother." Beth looked up at her, wide-eyed. Adriana could hear the abacus in Beth's brain, ticking over.

There was a soft knock on the door. Mr. Song entered, holding a tray of Styrofoam cups and cookies in individual paper bags. He sat down on the edge of Adriana's bed, handing her a coffee and a hot chocolate to Beth. They ate and drank, quietly, thinking their own thoughts. Mr. Song smiled, sad but satisfied that he had provided them with a meal that was more than tears.

After Beth and Mr. Song had gone home, Adriana sat back in bed, unfolding the note from Jazz. She was unsure of what to expect, so she prepared for the worst. If Jazz knew she'd attempted suicide, Adriana was pretty sure she'd be angry and upset. But it might be that Jazz only knew that she's ended up in the mental hospital because she was depressed.

The note was written on onion skin paper, as though it were an airmail letter. Adriana held it up to the window, and it glowed in the sunlight. *Hi Adriana*, it began, *I miss you, but I don't want to come to the hospital. You know I hate hospitals worse than fleas, dog dirt, and Oil of Olay mixed together. Please don't hold it against me.* Adriana couldn't blame Jazz. It wasn't exactly a laugh and a half in there, and Jazz wouldn't set foot in any hospital, anyway. Even when Jazz's grandfather was dying of cancer, she'd refused to go to his bedside; it was easier for her to go to the funeral, to view his corpse

I hope you feel better soon. I haven't been able to call. I've been busy is all.

Adriana knew Jazz would have called if she felt she had something to say—and she didn't blame her friend for not knowing what to say to her. Adriana wasn't sure she'd know what to say to Jazz either. She'd avoided calling her because she didn't know how to tell Jazz she'd tried to die by taking an overdose. The fact which loomed large between them, blocking the sunlight. Adriana was sure Jazz would be angry enough to kill her, if she knew.

She could picture Jazz, sitting at the kitchen table, gripping the phone in one hand and rubbing her brow with the other, as though she had a headache. Adriana felt her own forehead tense with the thought of having that conversation . Still, Adriana could have used the company, even just over the phone. She realized she felt like she was in a foreign country, one where she had no friends.

Adriana felt guilty about that thought. The other patients were as friendly as they could be given their situation. She let a curtain of hair fall over her face and her hands go limp.

The door to her bedroom opened a bit. Adriana looked up. It was Jeff, his eyes seriously dark. He slipped into her room and closed the door, putting a finger to his lips. Adriana felt a smattering of panic. What was he going to do to her?

Jeff whispered. "We're safe here. There's a layer of lead under the ceiling and walls which keep out the x-rays," he said. Noticing Adriana looked unconvinced, he scratched the wall paint slightly. "Look," he said. Sure enough the scratch revealed a dark grey colour, but Adriana didn't think it was lead. "This is the room where President Clinton stayed when the G8 summit happened in Halifax," Jeff continued. I doubt that, Adriana thought to herself, trying to keep her panic at bay. "He had women come to stay with him. It was like one big brothel," Jeff said, and his voice took on a hard edge. Adriana looked at him carefully.

"He was a fucking joke," Jeff said. "But he was safe here." Jeff sat down on the chair near the door. He looked exhausted. Adriana felt herself trembling. There was no way she could get out of the room without him stopping her.

Jeff's skin looked grey and his eyes glittered. In this moment he looked like an old man, but Adriana estimated he was about her age.

"Wanna play cards?" he asked, taking a packet from his jean pocket. Adriana wasn't sure what to answer, so she shrugged. "I know an Italian game," he said, coming to sit on the edge of her bed.

He began dealing out cards and creating piles, all the while explaining the rules. Adriana couldn't follow them and her hands shook. Then there was a knock on the door and Fiona's head appeared in the doorway. Jeff jumped up scattering cards everywhere and put his hands on his head as if to shield it from something—radiation? Adriana wondered.

Fiona smiled, her eyes glancing from Adriana to Jeff. "You guys are playing cards?" Jeff nodded, but Adriana discretely shook her head no.

Fiona got the message. "Jeff I think Adriana is pretty tired. Maybe you could play cards tomorrow?"

Jeff said nothing but scrambled to gather all the cards and put them in their plastic bag. Fiona stood in the doorway until Jeff left, then sat down in the chair near the door. "Jeff likes his card games," Fiona said, winking at Adriana. "He'll play anybody, whether they're sick or asleep." Adriana smiled weakly. "You've got some new meds tonight," Fiona told her. "Are you nervous?"

Adriana wasn't sure what to say. She was more anxious about the thought of the medication that someone was putting in her food than the official stuff. Fiona squinted at her. "What's wrong, hon?" She asked. Adriana put her face in her hands. Fiona, looking worried, came to sit at the foot of the bed.

"It's alright, you can tell me sweetie."

Adriana thought of mentioning to Fiona about the drugs in her food, but instead she said, "Jeff is afraid of the weather. He was watching the Weather Network, and he's frightened." Fiona squinted at her. "Don't worry about Jeff, darling. We're looking after him Are you sure there isn't anything else bothering you?"

Adriana wanted to shout and cry and throw things, but that was not the way she'd been brought up. In her family, it was her mother who was the angry and impassioned one and Adriana was the dutiful daughter. She shook her head at Fiona and rolled over, her face to the wall. Fiona got the message. "Alright, hon, I'll leave you be. But if you ever want to talk you know where to find me." Fiona closed the door behind her.

Adriana felt lonely, as soon as she was gone. Her room seemed small and cramped and claustrophobic, its dull colours filling her with dread and loathing. She wished there was something beyond the four walls of this room to look forward to but, out there on the unit, it was just one sick person after another, one screwed up human being after another.

Adriana closed her eyes and slept. In her dreams, she got out of bed and somehow all her molecules dispersed and she filtered through the window like sunlight. Outside, she floated into the lone tree that stood on the north end of the hospital grounds, near the swing set. She hid in that tree, branches sticking through her, as though she were a cloud. Adriana felt safe in there, where she could spy on any humans that made their way across the back lawn, but she also felt terribly lonely.

CHAPTER 18

Adriana woke up after dark, groggy from too much sleep, her hair stringy and damp with sweat. She heard the nurse yell, "Medications", so she knew she'd better get in line behind the others. There was Redgie, looking morose, and Marlene, dressed as usual in her red parka, though underneath she was wearing pyjamas and a pair of hospital slippers. Melvin was silent, glowering under his sunglasses. Jeff hung out at the back of the line, wearing an old tweed cap. He still had that haunted look, which made Adriana afraid for him.

Jeff turned to Adriana when she joined the back of the line. He tried to smile. "You must be someone special to get the room with the lead lining," he said quietly so the nurse wouldn't hear him. "If you're a spy for them, believe me, I will find out." Adriana stared at him. She wanted to scream that he was crazy, that everyone was crazy here, that she couldn't wait to get out. The line shuffled forward and Adriana said nothing to Jeff, merely turned away when he stared at her.

When he reached the counter in the half door that led to the medication room, Jeff held out his hand for the tiny plastic cup of pills and the cup of juice to swallow them with.

He swigged the liquid and opened his mouth to show the nurse he'd swallowed the pills. But when he turned to leave, he stuck out his tongue at Adriana. She thought it was an obscene gesture at first but then she saw the meds, stuck to the bottom of his tongue and realized it was actually a gesture of defiance.

Jeff would go to the bathroom and spit them out, Adriana thought. But instead he walked past the washroom door to his own room, which he didn't leave for the rest of the evening.

The nurse had handed Adriana a tiny cup with two white pills. "These are the antidepressant and the sleeping pill that Dr. Chen ordered. Would you like water or juice with those?"

Adriana held the cup of pills for a minute. "Why do I need the sleeping pill?" Adriana asked. Dr. Chen had said she slept too much.

"It's to help you sleep better at night, so maybe you won't need as much sleep in the daytime," the nurse explained.

Dr. Chen hadn't mentioned the sleeping pill to her. She panicked a little, wondering whether this was a ploy to get her to take poison. She stood with the tiny cup of pills in hand, as the nurse waited for her to swallow them. "Is there something wrong?" the nurse asked her. Adriana felt the nurse was looking at her strangely.

She turned and walked away without swallowing the pills. "Adriana," the nurse called. "You can't take those pills away. Swallow them here where I can see you."

Adriana turned around. She threw the cup of pills at the nurse. "I won't take your poison!" she yelled. People stood aside to let her pass, and someone clapped. The nurse had a stunned look.

Adriana went back to her room. Shakily, she sat on the bed and looked down at her slippers. No doubt someone would come by to talk to her soon. She took the slippers off and got under the covers. Eventually someone opened her door a crack and saw her lying there asleep, and closed the door.

The next day Adriana woke up groggy. She walked out to the washroom with her toothbrush and saw that Fiona's name wasn't on the board, meaning she wasn't on shift. Adriana felt disappointment and relief. She was pretty sure Fiona would have something to say to her about last night. It would no doubt be on her chart that she threw her pills at the nurse doling out meds. Adriana felt something akin to smugness, but she was also terrified. What if Fiona was in on the poisoning attempts? Somehow Adriana didn't think so, but it was impossible to tell.

Adriana knew the staff would be busy till about 9 a.m. while the doctors did their rounds, and she expected a knock on her door shortly. She tidied the newspapers and pens, put some clothes in her locker, but didn't get dressed. She figured they'd put her in TQ. Such a terrible thought.

There was a knock on her door and it opened a crack. The young student doctor, dressed in blue, nodded to her somewhat awkwardly and smiled. "Dr. Chen wanted me to introduce myself," he said brightly. "I'm Colin." Adriana looked at his shoes. They were slightly too long for him and turned up at the toes. "Can we have a chat?" he asked.

Adriana nodded once. Was he in on the poisoning too? She sat cross-legged on the bed, shoulders hunched and peered at him through narrowed eyes, as though challenging him to come closer. But he stood in the doorway and made no move to enter. Adriana motioned to the chair, and he finally sat down, leaving her door wide open.

"You like flowers?" he said, engagingly, leaning forward on his knees and nodding at the bouquet her father had brought her. The tiger lilies had drooped and shed pollen all over the window sill. Adriana shrugged. Didn't everyone like flowers? "I'm Colin," he said, straightening up, and arching his back slightly, as though it ached. "I'm a medical student, just doing a rotation here at the NS for a few weeks."

Adriana nodded. She wasn't going to give him any ground. He half-smiled. "You're Adriana." She looked at him, and waited.

Colin cleared his throat. "Um, last night," he said, "You were pretty upset." Adriana waited. "Do you want to talk about it?" She shook her head. "Because it might help us help you, if we knew what you were upset about."

Adriana crossed her arms and pouted. She felt slightly childish but also very afraid, almost wildly so. Her heart beat loudly, and she put her hands over her ears, so he wouldn't hear the blood pulsing through her. He looked concerned. "Do you hear something?" he asked. She shook her head.

His eyes were very blue, or maybe it was simply a reflection of his shirt. "Look, Adriana," he said, earnest and confiding, like a cop trying to get a suspect to talk, Adriana thought. "You're here in this place to get help, aren't you?" Adriana refused to look at him. "We can help," he said with confidence, "but you have to let us."

There was a commotion in the hall. A nurse ran by Adriana's door, shouting for help. Colin jumped to his feet. Then it seemed like a whole stream of people ran by in a stampede. Colin excused himself and stepped into the hall, closing her door behind him. Adriana made out from the shouts and stray exclamations that someone had taken an overdose. Soon paramedics were on the scene and someone was being taken away on a stretcher.

Adriana opened her door a crack, but a nurse in the hallway had motioned for her to stay back. She felt both trapped and exposed. What if someone came into her room and killed her while everyone was concentrating on helping the person who'd overdosed? Her mind felt hot and roiled as though it were boiling.

Adriana heard Redgie and Marlene walk by her door. "Such a damn shame," said Redgie. Adriana imagined him shaking his head. "Just a young man, in the prime of his life. Why'd he want to end it?" Adriana thought Marlene nodded, and spoke in a hoarse and quavery voice. Then she stopped not far from Adriana's door. Adriana pictured her patting Melvin, disconsolate and lonely, on the shoulder. "He'll be back, don't you worry. I saw his face."

Adriana pictured Jeff, pale and resigned, being carried away on the stretcher. Outside the rain was beginning to fall, and wind lashed the harbour-side of the hospital. He'd tried to outrun the storm but they'd pump his stomach and give him charcoal to drink, and the thing that terrified him would pass, leaving him to face the futility of delusions, and the emptiness of his life without them.

CHAPTER 19

Adriana sat down to breakfast. There was a oblong plastic bowl with grey porridge, a hard-boiled egg, a piece of toast, and a small plastic mug of hot water to make tea. Any of it could have been tampered with, except perhaps the egg, which was still intact. Adriana cracked the egg against the table top and peeled the shell. She carefully bit the top off the egg and tore open the little packages of salt and pepper to sprinkle on the remaining egg.

A male nurse was leaning against the kitchen countertop watching her. Adriana felt terribly self-conscious, and panicky. What if the nurse was in cahoots with the people who were poisoning her food? Adriana made a point of covering her toast and porridge with a paper napkin.

The nurse, a muscle-bound, dark haired man whose name tag said "Tony", took her tray. "You didn't eat much," he noted. Adriana felt a surge of anger but said nothing. If he wanted to make a note of the fact that she left her breakfast, let him, she thought. He couldn't force her to eat.

Melvin, wearing his sunglasses as usual, was looking down at her tray, as though mesmerized. "Are you hungry" she asked, in a hoarse whisper. Melvin nodded. Before she could say a word, he took the toast and porridge from her tray onto his. Adriana was terrified. "Don't,"she said loudly, gripping his wrist. He looked at her mildly, and the male nurse watched, from behind the counter, with eyes narrowed with concern.

Adriana bent her head toward Melvin. "They're poisoned", she said, feeling the words escape her lips like a snake. He looked at her for a moment, considering, then smiled. "I'll be okay," he said. That was the only thing she'd heard him say since she had been admitted, and the high, bell-like clarity of his voice surprised her. He made the sign of the cross and waved his hands over the food, laughing soundlessly. He began to eat and Adriana she felt half dread, half humiliation.

She went back to her bedroom to lie down. Something didn't feel right in her brain. She pictured her hippocampus, tethered but drifting. Her mind wandered over Jeff's delusion about the lead ceiling in her room—the idea of a man who had lost his bearings. Or was it?

Adriana thought she saw a glimmer above her in one of the small holes in the ceiling tile. Could it be a hidden camera? Or had she, like Jeff, slipped somewhere between the lining and the outer garment of reality? She felt hemmed in, narrow, constricted—it was impossible for her to get off the track her mind had taken, like a street car on its rails.

Even in turmoil, there was something sluggish, viscous, about her thoughts. What was wrong with her? Had the hippocampus, she panicked, shifted position? She could almost feel it, floating free in the porridge of her brain. There was an illness she'd heard of, something one contracted from a mosquito bite, that turned one's organs into mush, but Adriana thought it was a tropical disease. Anxiety clawed at the back of her throat.

Adriana lunged for the door. She was afraid her brains would begin to leak from her ears. Fiona was coming down the hall toward Adriana and smiled when she saw her. The nurse stopped at the door to an interview room and called out, "Adriana, my love, won't you come talk to me for a minute?"

Adriana nodded and hurried toward Fiona, who stepped aside, surprised. Adriana sat down near the window where a red geranium bloomed, vigorous and robust. She couldn't stop staring at it—it was a symbol of health and happiness, oblivious to her suffering.

Fiona flopped into one of the old vinyl chairs. "Whew, nice to get off my feet," she said. Adriana noticed for the first time that Fiona looked pregnant. She wasn't a tiny woman by any means but the thickening around her middle was more than the result of a few too many donairs.

Adriana looked at her hands. Fiona got down to business. "You didn't eat much breakfast today," she began. "You must be starving. Would you like a cookie?" Fiona pulled a chocolate chip cookie from her pocket. It was a cafeteria cookie, in a wax paper bag. Could be okay, or could be poison. Adriana shook her head.

Fiona leaned forward, a serious look in her eyes. "Are you worried about how safe the food is here?" she asked. Adriana looked at her, considering. "I mean the food is terrible, it's hospital food," Fiona said with a wave of her hand, "but have you had any thoughts that it might be contaminated?" Adriana opened her eyes widely. She could trust Fiona. She nodded.

Fiona nodded back. "We can make sure the food you get on your tray is pre-wrapped if you want. It means you'll get sandwiches when other people are eating hot meals but at least you'll know it's safe."

Adriana felt tears start to spill over her cheeks. It surprised her, how thankful she felt. Fiona patted her hand. "Don't worry, darlin', you're going to be just fine." They stood up to go. Adriana took one last look at the geranium and slipped past Fiona, who was holding the door open for her. She couldn't help brushing Fiona's belly. The nurse laughed, saying, "Sorry, love, I don't know my own size."

Adriana went to her room. She had meant to ask Fiona about Jeff, when she got waylaid by her questions about the food. How did Fiona know she was worried about that? she wondered. Then it struck her that maybe Jeff was right, about the lead lined room. Someone was monitoring her brainwaves and had told Fiona about her thoughts that the food was poisoned. Adriana had a painful jolt of realization that Fiona was in on the whole thing. She would have to be careful what she said around Fiona from now on. It was devastating, Adriana thought, to have no one to confide in.

Dr. Chen sat across from Adriana with Fiona by her side. Adriana thought she looked curious. The doctor asked Adriana the same questions that had been asked of her already, three or four times. Did she see anything that no one else could see, hear anything that other people couldn't hear? Did she experience any strange smells that no one else could smell? Did she have any thoughts that she had special powers? Did she believe the radio and television were sending her messages? Did she think anyone could read her thoughts or that she could put her own thoughts into other people's heads? All these questions, which she had answered "no" to in the past, and answered "no" to now, suddenly caused her to stop and think. It was true that she believed someone was monitoring her brain waves, but that wasn't quite the same thing as thinking they could read her thoughts. But what if she answered yes to that question, or to all of them, what would happen then?

Dr. Chen and Fiona were sitting looking at her. Adriana decided in a moment to tell them the truth. If she told them, they wouldn't know she knew they were in on the scheme. Her heart beat fast at this small act of manipulation. "There are hidden cameras in my room, and someone is trying to control my thoughts," she said. Her hands started to shake. Dr. Chen nodded, either in agreement or simply to indicate she should continue. "Someone is trying to poison my food." Adriana looked down, tears starting to spill down her cheeks. "They think I know something, but I'm just depressed."

Fiona handed Adriana the box of tissues on the table, her eyes sympathetic. Dr. Chen nodded, her short bob bouncing, and scribbled some notes on a yellow legal pad. She cleared her throat and seemed to be deliberating. Adriana felt her whole body was made of tears, that they would flow until there was nothing left of her.

Dr. Chen finally said, in a warmer voice that was still prim and now, pitying, "It's going to take a little time for you to get better, Adriana. You'll need other medications. We'll send you up to Mayflower, which is a unit where you can stay until you're well," she said.

Adriana knew about Mayflower. Redgie and Marlene had some visitors from that unit one day. When they left Marlene had said to Redgie in a low voice, "We'll be out before they are."

Adriana shook her head. Dr. Chen asked, "Does that mean you don't want to go to Mayflower?" Adriana shook her head again. She wasn't protesting, just shaking her head, unable to believe the dread she felt. She'd been feeling better and somehow hoped they were going to discharge her and now they were telling her she was going upstairs. Suddenly, a nameless panic seized Adriana and she felt the need to flee. She stood up abruptly and left the room, running out the door of Short Stay in her slippers. They came off her feet in the hall of the assessment unit and she ran in her socks, up the hall to the front doors and then out into the parking lot and across the street, where there were several empty lots covered in weeds. She was headed up the highway toward home, where her father's worry and her sister's trauma were more than she could face. But where else was there to go?

Suddenly there were shouts and sirens behind her. She ducked among some cars in the parking lot, flattening herself to the ground. The police cars stopped, one ahead of her and one behind, hemming her in.

Four policemen got out of their cars and stood watching Adriana. She lay as heavily as she could, her body sinking into the ground. If they wanted to move her, they'd have to contend with a dead weight. It felt to her that this was the end of something. If only they'd shoot her, she thought. Death was preferable to whatever came next—a long stay in hospital, and then what? An existence without any shape she could imagine, a fuzzy, faded, formless life.

One of the policemen had radioed for an ambulance, which pulled up on the gravel behind the police cars. Adriana looked at her hands—the palms were raw and bloody, as though she'd braked with them when she slid down between the cars. She rolled on to her back and put her hands in the air, surrendering. Two of the policemen picked her up and put her on a stretcher the paramedics pulled out of the back of the ambulance.

A young officer sat in front of the ambulance with one of the paramedics, while the other and a stocky, middle-aged policeman, rode with her in the back for the short return trip to the hospital. "Why'd you run?" the older man asked. He was chewing a piece of gum and monitoring his radio. Adriana stared up at the ceiling of the ambulance, then closed her eyes. There was no law that said she had to talk to him.

At the hospital, the two paramedics carried Adriana onto Short Stay on the stretcher, while the police men walked beside them. Adriana wished they would disappear. When they stopped at the nursing station. Adriana saw Fiona walking toward her, a worried look on her face. The paramedics put the stretcher on the floor and Adriana noticed they too had radios. There were intermittent bursts of sound, a dispatcher talking in some sort of code. Adriana's brain sloshed as though on rinse cycle. The policeman turned away from her to answer his radio, while the paramedics spoke to Fiona.

Redgie and Marlene were sitting in the common room, staring at her. Marlene shook her head and clucked. Melvin, from his chair in the corner, chuckled, his teeth brilliant against the black of his face. Since Jeff had been taken away, Melvin had been acting strangely—voluble, muttering as he paced the halls, laughing at nothing.

Fiona noticed Adriana's hands. "Oh my, love," she said. "We're going to have to clean up those hands before anything else." Fiona took her hand and examined it gently. "You've got enough gravel in there to cover my driveway back home," she said. Adriana felt tears seeping down her face, dampening the neck of her johnny shirt. Fiona smoothed the hair from her forehead. "Don't cry, hon," she soothed. "You're going to be just fine."

Adriana couldn't imagine it. She wasn't sure she knew what fine was anymore. Even while running, ostensibly toward home, she had felt she was sinking into something— an oil spill, something that sucked her under and made it impossible to breathe. She knew that, like her mother, she was between worlds, and didn't really have a home.

CHAPTER 20

One of the paramedics helped Adriana off the stretcher. He was a well-fed young man, dressed in a dark blue, wearing white gloves, and he smiled at her sympathetically. Adriana looked down. Her Johnny shirt was covered with streaks of dirt and her white sports socks were brown. She knew her hair was a tangled mess. Her father would weep to see her like this. It made her stomach ache to think about explaining herself to him.

Fiona took Adriana to a room with an examination table and helped her to sit on it. With tweezers, she picked pebbles from Adriana's hands. The palms were raw and burned, but Adriana hardly felt them.

Colin, the student doctor appeared in the doorway. Tentatively, he asked, "Mind if I come in?" Adriana shrugged, and closed her eyes. It was easier to imagine she was alone.

As Fiona picked the last of the gravel out of her hands, Colin leaned over to examine them. Adriana held her hands toward him, as though she were presenting him with a precious object. He turned her wrists with such gentleness that she began to shake. He was barely out of childhood himself, she thought, the bright film of idealism still clinging to his eyes. If she had met him in normal life, she wondered, would he smile at her this way?

Fiona looked worried. "She's fine, isn't she?" he asked. Fiona, relieved, nodded.

"You're fine," he told Adriana, and to Fiona said, "You can just clean them up and bandage them I guess."

Colin sat down in a chair and Adriana closed her eyes. She wished he would leave so she could just face her sadness by herself. His curiosity reminded her of Jazz, except that he wasn't cool, but warm with concern. "Does it hurt?" he asked quietly. Adriana nodded, then shook her head. She felt numb. Colin stood up and squeezed her shoulder, while Fiona glared at him with mock irritation. "Shoo," She said and Colin, ducking his head and shrinking his tall thin frame in an elaborate apology, left the room.

Fiona took rubbing alcohol and cotton balls from a cabinet on the wall above the sink. Adriana cringed. "It's going to sting, my love," Fiona warned. Adriana closed her eyes. It occurred to her that even her desire to die had not been able to supersede her fear of pain. She had too much imagination, and too keen a memory not to be filled with dread. But strangely, the sting felt dampened, filled with melancholy, not the burning she'd feared.

Fiona squinted at her. "Adriana, Dr. Chen is going to want to ask you why you ran today. Do you want to tell me about it now?" She sat down in the orange plastic chair across from the examining table. Adriana looked down at Fiona's sneakers, which were clean and white, as though she'd never worn them outside.

Fiona repressed a sigh. "Listen, you. You gave us a big scare running out like that, in your sock feet and all. You could have been hit by a car or wouldn't have made it far down the highway anyway... Not many decent folk would pick up a hitchhiker in a Johnny shirt."

Fiona peered into Adriana's face. It was clear from her downcast eyes that she was barely listening.

Adriana was thinking about the road with the oily slick of water on its surface. If only she could lie down on it and disappear, blending into the asphalt like a puddle.

Fiona stood up. "Adriana," she said in a low voice. Adriana looked up at Fiona shaking her head, the angry red spots on her cheeks. "You have a father that loves you. Many people here are not so fortunate. For the love of God, girl, you've got to start thinking about that. Think about all the positive things in your life and where you want to go from here." Adriana looked down at her knees. Fiona got up and opened the door.

"Go on now" she said more gently. "I'll let you know when Dr. Chen wants see you."

When Adriana reached the door of her room, she saw Marlene coming out of the washroom. Marlene stopped and waved, and Adriana, not knowing what else to do, waved back. "You'll be alright, hon," Marlene said in a loud, almost operatic voice. For some reason it reassured Adriana. Marlene ambled around the corner of the nurses' station into the common room. Adriana could hear the blast of a television commercial but couldn't make out the words.

Her room was as she'd left it. The window was slightly open, and there were drops of water on the window sill. Jeff's storm had come and gone as a shower. She pushed the window shut with her forearm and got into bed. The holes in her ceiling tiles gazed down at her. Was it really a glint of a camera she'd seen before? Adriana squinted her eyes at the tiles above her. She could see nothing, but thought she heard a soft whirring sound. Perhaps it was an audio recorder?

Adriana fell asleep, her bandaged hands on either side of her head. When Mr. Song entered her room, he thought she looked like she was surrendering. He'd left Beth home alone, watching cartoons on TV, precisely because he didn't want her to see Adriana like this. Beth never smiled, but sat twisting her hands together—she didn't need another worry. Mr. Song was a little nervous about leaving her alone, but he'd told her not to answer the door, and that he'd be back in an hour. She had nodded, her eyes glued to the black cat who always tried and failed to catch the little yellow bird. Mr. Song didn't know what the cartoon was called but he'd watched it himself after his wife died. He'd spent hours in front of the TV the month after her passing, his head full of clouds of grief.

Adriana stirred a little but didn't wake up. Mr. Song stretched out his legs, and looked down at his shoes. These were the same shoes he'd worn to his wife's funeral; when had he started wearing them every day? He couldn't remember, but he wondered whether they were an advertisement of mourning. They were a little worn, but still serviceable and he polished them every Sunday.

Adriana was staring at him when he looked up. Her eyes were dark slits and her cheeks looked slightly swollen, whether from crying he couldn't tell. He got up from his chair to give her an awkward shoulder hug. Adriana didn't hug back but didn't resist either. Encouraged, he took her bandaged hands in his own. They were like two big white lobster claws, he thought, and smiled. He pulled his chair close to the head of the bed so he could hear Adriana, who spoke in a whisper. "I don't want to go to Mayflower," she said.

Fiona had briefed Mr. Song. Adriana would probably be made an involuntary patient now, which meant she would have to stay in hospital, even if it were against her will. He knew if it were him, he'd feel claustrophobic, and the thought of freedom would gnaw at him like a rodent, but at least she'd be safe.

"Darling, Mayflower is just another place to get better," Mr. Song said. Adriana looked down at her hands. Boxing gloves, she thought. Her father leaned over and touched her head with his hand. "You will get better." She could tell he believed it—he radiated a kind of calm benevolence, which told Adriana that he was at peace with the idea.

Fiona knocked on the door. Dr. Chen was with her, and they both smiled at Mr. Song. Adriana felt something momentous was about to happen. "Dr. Chen will see you now Adriana. Mr. Song, we'd like you to come too." Mr. Song stood up and, looking slightly unsure of himself, waited for Adriana to get out of bed. It took her a little while, since she couldn't use her hands, and the sheets were tangled. Mr. Song held her elbow until she was finally able to stand, free of bedding.

Adriana felt she and her father were like survivors of an airplane wreck, holding on to one another as they climbed out of the ashes. Fiona and Dr. Chen parted for them at the door. Mr. Song put his arm around Adriana's shoulders. She felt so thin, he thought. Her shoulder blades stuck out like antlers.

Fiona led the way to the interview room. It was a different one than Adriana had been in before—bigger, with windows on to the hallway. Redgie walked past, limping slightly. He saluted Adriana with a serious face and continued on his way.

Dr. Chen shook hands with Mr. Song. "Thanks for coming in," she said and Mr. Song looked slightly confused. Fiona cleared her throat. "Dr. Chen asked me to phone you about meeting with her, but I couldn't reach you—you must already have been on your way."

Dr. Chen got down to business. "Mr. Song, as you know, Adriana ran from the hospital today in her sock feet. "Mr. Song nodded. "She has also been concerned about the safety of the food served here." Adriana looked down. Mr. Song appeared confused. Fiona explained, eyelashes fluttering nervously. "She's worried that someone has contaminated the food in order to harm her." Adriana noticed she didn't use the word "poisoned". Mr. Song looked as though he'd been struck by lightning.

"We think she needs a longer stay in hospital and so we'd like to move her to Mayflower, upstairs." Dr. Chen continued. "We are in the process of adding another medication to her antidepressant which we think will help with the paranoia."

Adriana looked at Dr. Chen, and at her father. "I'm not paranoid," she said quietly. Dr. Chen, smiling briefly, wrote something on her clipboard. Fiona looked like she was aching to say something, but thought the better of it.

Mr. Song patted Adriana on the shoulder. His face looked troubled. Fiona reached over and took one of Adriana's hands in hers. "Mayflower is not really different from here," she said. "Only there you can stay longer." Adriana despaired at the thought. She couldn't imagine anywhere she liked less than here.

Adriana and her father retreated to her room. Mr. Song stroked his invisible goatee. She looked up at the ceiling. Was the camera on? There was no glimmer of metal above her, so she decided it wasn't. Adriana leaned toward her father and whispered, "Dad." He looked up. "They're killing me in here." Mr. Song's eyes widened. "I want to go home," she whimpered, rocking back and forth.

Mr. Song's face was a blur. Adriana didn't even realize she was crying, until her father came to stand beside her and offer her a tissue. Mr. Song rubbed her back. "They're trying to help you Adriana," he said. "They wouldn't do anything to hurt you. I wouldn't let them," he said. Adriana thought of Beth sitting at home in front of the television, eyes glazed. That was a hurt.

At this moment, Mr. Song thought of Beth too. The cartoon would be over and Beth would be watching whatever was on next, barely conscious of the room around her. He stood up straight as though he were a soldier at attention. "I have to go, sweetie," he said, his voice full of regret. "Beth's home alone."

Adriana put her head down and let her hair fall around her face. She thought about her sister's terrified eyes, staring at nothing, Adriana shut her own eyes and saw her mother's face, staring back at her. She looked, Adriana thought, worried.

Adriana slept for a long time and only woke up when there was a knock at the door. Fiona and Joanne entered the room, and Fiona smiled. Adriana wasn't about to trust her this time. Fiona had given away her secrets and was clearly in cahoots with Dr. Chen. Adriana looked away.

"Rise and shine, hon. You're moving up to Mayflower," Fiona said, her voice slightly troubled. Adriana looked at her sharply, her eyes narrowed.

Fiona looked startled, and then hurt. Adriana turned her face to the wall. Joanne, her blonde perm hair-sprayed stiffly into place, said briskly, "You're going to have to get up, dear."

Adriana stood, with a blanket around her shoulders. She

watched as Fiona and Joanne piled her things into plastic bags and set them on the bed. Her own hands stung as though she'd dipped them in salt water and she realized why Fiona hadn't asked her to get her things ready herself.

Adriana felt helpless, watching her worldly belongings accumulate in a pile. They were the things her father had brought her—practical things—clothing, a hairbrush. She was conscious of the fact that things that were important to her were missing from the pile. They were at home. The family photos and the old school projects, the ribbons her mother had given her for her hair when she was younger than Beth was. Things she didn't often look at but kept squirreled away in a box under her bed. Sometimes as she lay there, she would feel the heat of the box beneath her, glowing in the night.

Fiona and Joanne were finished. "We'll help you take these things upstairs," said Fiona, her face turned away from Adriana. Joanne went to find a trolley, and Fiona stood in the doorway. "Adriana," she said. "I'm sorry you're upset with me. I did what I thought was best for you. What I had to do, as your nurse." Adriana remained silent. "Anyway," Fiona hurried along, sounding as though she might cry, "Mayflower is where you'll get the treatment you need."

Adriana looked at Fiona as though a harsh new light shone on her, Fiona wasn't so impervious to pain, then. Her golden life was maybe not so golden after all.

All Adriana's things were loaded on a trolley, and squished into the elevator with Adriana and Fiona. They didn't speak on the way up to the fourth floor, but the silence wasn't un-comfortable. Adriana was anxious about what she'd find on Mayflower, and Fiona was lost in her own thoughts.

When they reached the fourth floor, Fiona backed out of the elevator into a noisy hallway, pulling the trolley with her while Adriana rested her hands on it, afraid to let go. Fiona looked at her with warmth and pity. "It's going to be alright," she said, and Adriana nodded, trying to convince herself, ignoring the pity. Fiona smiled, knowing she was forgiven, or at least, that the question in Adriana's mind about Fiona's trustworthiness had taken a back seat to what was happening in her life right now.

In the common room, the TV blared, just as it had on Short Stay. This was a larger unit though, taking up the whole south side of the floor. Adriana could see from where she stood that it was as big as Short Stay and the assessment unit combined. Adriana knew from hearing Marlene and Redgie talk that Laurel Unit— where people who were getting ready to be released back into the community were transferred after Mayflower—was across the hall. She dreaded the idea.

In the past she knew the hospital housed maybe four times as many units plus the forensic unit on the fifth floor. Nowadays though, people were treated in the community as much as possible, and the hospital had shrunk in on itself. It made Adriana's spirit dwindle to think she was one of those who still needed care in this relic of another age. She felt her mother's grey eyes on her, as though to say, you are one of the weak ones.

In the common room, Adriana noticed Jeff sitting in a rocker, unmoving, his hands pressed together as if in prayer. Adriana was glad to see a familiar face, but Jeff looked pale and less well than when he was downstairs. Adriana waved in his direction but he didn't seem to see her.

Fiona had stopped at the nursing station and had put

on her best Newfoundland accent. "Good to see you, my duck. I brought you another." She winked at Adriana, as the serious young woman consulted her papers. "She's with Elspeth," the orderly said, without cracking a smile. Adriana thought of her face exercises from Jazz—she hadn't done them since she came to hospital and she felt her face sagging. But Fiona was bright and cheerful, and told Adriana, "Elspeth! My girl, you've won the lotto. She's a handful of cherries." A nurse stuck her head out from the office where Adriana could see the nurses working on computers. She was a big square-jawed woman with wavy greying hair pushed back with a plastic hair band with teeth. She smiled at Fiona. "Who have you brought me today, Fifi?" she asked, consulting her clipboard. Her voice was calm and intelligent. Elspeth looked up at her. "Adriana Song? Why, that's a beautiful name. Can you sing?" Adriana shook her head no. "Because there's chapel service on Sunday and they could probably use a soprano." She set her clip board down carefully. Adriana was anxious about this woman, who seemed slow moving and strange—but if Fiona liked her, maybe she was okay.

Fiona chatted away to Elspeth while they walked Adriana to her room at the southern end of the unit. She was on the side of the hall away from the harbour this time, and felt as though she'd moved to the wrong side of the tracks, away from the ocean view.

There were four beds in the room, three beds made up neatly and one a mess of blankets and clothes. For privacy, it was possible to draw a curtain around each bed but it was clear whoever was in the other bed didn't care much about that.

Fiona and Elspeth unloaded the bags of Adriana's stuff

from the trolley. Adriana sat down on the bed, exhausted. She would deal with her things later. The nurses looked at her with understanding eyes. "You rest," said Elspeth kindly, "We'll talk later."

Fiona gave Adriana a hug, Adriana was tempted to hold on, to beg Fiona not to leave her. But she didn't. "You'll be just fine, my lovely," she told Adriana. "Elspeth will take care of you." She patted Adriana's arm. "Now I'm going to leave you be," she said.

Adriana watched Fiona close the door behind her. She lay on the bed, and felt her brain sloshing slowly around, as though caught in a whirlpool. She stared upward. The ceiling was the same as downstairs in Short Stay, white tiles with holes in them. She didn't see anything like the glimmer of a camera. Maybe there weren't any.

CHAPTER 21

Adriana slept and dreamed that a woodpecker was knocking on her skull. When she awoke, she realized the woodpecker was actually an enormous woman counting change from a small change purse onto the table beside the messy bed. She must be over 6 feet tall, Adriana thought. The woman turned to her and smiled, and Adriana realized her roommate was practically a senior citizen, though she had the build of a hockey player. "Did you sleep well?" the woman asked, with a throaty trill that reminded Adriana of Julia Child.

Still befuddled with sleep, Adriana nodded. The woman went back to counting change. Eventually she sighed and scooped the coins into her hand, with a flourish "Just enough for a Coke!" she thrilled. "Do you want something? If you have the money I'll get it for you. I'm Samantha, by the way." In two strides she reached Adriana's bed, hand extended. Adriana shrank back involuntarily. "Pleased to meet you," Samantha said, obviously hurt, and yet apologetic. She smiled briefly and said, "I'll be back in a jiffy." Adriana felt ashamed of herself, but Samantha frightened her. She looked like something from another planet.

Adriana took stock of her neighbour's possessions. There

were clothes strewn on the bed and a faded poster of Barbara Streisand above it. On the bedside table sat an accordion, a makeup bag and a package of rice cakes. Adriana smiled drearily in spite of herself and shook her head. What kind of creature was this Samantha?

Five minutes later, a can of diet cola almost hidden in her massive hand, Samantha reappeared and smiled shyly at Adriana. She sat on the edge of her own bed while Adriana sat up, wakeful and alert. Samantha took a swig of Coke, staring out the window at a couple of crows. They looked cocky and gleamed as though they'd been polished.

Samantha smiled and pointed her pop can at them. "Two crows: joy," she said happily. Adriana took a breath and asked, in a voice croaky from disuse, "How did you learn to play the accordion?"

Samantha turned toward her. Her nose was long with a Roman bump, and her eyes looked sad. "I was part of the Salvation Army band," she said in a slightly pained voice, "in England. But here in the Americas it's all brass." She did have a slightly English accent, Adriana thought.

"I came to Canada in the 1970s. Following my love," Samantha said. She took a framed photo from the drawer of her side table and held it up in front her chest, so Adriana could see it. It was a photo of Samantha bending down over the shoulder of a short bespectacled man in a white button down shirt and expensive looking trousers and shoes. He was grinning proudly for the camera as a younger, more slender Samantha, in a minidress that just covered her massive thighs and a pill box hat, smiled as though she would never stop.

Adriana doubted it was Samantha's boyfriend. But she nodded her head and tried to smile, her eyes wary. Samantha sighed. "He was the love of my life." Wiping a tear from the corner of her eyes, she asked, "Are you too young or have you ever had a special someone?"

Adriana was taken aback. Was this giant of a woman really asking her about her love life? She shook her head and mumbled something non-committal, then rolled onto her side, as if to go back to sleep. Samantha hummed a tune in a wavery contralto, and Adriana drifted off despite herself.

The next morning Adriana stood in the hallway a moment to get her bearings. There was a south facing window to her left, from which she could see the oil refinery in the distance. Its convoluted structure reminded her of a musical instrument crossed with a blow torch, with a flame rising from a thin chimney. It was a depressing sight . She turned away from it and walked toward the nursing station. No one was in the hall, and the TV was blaring as usual in the empty common room. Outside it was a beautiful day—maybe everyone had gone for a smoke.

Adriana turned off the TV and sat down in the rocker. The nurses were tucked away in their office, where she could hear them laughing every so often, playing their video games. She felt at peace for the first time in weeks. A silent square of sunlight crept across the common room floor toward her feet. Adriana imagined that when it reached her she would—as though touched by King Midas—turn to gold, starting with her feet and slowly spreading upward. That would be a desirable way to die.

Elspeth was standing beside her before Adriana noticed her. The nurse sat down in a chair facing Adriana, her heavy body causing the chair's vinyl cover to exude a gust of air. Elspeth sighed, and brushed hair off her temple, smiling at Adriana but saying nothing at first. Adriana looked down at her hands and kept rocking. For some reason, at this moment, she thought of her mother, whose grey eyes were looking not at her daughter, but dreamily out at the sea. Adriana was surprised, even slightly anxious, that her mother wasn't paying her more attention.

"You know, I had a half-Chinese friend when I was young," Elspeth said. "Her father owned a restaurant and he married one of the waitresses. Kids used to throw rocks at the windows until he chased them away." Adriana nodded, still looking down. "My friend—her name was Stacey—always fed me chicken balls. She told me they weren't real Chinese food, but she liked them anyway. She said they were like her brother, yellow on the outside, chicken on the inside. "

Adriana smiled drearily. Her father would like that, she thought. He always enjoyed good-natured Chinese jokes, the cornier the better.

Elspeth looked up at the ceiling. "I always thought Stacey should be a stand-up comedian, but she became a lawyer." She shook her head and smiled. "Such a waste."

Adriana looked at Elspeth—greying, middle-aged, otherwise non-discript. She didn't wear a wedding ring, but looked like a grandmother. Adriana's bare feet felt warm. The sun had reached and covered them, like a pair of socks. She surprised herself by wanting to stop at this moment, let time go on ahead and remain here in the common room with Elspeth, her feet bathed in gold.

Elspeth breathed and got up from the vinyl covered couch with difficulty. Adriana twinged with disappointment, but Elspeth walked stiffly over to her chair and touched her lightly on the shoulder. "You'll see the doc tomorrow," she said, patting her shoulder kindly, "but if you ever want to talk, you know where to find me."

Adriana felt an edge of desperation. "Could we talk now?" she asked.

Elspeth looked mildly surprised and smiled. "Let's find an interview room," she said.

All the rooms were empty. Adriana entered the first one, and sat on a chair close to the window, while Elspeth plumped herself down near the door. Adriana knew that was the policy, that the medical staff should be closest to the door in case the patient became threatening. She had heard it from someone on Short Stay. She couldn't remember who. It sounded like the kind of thing Jazz would know. Adriana missed her, with a gnawing ache. She'd been too numb and too wrapped in illness until now to really care. But the move to Mayflower had stirred something up in her. She felt a kind of melting and a movement, as though she'd been encased in ice that was beginning to thaw. It wasn't exactly hope, but it was something.

Elspeth took off her hair band, and her greying hair fell wavy beside her face. She looked simultaneously younger and older—less severe and yet plainer, if that were possible. She looked like a person Adriana would pass on the street without a second thought.

Elspeth leaned back in her chair. 'So..." she said. Adriana looked down. "Would you like to start?" Elspeth asked. Adriana shook her head, furious with herself for the tears dripping off the ends of her nose and her hair.

Elspeth sat back, considering, then leaned forward. "I know someone with a daughter," she said, "about your age. The daughter had a baby last year." Adriana looked up bleary-eyed. "She thought having a baby would complete her. Now she's a stay-at-home mom and depressed to boot.

Actually, she's a stay-in-bed mom. My friend takes care of her grandson."

Adriana tried to imagine why Elspeth was telling her this. Was it to make her realize how lucky she was? That she should pull herself up by her bootstraps? Elspeth's face looked slightly pained, but she was smiling.

"I want you to know that I think you did the right thing, coming here," Elspeth said. I wish my friend's daughter had done the same. Sometimes I ask myself, what if my friend hadn't been working as a psych nurse—would her daughter have felt differently about coming here for help? Could my friend have done anything else to get her daughter to see someone? But in the end, she's a bright girl, like you are, and she wanted to do things her own way. She just made a bad choice. I think you made the right one." Adriana couldn't imagine that she'd made the right choice. How many wrong turns do you have to make to end up in the mental hospital? But she admitted to herself that having a baby to cure depression was like swallowing a bottle of insect repellent to keep mosquitoes away. How did she know that? Perhaps it was from her mother, who never hid from Adriana that having children had turned her life upside down.

Adriana gazed at Elspeth. Was this friend of hers, the psych nurse, actually Elspeth herself? Adriana couldn't imagine her, carrying a baby on her hip as she poured tea to bring to her depressed teenage daughter.

Elspeth leaned forward. "So Adriana, I'm listening. What did you want to talk about?" Adriana looked at Elspeth's hands. They sat in her lap, free of any ornament. They looked like they belonged to a baker or someone who worked at manual labour, strong square hands with nails cut short.

"I don't know what I'm doing," Adriana said. That was all she could think of. She shook her head helplessly. "I don't know what I'm doing."

Elspeth leaned in. "It sounds like maybe you're having the same kind of problem that a lot of people your age have," she said. "Just because you have a mental health difficulty doesn't mean you're not facing the same problems your peers are." Adriana wasn't sure what to think— it hadn't occurred to her that what she was feeling was typical in any way.

Elspeth handed her a tissue, and Adriana wiped her face. She felt just a tiny bit better, somehow, but she still didn't know the words to use. "I don't know how to take the next step," Adriana said. "I don't know what the next step is."

Elspeth thought for a moment. "It's hard to take the next step when you don't know where you want to end up." Adriana waited, considering those words. "Maybe," said Elspeth, "you need to be able to picture what you're aiming for." Adriana closed her eyes. She had no idea what she was aiming for.

"Do you have a faith Adriana?" It seemed like a strange question. Elspeth continued, "I mean, what do you believe in... or what don't you believe in?" Adriana couldn't say. In high school she'd gone to Bible class with a friend who turned out to be a two-faced liar. After that she started hanging out with Jazz and the other girls who smoked around the front door of the school building. She never really felt comfortable there, but she didn't feel comfortable anywhere, so it didn't occur to her to look elsewhere. And Jazz had become her best friend, in fact the best friend she'd ever had. She believed in Jazz.

Adriana hung her head. Elspeth continued. "We all believe in something. Maybe you just haven't figured it out yet. A lot of people are really helped by defining what they believe in, and what they're aiming for, and setting some realistic goals. It's like putting on a pair of glasses when you've been struggling to see clearly. I'm not saying that medication and psychotherapy won't help, but you might be surprised how much you can do for yourself."

It seemed too straightforward to be true, Adriana thought. But she nodded her head, and Elspeth patted her hand. "It's not easy to be young," she said, sympathetically. "If it's any consolation, in my experience, life gets easier as you get older. That is aging's one saving grace." Adriana didn't believe her. She thought aging was a matter of loss and regret, and how could the sorrows of old age not be felt as deeply as those of youth? We're the same people at 70 as 20, she thought.

Adriana looked at Elspeth's hands, resting in her lap. They seemed peaceful and Adriana wished for that kind of peace. "You have a younger sister," Elspeth said. Adriana looked up at her face, surprised. "I understand that she's struggling too. Fiona told me that you both recently lost your aunt." Adriana nodded. Not that she'd given much thought to Beth's feelings. "Are you glad to have her back in your life?" Adriana shook her head, her eyes downcast. She didn't think Elspeth would judge her. "Why not?" Elspeth asked. Her eyes were warm and intelligent, Adriana thought. She felt a pang of regret, and a sudden shyness. She shook her head again and her cheeks reddened

They sat quietly for a minute, Adriana struggling for something to say. Then Elspeth, smoothing the skirt of her dress, said, "Tell me about your mother. What do you remember about her?"

In a moment of stunned silence, Adriana's mind adjusted itself to Elspeth's question. She thought of sitting at the kitchen table, barely tall enough for her chin to reach the tabletop, eating a peanut butter cookie her mother had made. Her mother had smiled at her, her eyes crinkled with happiness, her long curly hair swinging as she leaned forward to give Adriana a glass of milk. It was a surprising memory, one she had not thought of for a long time.

Elspeth smiled at her. "All in good time," she said. Adriana wasn't sure but she thought Elspeth was letting her off the hook. They sat together quietly, Adriana caught up in her own thoughts and Elspeth, patiently waiting. Adriana wondered how she had learned to sit so quietly, and whether the wait was worth it in the end.

Something came to her, suddenly—a memory she had forgotten, that had been squeezed out of her by the pain of adolescence.

Her mother stood, backlit, in a summer dress. Her angular face pinched looking, with the effort of picking blueberries. Adriana's margarine container had filled nearly to the brim. Her mother beckoned for Adriana to come to her, to pour the contents of her small container into a larger one. Adriana wasn't sure she wanted to give up her berries but was too timid to tell her mother. She watched the beautiful, smoky blue of the small fruit tumble into her mother's bucket. A noise startled her and her hand jerked sideways, the remaining berries spilling to the ground. Adriana sat down where she stood and started crying. Her mother looked at her, startled, then yanked her by the hand. "Don't cry, don't cry," she muttered as she hurried Adriana to the path that led in one direction to the lake and, in the other, toward home. As Adriana's mother pulled her away, she looked back at the blueberry patch and saw a man standing at the edge of the woods, his hair as blonde as an angel's. His pants were open and Adriana could see that he was exposing himself.

Her mother tugged violently at her hand. "Hurry up!" she hissed. Adriana didn't know whether her mother had seen the man, standing peacefully by the edge the trees. But later, she heard her mother telling her father about it in a low voice, punctuated by titters of nervous laughter. Mr. Song held her hand and nodded, his eyes concerned. And for the first time Adriana could remember, she thought her mother was going to cry. But she didn't—instead she got up and busied herself putting away dishes from the dish drainer.

Adriana wondered if her mother were angry with her. She had seemed so, as she dragged Adriana by her hand on the path to home. As usual, her mother walked faster than she did, always tugging on Adriana's arm to hurry her up. When they hit the main road, her mother slowed down. There were cars, and people. Adriana looked over her shoulder and saw that the man hadn't followed them. She was glad, because she knew her mother would be furious. That night at bedtime, her mother hugged her hard and kissed her on the forehead. "You forget about today, *rozumiesh*?" she demanded. "We no pick blueberries again without your father."

Adriana, dazed, slouched in her chair. Elspeth nodded. "You remembered something?" Adriana shook her head, then nodded. She wasn't sure whether you would call what she'd seen in her mind, a memory—it was more like a paint chip, one among many small samples of colour. Yes, it was like a sample. There were many more of them waiting to be picked up, fingered and kept or discarded. As if there were only one that she would choose to keep in the end, and that sample would colour the whole of her later existence.

Elspeth was smiling, a warm and yet unobtrusive smile. Adriana smiled back tentatively. Elspeth had helped her claim something, though she wasn't sure what yet.

CHAPTER 22

Samantha was snoring when Adriana went for breakfast the next day. Adriana sat down at a table with the weepy woman who combed her hair all the time—evidently she too had been moved up to the purgatory that was Mayflower. It seemed like the same men and women as had been in Short Stay sat around the tables eating porridge, some of them barely able to lift spoons to their mouths.

Adriana made herself a cup of tea at the hot water dispenser by the sink and sat down to eat a tea biscuit wrapped in Saran Wrap. Jeff sat at the table across from her and looked at her as though seeing her for the first time, as if he'd just woken up and was confused to see her sitting there.

"I've seen you before," he said.

Adriana nodded. "We were both on Short Stay," she ventured.

Jeff frowned, trying to think. "No I don't think it was Short Stay. I think it was somewhere else. Maybe Vietnam?"

Adriana smiled. "I've never been to Vietnam," she said. She doubted Jeff had either.

Jeff shook his head. "Maybe it was China," he muttered, "It looks like China in here." Adriana felt a sting, like a bee had collided with her heart. Jeff was staring out the window. "Even the trees are Chinese," he said, rubbing his forehead.

Jeff stood up and walked to the window. "There's a storm coming," he said. The sky was blue with a few puffy white clouds. He looked forlornly out the window, resigned, it seemed, to something terrible. To Adriana, it was as if Jeff stood between two mirrors, his reflection multiplying to infinity, trapped forever.

Adriana had a lump in her stomach. She wanted to go curl up under the blankets and sleep off the feeling of futility emanating from her gut. It was as though, after the talk with Elspeth, something should have changed—but she was still bleak inside, still stuck with herself in this terrible hospital. Adriana looked at Jeff's thin shoulders. He was so absolutely alone.

Adriana stood up straight, as though she had made some kind of decision. She walked out of the kitchen and down the hall to her bedroom. Adriana went straight for her locker, and began to empty it of clothes and the other things her father had brought her—shoes, books, pens and paper, deodorant, CDs. She stuffed them all in her knapsack and a couple of plastic grocery bags.

Samantha opened one eye. "Leaving, hon?" she asked. Adriana nodded. Samantha pulled the blanket up to her chin, a contented smile on her face.

Adriana walked down the hall of the unit to where the open door beckoned. No one was stopping her. Her heart beat fast as she exited the unit and stood at the elevator. It didn't seem like Samantha would tell the nurses she was leaving. Adriana stepped on the elevator and the doors closed the way a hand closes into a fist. She felt safe there, somehow. She wished the elevator would keep going, down into the earth until she emerged on the other side of the world—as far away from the hospital as possible.

She left through the front door, and quickly crossed the grounds to the bus stop. No one came for her, but the hospital loomed, massive as a mountain face, the people inside hidden from view. It occurred to Adriana that the building was like a brain, and the people inside like part of a communal mind. She herself was a rogue thought of escape.

The bus arrived and Adriana hesitated before mounting the steps to where the driver sat, looking at her, guardedly, she thought. She felt the stares of the other passengers. Did they know she was a mental patient? It would be hard to think otherwise, as she was carrying her clothing in plastic grocery bags. She sat at the front of the bus and stared straight ahead.

She would go to Jazz's house. Jazz and her mother wouldn't be there, but Adriana knew where Jazz hid the key, under a particular stone in the rock garden out back. When she arrived at the O'Connell's subdivision, she slipped through the gate to the backyard, looked around to make sure no one was watching and let herself into the basement where Jazz's bedroom was.

Jazz's cat, Maestro, was curled up on her bed, his yellow eyes blinking slowly and inscrutably. Adriana gently pushed him to one side and crawled into bed, Jazz's scent on the sheets. She wouldn't mind, Adriana thought. She had often let Adriana sleep in her bed when they were younger.

Adriana fell asleep to the sound of purring, a low electric hum. She dreamed a door opened, but no one was there. Dressed in a johnny shirt with a blanket around her, Adriana went through the door into an empty corridor. It was like the hospital, but also like a funeral parlour. There were flower arrangements in shallow bowls and a casket in front of the nurses' station. Adriana approached it, knowing who she would see inside. It was her mother lying there, long curls spread across the pillow, hands crossed on her chest. But strangely Adriana wasn't afraid. Her mother looked like a china doll, her face serene and peaceful, almost blending in with the ivory satin lining the casket.

Adriana woke with a start. There was a noise above her. Someone was home. For the first time she felt uncomfortable about having let herself in. It occurred to her she should try to leave without them knowing she'd been there, but her limbs felt heavy and paralyzed, as though she were in quicksand. Adriana heard footsteps coming downstairs, and the door swung open. Jazz gave a little scream, her hand over her mouth.

Adriana smiled weakly. Jazz looked angry. "Shit, Adriana. You scared me. You look like a corpse lying there." Adriana couldn't speak. She hadn't seen Jazz in a few weeks. "Are you out of the hospital now," Jazz asked, diffident, pulling her sling bag off her shoulder on to the floor.

Adriana croaked, "No." She wasn't sure why Jazz was acting so casually. She thought she'd be happier to see her.

Jazz straddled the chair at her desk, arms folded over its ladder back. "Did you run away?" Jazz asked, coolly, Adriana thought. Even clinically.

"Yes." She never lied to Jazz. She'd never had to.

"Your dad will be looking for you," Jazz said. Adriana nodded. Finally she was crying, the hair that framed her face damp with tears.

"Okay. It's okay," Jazz said, softer now. She sat down on the bed next to Adriana. "It's going to be fine," she said, stroking Adriana's hair. Jazz took a deep breath. Adriana looked up at her and saw that Jazz had dark circles under her eyes.

The two of them sat there, with Maestro making a figure eight around them. Adriana felt emptied. The strength she'd had when she walked out of hospital had evaporated.

Jazz put her arm around her shoulders. "Want breakfast?" she asked. Adriana felt confused. Wasn't it late afternoon? Jazz smiled. "I was just testing to see if you knew what time it was." She said. Her face turned serious. "Who's the prime minister?" she asked, then laughed. It was a mirthless sound, dark and heavy.

Adriana had thought she would feel better with Jazz, but she didn't. It was as if a shadowy membrane stood between them. On her side Adriana was submerged in liquid, struggling simply to move. She envied Jazz her freedom. If they had been walking side by side, Jazz would be miles ahead by now.

But there was something different about Jazz. She didn't look happy. In fact, she looked kind of miserable. Adriana put her hand on Jazz's. "I missed you," she said, quaking.

Jazz hugged her shoulders hard and seemed to brighten. "I missed you too, potato head."

They climbed the stairs to the kitchen, a spotless place with a bowl of fruit on the island counter. Jazz grabbed a banana and handed it to Adriana, and then an orange too. "You look like you need vitamins," she said. Adriana thought the same thing about Jazz but didn't feel up to bantering.

They sat on the bar stools at the counter. Adriana handed half the orange to Jazz, who took it without saying anything. Adriana looked at Jazz who stared straight ahead. "Is something wrong?" Adriana asked, her voice sounding tiny in the kitchen, immaculate as a museum. Jazz looked at Adriana with something bordering on disdain. Adriana stopped chewing. "Jazz, what's wrong?"

Jazz's face closed, before it started crumbling. Adriana put her hand on Jazz's. Adriana had never seen her like this before and it frightened her, more than the hospital ever had.

"I'm pregnant," Jazz told her.

Adriana's mouth hung open. Jazz screwed up her face. "Shut up." She said. "Don't say anything. I can't..." Jazz rubbed her eyes with the heels of her hands.

For some reason, Adriana pictures Jazz's mother, hanging the delicates she washed by hand on the wooden rack in the bathtub, when she gets the news.

"My mother doesn't know," Jazz said. She took a fierce bite of banana. "I can't tell her." Adriana wondered, but didn't ask, who the father was. That was clearly not something Jazz thought was important to mention. Another image wandered across Adriana's mind, of Jazz in her pale blue underwear and undershirt, sitting on a kitchen chair, smoking a cigarette. There is a guy lying under a blanket on the living room couch but she can't see his face, just his muscular arms hugging the covers. Adriana didn't even know Jazz had a boyfriend.

Jazz hung her head. "I just found out this week. I have an appointment for an abortion tomorrow," she said. Adriana gaped.

Jazz whispered something. Adriana bent her head close. "I don't want to go," she said. "I'm scared." Adriana put her hand on Jazz's hands, which were twisting the front of her shirt in knots. She whispered, "I'll go with you."

Jazz smiled weakly. "You'd do that? I would have thought you'd had enough of hospitals." She put her arm around Adriana's shoulders. "I'm sorry that I didn't visit you." Adriana shook her head. There were dozens of questions she wanted to ask but they all had hooks. Jazz didn't need any more pain. They sat quietly, finishing their bananas. Jazz got down from the bar stool, her hand on her stomach. "I've been feeling so queasy," she said, rubbing her gut. "Bananas are about all I can handle"

"Can I stay here tonight?" Adriana knew it was a lot to ask. Jazz frowned, thinking.

"Mom can't know," she said. "You'd have to be quiet and stay downstairs." Adriana nodded. She thought of Samantha, alone in the bedroom at the hospital, looking up at the ceiling. Adriana didn't think Samantha would tell the nurses anything.

They went downstairs and made Adriana a place to sleep on the floor. Jazz sat down wearily on the edge of her bed. "I have sociology today and I feel like shit," she said. Adriana wanted to say don't go. But she knew that for Jazz, it was better to behave as though nothing was wrong, to plough through the day, and come home exhausted. Then, she would sleep, and tomorrow would come. That's what always seemed to work for Jazz—pretend a problem doesn't exist and then it passes without much fanfare.

Adriana put her hand on Jazz's back. "Go now," she sang, giving Jazz a little push "before you see me cry."

Jazz smiled. "You're such a ham. What are you doing in the mental hospital?"

Adriana shook her head and put her hands over her ears. She wanted to hold her head and scream.

Once she heard the storm door bang shut, she knew she was alone. Even the walls looked sad, a dreary battleship grey in the muted light. Adriana settled into Jazz's bed, with a book from her bookshelf. It was the first year psychology textbook, a copy of which she knew lay open on her desk at home. She opened it to the familiar picture of the bisected brain, the labels spiking out from the various parts, and felt a strange longing, for her old life, the life of a university student. She'd never much appreciated it at the time, but it beat being in the mental hospital hands down.

She turned to the chapter on abnormal psychology. She had dutifully read this section of the book last year, without a great deal of interest, but now it was like being struck by lightning. There in black and white were several possible diagnoses with symptoms that seemed to match hers. With a sinking feeling, she read about schizophrenia, delusional disorders, and schizoaffective disorder. People with schizophrenia often experienced paranoia, thinking that someone was trying to harm them, reading their thoughts and contaminating their food. It was like a thief, stealing a person from themselves. She wavered between chucking the book at the wall in anger, and crumbling onto the floor. She wanted to talk to someone. Someone like Elspeth.

Jazz wouldn't be home until the late afternoon. Adriana would return to the hospital, hopefully without anyone knowing she'd gone missing, and come back tonight. She'd leave Jazz a note, saying she'd be back, and to wait for her. Adriana thought about leaving her knapsack and bags of clothes but what if Jazz's mother found them? She scooped them into her arms and headed out the door.

At the bus stop she had second thoughts all of a sudden. The plan seemed too smooth. There were always wrinkles that no amount of massaging and face exercises could do away with. Uncharacteristically, Adriana made the choice Jazz would make, and decided not to think about it.

During the twenty minute bus ride to the hospital, Adriana considered what she'd read in the psychology textbook. Panic rose in her throat, threatening to swamp her. She couldn't scream and cry on this city bus full of people. Adriana leaned her forehead against the bus window, struggling to keep her face as smooth as possible. But what about her mother? What if she forgot about her mother? Adriana sat bolt upright. Her mother had been surprisingly absent from her thoughts the last few days, or could it be weeks. Except for the talk she'd had with Elspeth, and the dream of her funeral, she'd hardly thought of Viera at all. Adriana tried to picture her mother's grey eyes staring stonily at her but all she could muster was a pale face, with a weak smile that looked pasted on. What had happened? Was it the drugs that had turned her mother into a faded, watered-down version of herself? Or had her brain shrunk and shrivelled over the past few weeks from depression, the way her heart had?

Adriana rested her forehead on the window again. Some of the hospital buildings came into view—the brick laundry facility, the cafeteria building and the newer Mount Hope, which had units for longer term patients and senior citizens. Some people lived out their lives here, she thought, with a sick feeling.

A man just past middle age, with the red and porous nose of an alcoholic and suspenders under his jacket, stood up to get off the bus. He carried a grocery bag of books in his hand. Several other downtrodden looking people shuffled off the bus, lighting up cigarettes almost immediately. Adriana quickly exited out the back door, feeling the eyes of the other passengers on her.

She passed the smokers and entered the Purdy building. Just as she got on the elevator, Samantha appeared from the door to the basement, holding a bag of chips and a can of Coke. She smiled as she stuck her foot out to keep the elevator door open. "You're back? Couldn't stay away, eh?" she chortled. Adriana nodded grimly. Samantha hummed to herself as the elevator reached Mayflower on the third floor. "Well, I missed you," Samantha said, with a shy smile. Adriana's eyes opened wide. Perhaps Samantha considered her a friend.

As they walked down the hall to the nurses' station, she saw one of the staff staring at her from the back office, and soon, all their heads were turned in her direction. Elspeth appeared in the doorway, her face grim. Adriana tried to smile but it was obvious Elspeth was not pleased. "Adriana we've been looking for you. You are an involuntary patient now and not allowed to leave the hospital grounds." Adriana set her bags down and tried to explain, but the words got caught in her throat. Elspeth was waiting for her to say something.

Adriana blurted, "Am I schizophrenic?"

Elspeth's frown deepened. "Go put your bags away and then we'll talk," she said. "The doctor wants to see you also."

Samantha was lying in bed, delicately eating one potato chip at a time and sipping her cola. Adriana put her things in the locker, without thinking, and took her shoes off so she could put on the boat-shaped hospital slippers. "They gave me the third degree," Samantha said. "I didn't tell them anything," she added with satisfaction.

"Thank you," Adriana said, though she didn't think Samantha could have told them much anyway.

Elspeth was waiting for Adriana down the hall. She had softened a little. "Dr. Burke will join us in a while," she said, and she opened the door to the interview room. Adriana took the seat near the window. That much of the drill she knew. Elspeth was silent, waiting for Adriana to begin. Adriana hung her head. "I needed to get out of here," was all she said.

Elspeth nodded. "I can appreciate it's difficult to be here, Adriana," she said, "but you are here to get help, and we need you to stick around so we can give you that help." Adriana looked at her feet. "Why did you come back?" Elspeth asked.

Adriana was surprised by the question. She thought Elspeth would ask why she had left. "I went to my friend's house. I was worried about her," Adriana said, realizing even as the words left her that she hadn't known about Jazz's predicament when she left the hospital. "I read about psychosis in her psychology textbook, and I came back so I could ask you whether you think that's what's wrong with me."

"And what made you worried?" Elspeth asked.

Adriana quaked. "I... Jeff was... I had a bad feeling, about Jeff and the storm." Adriana couldn't tell her, that she had had a sudden overwhelming need to flee—that would just make things worse. Elspeth seemed to take note of it, but said nothing. Adriana held her breath for a few seconds. "She's pregnant," Adriana said and put her face in her hands. "My friend. I want to go with her to the hospital tomorrow for the abortion."

Elspeth softened. "Adriana, you'll have to talk to the doctor about that," she said.

As if on cue, there was a knock at the door, and Dr. Burke entered. He was a short, thin man with dark curly hair and a beard. Adriana twisted her hands in her lap. Dr. Burke looked sombre. "Hello, Adriana," he said and, without waiting for her to greet him, said "We've been concerned about you. So has your father." Adriana felt something collapse. She hadn't thought about her father. "So what made you run this morning?"

"I didn't run," she protested, but her stomach was weak. "I walked out." Dr. Burke smiled, his eyes kind. "Okay, what made you walk?" he asked. Adriana was going to tell him about her dream but suddenly it sounded ridiculous. She looked at the ceiling, and her anxiety about hidden cameras kicked in, but she wondered whether that was ridiculous too.

Adriana felt completely demoralized. "Do I have schizophrenia?" she asked. Dr. Burke sat back in his chair, considering. Adriana put her face in her hands.

Dr. Burke leaned forward. "Adriana," he said. "A diagnosis of schizophrenia is not made easily and often not the first time someone ends up in hospital."

Adriana kept her hands over her eyes. "But what's wrong with me?" she asked. Dr. Burke cleared his throat.

"Dr. Chen does think you have some psychosis," he said. "We're not sure when it started, whether in hospital or before. I am going to consult with her today, and later we can chat about all this."

Adriana's mother watched her, as she used to from the door to the kitchen. She leaned her shoulder against the sill, arms folded. Adriana felt a rush of relief that her mother had returned, though she was still a pale version of herself.

Dr. Burke was watching her, his head tipped to one side, as if he were asking a question. Adriana knew he wouldn't let her go back to Jazz's place, but she had to ask.

"My friend is going through a difficult time," she said as calmly as she could manage. "I wanted to be with her. Tomorrow she's having an operation at the hospital. Can I go with her?" Dr. Burke looked at Adriana, considering. "You know, Adriana, it is a good sign that you're able to think about helping your friend, but you need to put your own medical treatment first. You're not going to be able to help anyone if you remain ill."

She crumbled when she thought of Jazz making her way alone to the abortion clinic. Adriana knew stepping inside a hospital would undo her, even before she lay on the operating table. Adriana began to weep, loudly and hopelessly. Dr. Burke stood up. Elspeth nodded to the doctor, who left them. Elspeth put her hand on Adriana's shoulder, which made her cry even harder. "Adriana," she said. "Whether or not you are with your friend tomorrow, she'll know you care. That you wanted to be there. And that will mean a lot to her," she said. Adriana knew that was true. She wished she could curl up like a baby in Elspeth's lap and go to sleep. Instead she wiped her nose on her sleeve, and hiccupped.

Elspeth smiled and handed her the tissue box on the coffee table. Adriana realized that in all the years since her mother's death, she'd never had an impulse like that, had never wished for her mother to hold her.

"I dreamt my mother was in a coffin, at the nursing station." Adriana didn't know why she said that. Elspeth nodded. "She looked like she was asleep." Elspeth smiled. Adriana realized she felt something, as though she'd unclenched her fist, and let something go, her palm still warm from the friction of it.

CHAPTER 23

Adriana went to the kitchen, where the patient phone re-served for making outgoing calls sat on the counter. Jazz would be in class, but she couldn't leave a message that would alert Jazz's mother to what was going to happen tomorrow. Jazz didn't own a cell phone because she didn't want her mother to be able to track her down. Maybe if Adriana called the Admissions office they could get a mes-sage to her. But that seemed too drastic a move. She would just have to wait until Jazz got home around 4 p.m.

Adriana sat with the telephone receiver in her hand. She decided to call home to leave a message for her father, as it was likely he had heard about her leaving the hospital and would be worried. He'd be home at noon, to give Beth her lunch. She felt strange dialing her own number. "Hello?" said a young girl's voice on the end of the line. It was Beth.

Adriana answered quakily, "Hi Beth." There was silence on the other end. "It's Adriana. Can I speak to Dad?" Again, silence.

"He's not home," Beth said in a small voice.

Adriana felt sorry for her. "Could you ask him to give me a call at the hospital?" Adriana asked. Beth seemed to hesitate. "Beth? Are you there?"

"Yes," Beth said. Her voice took on a higher pitch. "Dad said you ran away." Adriana's forehead wrinkled.

"I didn't," she said. "It was just a mistake. I went to see my friend Jazz. But I'm back now."

Adriana wasn't sure that Beth was convinced. "Don't worry, okay?" She said. "Dad will be home soon." Jeff drifted into the kitchen and sat down, ghostly pale. His eyes looked haunted. Adriana turned away from him "Let Dad know I called." She hung up the phone, and sat there for awhile, her head swirling. She felt a bit dizzy, as though she were going to faint.

Adriana looked up at the clock—lunch wasn't for another half hour. "Can I use the phone?" Jeff asked, in a hollow voice. Adriana nodded. Jeff dialed a number and waited, listening. Adriana could hear an automated voice come on at the other end. Jeff nodded and whispered something, before hanging up. Adriana looked at him cautiously, trying to decide what to say. Jeff volunteered, "It's the weather number," as if that explained everything. Adriana nodded.

"Soon, there's going to be a big storm headed our way," said Jeff. Adriana had heard that earlier, on the Weather Channel. She nodded, and because she didn't want to look at him, she examined her hands. Her fingernails were gnawed short, without polish. She wondered when she'd started biting them again.

"It could be a hurricane," Jeff said, more to himself than anyone else. "I'm watching it. I'll try to stop it but I don't know if I'm strong enough," he said. Adriana gazed at him. She could see he was dead serious.

Marlene in her red parka ambled into the kitchen. "Phone's busy downstairs," she said, pushing past Jeff and

Adriana. Jeff stared at the floor, something turning over in his brain. Adriana stood up. She figured there wasn't anything else she could do but wait till her father called. Suddenly she felt a weight on her shoulders as if a gigantic hand had placed a boulder there.

She went to her room to lie down. There was a book on her bedside table, *Out on a Limb*, by Shirley MacLaine. Adriana picked it up, examined the spine, and put it down again. Samantha, who had finished her snack, smiled beseechingly. "I love Shirley MacLaine," she trilled. "I hope you'll like the book. It's a gift." Adriana nodded, staring at the cover. Shirley MacLaine sat in a tree, her long legs stretched elegantly out in front of her. "Did they give you the third degree?" Samantha asked. Adriana shook her head and got under her covers. She didn't feel like talking to Samantha or anyone else. Instead, she closed her eyes and fell asleep in a matter of minutes. Samantha watched her, a cloud of something indistinguishable passing over her face.

When Adriana opened her eyes and saw Beth standing in her doorway, she sat up as though she'd been shot. "Where's Dad?" she asked. Beth shook her head. Adriana threw the covers off her. "He'll be worried about you," Adriana scolded, anxiety gripping her. Beth looked terrified. "It's okay," Adriana said. "I'll call him."

She pulled Beth by the arm, down the hall to the kitchen. Marlene was still on the phone. She waved at Adriana with an unlit cigarette. "I'm almost done," she called out.

Adriana and Beth sat down at the table, facing one another. Beth looked miserable and her long kinky hair hadn't been combed. Beth, who had come all this way, alone, to find her. "Wait here," Adriana commanded, and returned

to her room to get her brush. Samantha seemed peacefully asleep, her head tipped sideways on her shoulder, her
mouth hung open.

Adriana reached the kitchen just as Marlene hung up the
phone. Adriana dialed home, but no one answered. She's
tried her father's workplace but the secretary said he'd left
half an hour ago. If he was in the car, he'd have his cell, she
thought. It made her anxious to think of reaching him
while driving—she was afraid he'd go off the road, but she
dialed the number. Someone answered right away with a
breathless, "Hello?"

Adriana wasn't sure it was her dad. It didn't sound like
him. Then she realized it must be Madeleine, the neighbour
woman with the red hair and a crush on her dad. "Hi Madeleine," she said, "It's Adriana."

"Adriana! Your dad's been so worried." She heard a squeal
and the sound of braking.

Then Adriana heard her father's voice. "Adriana!" he
shouted into the phone.

"Yes, Dad. I'm at the hospital. Beth's here too," she said,
meekly.

Her father gasped. "Oh my God, Beth." He began to
choke with laughter and tears. "I forgot about Beth," Adriana heard him say to Madeleine. He was sobbing now.
Madeleine came on the phone.

"Adriana, I'll drive your dad over," she said. "We've been
looking everywhere for you."

Adriana detected no judgement in her voice, just concern. "I'm okay Madeleine," she said. "And Beth's okay too."
Actually Beth looked less okay—her nose was runny and
her eyes were puffy.

Elspeth came into the kitchen as Adriana hung up. "I

called Dad," she said before Elspeth could say a word.

Her face looked relieved. "Oh good, we've been trying to reach him," she said. Adriana put her arm around Beth's shoulders They were equally miserable, she thought. Elspeth smiled. "You look like you could use a hot chocolate," she said to Beth.

Beth looked stricken, so Adriana answered for her. "Yes, she'd like that."

Adriana stood behind Beth and started to brush her hair. It felt softer than she thought. In her hands, the kinks lay limp and docile. She tugged gently from her sister's forehead backward and continued the stroke down to the end of her locks. The kinks softened and expanded into waves. Beth closed her eyes and let Adriana brush a hundred strokes.

Adriana held her breath. Jazz had brushed her hair before and she knew how soothing it felt, but it had always provoked anxiety in Adriana to brush someone else's hair. Her hands remembered her mother's hair, flowing through them as Adriana brushed it. Her mother sat in front of the mirror on her bedroom vanity and Adriana stood behind her, brushing carefully so she didn't hurt her mother. Every so often, Viera would flick a handkerchief at Adriana and tell her not to pull so hard. She closed her eyes, serenely. Adriana couldn't help but feel, as she stood looking into the mirror, that she looked like a Chinese maid to her white-skinned mother.

Beth opened her eyes when Elspeth put a cup of hot chocolate in front of her. They had an unfocussed, faraway look. Adriana stopped brushing and Beth let her head flop forward, hair covering her eyes. Adriana patted her shoulders, and sat down opposite her, with her own cup of hot chocolate. Elspeth left them. Marlene was cleaning the kitchen, running a damp cloth slowly over the stainless steel counters. Adriana smiled at Beth. She really was just a little girl, although at 12 years old, and almost five feet tall, with budding breasts, she could be mistaken for a teenager.

A ghost of a smile appeared on Beth's face. It made her look younger, her cheeks fuller and prettier. Adriana thought. It was the first time she'd seen Beth smile since she arrived. She wanted to show Beth pictures of their mother, to help her understand where she came from, and why Adriana had a difficult time separating Beth from her. Adriana gulped a mouthful of air, struck by this idea with fresh force. Was that why she had had such a problem with her sister?

Beth looked in need of a nap. Adriana led her up the hall to her bedroom, and tucked her into her own bed. Samantha, awake now, watched benevolently from her side of the room. Adriana nodded to her and sat in the chair by her bed to wait for her father. As Beth fell asleep, Adriana thought about her own brain, shape-shifting like desert dunes.

Mr. Song, dishevelled and wild-looking, strode down the hall to the nursing station. Elspeth greeted him and tried to explain that everything was okay, that his daughters were resting. She asked to speak with him privately, and he nodded reluctantly. Elspeth smiled and sat in the chair near the window of the narrow interview room. Mr. Song, exhausted, slumped opposite her.

"Adriana is fine," she began. "Beth came here looking for her, and Adriana brushed her hair and she fell asleep. It's a bit of a breakthrough, don't you think?"

Mr. Song looked confused and slightly stunned. Elspeth nodded at him encouragingly. "Do you mean... what do you mean?" he asked. Elspeth looked at him questioningly. "I always... I thought they got along alright," he said haltingly. Elspeth shook her head. Mr. Song looked at his shoes. "Well, they're sisters. They aren't always going to like each other," he said, more to himself than Elspeth, who smiled and shrugged.

"I hope Adriana's change of heart lasts a good long time," she said. "They need each other."

Mr. Song hadn't heard it put in those words before, but he knew she was right. He stood up and Elspeth also got to her feet. "Can I see them now?" Mr. Song asked. Elspeth nodded.

Mr. Song stood in the doorway of Adriana's room. Samantha was snoring loudly, but Adriana and Beth, also asleep, were not disturbed by the noise. Between snores, he could hear the sound of their soft breathing.

Adriana still looked too pale and thin, with dark circles under her eyes. Mr. Song wanted to shake her free of whatever it was that held her in its spell, but he realized that she had been making progress. Elspeth told him she was eating, though only the boiled eggs, plastic wrapped cookies and pre-packaged sandwiches that came for her at every meal now. She was also getting medication for her paranoia. The very word was a stab to his heart. He knew that his daughter was ill in a way that he couldn't understand—she was not just down or blue, something was wrong that put her even further out of his reach than Viera had been, at her darkest.

Adriana shifted and opened her eyes. It took her a moment to focus, but when she saw her father in the doorway, she turned her head away, unable to look him in the eye. Mr. Song took a few strides forward and hugged her hard. "I'm sorry Dad," was all she said.

"It's alright," he said gruffly, "It's alright."

Beth stirred in her sleep and moaned quietly. It was a lost sound, like a seal pup looking for its mother. Adriana put her hand on Beth's shoulder and Mr. Song smiled gratefully. "Beth must be having a bad dream," Adriana said, her brow furrowing. "Should we wake her up or wait for it to get better?" She personally thought they should ride it out. Waking from a bad dream could be a terrible experience.

Mr. Song started singing a Chinese song that he sometimes sang for Adriana when she was younger. She never understood the words but always liked the rhythm, like riding on a cart drawn by a donkey. The recording her Dad had of it included the jingle of harness bells. She knew Beth had probably heard it too, from Aunt Penny.

Beth awoke, bleary-eyed. She lay quietly, her eyes slowly adjusting to the dim light. Adriana wondered if Beth would be disappointed that it was their father and not Aunt Penny before her. But she saw a small smile lift the corners of Beth's mouth. Mr. Song continued to sing, even twirling around at one point, his elbows thrusting energetically. He finished with a grand sweep of both arms, bending onto one knee—like a dancer, Adriana thought. Beth giggled, and then put her hand to her mouth.

Mr. Song's eyes shone happily. He was breathing hard, after his performance. Elspeth stepped quietly backwards out the bedroom door and closed it.

Samantha was awake, watching. Her mouth smiled, but her eyes were sad. Adriana waved at her, and Mr. Song turned around, and dipped his head toward Samantha. She cackled behind her hand, which made Beth giggle even harder.

Mr. Song sat on the edge of the bed. "How would you girls like to go for milkshakes at John's Lunch?" he asked. Milkshakes were his favourite, but he always saved them for special occasions. Adriana nodded, but she realized she was exhausted. She lifted her hand. "You guys go," she said weakly. "I need to sleep." She saw how disappointed her father was. "But can you bring me back a strawberry shake?" she asked. Mr. Song smiled and nodded. "And one for Samantha?" Adriana whispered.

Beth scrunched the covers of the bed up and put her feet on the floor. It seemed she was almost reluctant to get up, which Adriana thought was strange, considering it was a bed in a mental hospital she was getting up from. Adriana gave her sister's shoulder a squeeze and then climbed under the covers. She could barely wait to go back to sleep. Her father and Beth hung on for awhile, watching as her eyelids closed. Adriana had a strange sensation, that she was being pulled away from them by a tide, into an illimitable ocean. Her father's shirt was the last thing she saw, its mother-of-pearl buttons glinting at her from the shore.

CHAPTER 24

When Adriana awoke, she was alone in the room, a strawberry milkshake sitting on the side table. She sat up on her elbows. Samantha was gone, and dusk was falling. Adriana drank the milkshake quickly, as though she were making up for all the calories she'd missed over the past couple weeks. She thought of charcoal, as she sucked on the straw, and shuddered.

Adriana felt alone in her room, which was darkening quickly. Summer had gone extinct, and October was almost upon them. She'd been in hospital three weeks now, while all the university students had their noses in their books. Except for her, of course, and Jazz, who was having an abortion tomorrow. Adriana felt flat, realizing she wasn't going to be there, and that she had better call Jazz now. She climbed out of bed, rubbing the goose bumps on her arms.

The hall seemed full of people pacing and nurses hurrying back and forth. Jeff sat glued to the Weather Channel, while Redgie and Marlene, who had also been transferred to Mayflower to make room on Short Stay, talked quietly in the background. Redgie looked glum, resigned to his fate. Marlene glanced up as Adriana walked by, raising a hand in greeting. Adriana lifted her own hand. She felt like a ghost, gliding among the living.

A few people sat in the kitchen finishing up their supper. The phone was free but a male nurse was standing beside it, his arms resting on the counter. Adriana sat down in the seat near the phone and the nurse moved sideways to give her room, but didn't leave.

Adriana dialed Jazz's number with a shaky hand. She'd be back by now, probably making dinner for when her mother got home. "Hello?" Jazz answered breathlessly. Adriana hesitated a moment.

"It's me," she said. Jazz's voice went hard.

"Where the hell are you?" Adriana knew she was worried.

"I came back to the hospital." She could hear Jazz's brain ticking over.

"Why?" Jazz asked calmly, with that cool curiosity that Adriana hated.

"It doesn't matter," she said. "They won't let me come with you tomorrow." Adriana felt a stab of pain in her own heart.

Jazz said finally, "It's okay."

Adriana sat rigid in her chair. She knew Jazz was struggling. "Jazz," she said, "everything will be alright." She wanted to add that an abortion was routine, like having cataract surgery, but she didn't think it would help Jazz to hear it. "I'll pray for you," Adriana said in a quavery voice. She felt stunned. Where had that come from, she wondered.

Jazz snorted, sounding like herself again, Adriana thought with relief, but all she said was, "Thanks, Adriana," in a small, flat voice that Adriana knew meant she was resigned to the worst.

When Jazz hung up the phone, Adriana felt like crying. But instead she went back to her bedroom and sat on her bed. *Please, God,* she prayed, *Make everything okay for Jazz, help her to not be afraid.* It didn't matter that Adriana didn't believe in God. He was what was left to her, now that there was no one else.

Adriana woke up groggy the next morning when Samantha came into the room, her hair short and puffed, looking almost like a wig. She sparkled, as though she had a happy secret. Adriana nodded. "Nice hair," she ventured. Samantha laughed giddily.

"The hairdresser was in today. I've been waiting for a month!" Samantha said. Adriana thought about that. How long had it been since Jazz had cut her hair?

"And I have a date tonight," she sang, "with that hunky nurse with the earring," she said. "He's going to take me to church!" The hospital chapel was having a performance by a local choir. Adriana happened to know that the nurse with the earring was accompanying anyone from Mayflower who wanted to go to the concert. Still, she nodded. Why burst Samantha's bubble?

Samantha was sashaying and singing to herself. She opened her locker. There was her other dress, the clean one, hanging there. Adriana wished she had something to lend Samantha to go with her outfit. She hadn't brought anything to the hospital except sweatshirts and jeans.

Samantha took the dress from the locker, saying, "I'll just have to give this a good iron." She draped the dress on its hanger over her arm. Adriana wanted to say something— good luck, or best wishes, or knock him dead—something to acknowledge Samantha's excitement and anticipation, but everything she thought of sounded lame.

Elspeth poked her head in the door. "Adriana, can the

doctor see you for a moment?" Samantha held up her dress and swished a little. Elspeth smiled. "Don't we look nice today?" she said without a trace of sarcasm. Samantha beamed.

Adriana crept out of bed, her blanket wrapped around herself. "Are you cold?" Elspeth asked. Adriana nodded. She didn't want to have to explain that she felt weak and in need of protection. She followed Elspeth's sturdy frame. She thought of a baby elephant holding on to its mother's tail with its trunk.

Jeff was pacing back and forth in front of the nursing station. He knocked on the wooden half door to try to get the nurses' attention. "I'm busy, Jeff" came an angry voice. "I've talked to you twice in the past two hours. Now unless you want to take something for that anxiety, I suggest you go lie down and try to rest." Jeff stood stock still, eyes dark and glittering. He looked like he was struggling to say something but nothing came out.

Dr. Burke met them at the door to the interview room. He ushered them inside and closed the door. Adriana sat by the window as usual. "So Adriana," he began. Adriana looked at his hands, clasped on his knees in front of him. "How are you feeling now?"

Adriana looked at her own hands, pale and twisting. "I want to know what's wrong with me," she said.

Dr. Burke sat back. "Well, what do you think is wrong with you?" he asked.

Adriana hesitated. Was this some kind of a trap? "I think I'm depressed," she said.

"We've established that," Dr. Burke said, nodding.

Adriana took a deep breath. "And I'm psychotic," she

said. Dr. Burke nodded. "I mean I think I'm paranoid. And I'm scared I have schizophrenia."

Dr. Burke leaned forward. "Adriana, in my professional opinion, schizophrenia is unlikely," he said. Adriana felt a trickle of relief. "But I think you're right about the psychosis, the paranoia," he said. "When did you first notice something was wrong?" he asked.

Adriana thought for a moment. It had been on Short Stay that she started thinking that there were cameras in the ceiling.

Dr. Burke leaned in. "Adriana, when you were on Short Stay, you talked to Fiona about your mother, who appears to you to chastise you." Adriana was shocked. Had she mentioned her mother? Then she recalled, with some embarrassment, an outpouring of confidences, into Fiona's sympathetic ear. Dr. Burke looked thoughtful. "We aren't sure if your visions of your mother are part of your psychosis and whether you've had a bit of it since you were quite young."

Adriana felt stunned. Was it possible, that she'd been ill since her mother died? Viera hadn't been around much of late—and it had already occurred to Adriana that the meds might have something to do with it.

"A traumatic experience like losing your mother at an early age could be stressful enough to cause a break with reality," the doctor said. Adriana turned those words ever in her mind. What did they mean, really?

Dr. Burke continued. "You told Fiona that you saw your mother in the back of your head. That she spoke to you and that sometimes you even smelled her cigarettes. This could be psychosis," he said. "Your symptoms in this regard seem to have abated since you started taking a major tranquilizer, or, as they are commonly called, an anti-psychotic. Am I right about that?"

Adriana didn't know, and didn't know what to answer. If she said yes, would that mean she was mad? But maybe it would also mean she was making progress, to the doctor's way of looking at things. She slumped in her chair. If her mother's appearance was merely a symptom, did that mean she wasn't really looking down on Adriana, wasn't coaching and chastising her, wasn't with her all those times when Adriana thought she was?

Dr. Burke remained quiet, peering at her. The sky had clouded over and the interview room had grown quite dark. Elspeth's face had taken on a haggard look. She's tired, Adriana thought. She pictured Elspeth, granddaughter on her hip, bringing her daughter supper in bed after a full day's work. Suddenly it didn't seem so implausible.

"We think you are doing well on this medication," Dr. Burke said, "and it seems you are tolerating it well... do you notice any side effects?" Adriana shook her head. Nothing, no tremors, restless legs, only a mildly dry mouth. She was one of the lucky ones, as bitter as that thought was.

"I'm going to increase your privileges, so you can go out on the hospital grounds for 15 minutes at a time. We'll see how you manage. I realize that it's not what you'd hoped for, but it's what I feel I can offer right now." Adriana nodded, eyes downcast. She knew it was more than she might have expected, but not enough to see Jazz.

"Maybe you should get some rest, Adriana." Dr. Burke offered. "Big storm's coming tonight. I don't know if any of us are going to be able to sleep."

He stood up and Elspeth stood with him. Adriana's eyes flickered up at them, slightly frantic. Elspeth put her hand on Adriana's shoulder. "Have faith Adriana. People get better all the time," she said.

Adriana left the interview room for the common area. Jeff, as usual was glued to the Weather Channel. Marlene and Redgie rocked in their chairs, also listening intently to the TV. An old man was snoozing upright on one of the sofas.

"Hurricane's coming," Redgie informed Adriana, in a hushed voice. Adriana could see the huge clot of white, swirling up from the Gulf of Mexico. "The boy's gonna flip," Redgie said, inclining his head toward Jeff. Jeff had a look of fascinated horror on his face as he tracked the storm. His hands twisted a white hospital issue facecloth which he used every so often to wipe the sweat from his upper lip.

Adriana felt Jeff's terror. She wished she could say something helpful but she knew the black abacus inside his brain was clicking over, calculating the possible damages this storm would visit upon him and the people around him.

To escape from the tension in the common room, Adriana decided she would go outside for her quarter hour. The field in back of the hospital, above the harbour, would be full of goldenrod and asters. The crickets sang all day and into the night she imagined. Sometimes Adriana would see people wading through the grass and weeds, as though they were looking for something. Were they collecting bugs, she wondered, or plants? Maybe they merely wished to stand in this tangled patch of unmown wilderness, this island of unregulated growth, to feel the sun on their hair, as it shone down just as it had for billions of years. There was something warm and stupefying about the field that made Adriana want to lie down in it, to bury her head among the roots and become a part of the flora.

As she walked back to her room to put on her sneakers, Adriana wondered if Jeff had ever had a pet to comfort him.

She imagined him with a big slender dog, a cross between an Irish setter and a wolf hound, with mottled fur and freckles. There was no chance of him having one here in hospital, but maybe he'd like a stuffed animal? She dismissed the idea. Too embarrassing for a grown man. It occurred to Adriana that she could catch him a cricket. She had a glass jar from some peanuts her father had brought her, with a screw-on lid, which she could poke holes in.

Adriana went outside clutching her jar. The grasses were thicker and more tangled than she expected, so she bypassed them for the lower part of the field where someone had mowed with a ride-on machine. She could hear cricket song but couldn't see them. Overturning a stone, she found a black insect with grasshopper legs and a creaky voice. She cupped it in her hands and released it into the jar, threw in some grass and screwed on the lid. With an old nail and a stone for a hammer, she punctured the lid full of holes. So that took care of ventilation but what about water? She wasn't sure if crickets drank water. Perhaps they got enough moisture from eating grass? She was a little worried about how to care for this small creature. Her father had told her when he was a boy in China, children caught crickets and made tiny carts for them to pull. They were kept as pets, so presumably her father would know about their needs. She made a note to call him.

Hiding the jar under her jacket, she entered the hospital, took the elevator up to Mayflower and walked quickly down the hall to the common room. Jeff was no longer there, but a crowd of nurses and patients were watching the news of the hurricane on TV. She continued down the hall to Jeff's room, where he lay in bed, staring at the ceiling. He looked pale and forlorn, orphaned even. Adriana realized that was probably how she looked too, but Jeff didn't have visits from his family or anyone else. She felt suddenly ashamed.

Adriana took the jar from her jacket and thrust it toward Jeff. "Here," she said, with no preamble. Jeff's eyes turned toward her while his body remained where it was. He didn't stretch out his hands. Adriana put the jar on his bedside table. Embarrassed, she mumbled "It's a cricket."

Jeff slowly sat up on the edge of his bed and took the jar in his hands, turning it slowly to look at the cricket from all angles. It made its creaking sound, and a smile, at first tentative, spread across Jeff's colourless face. "Thanks," he said in a hoarse whisper. Adriana smiled quickly and left the room.

Later Adriana passed Jeff's room and glimpsed him lying on his bed, still examining the cricket in the jar. Its song seemed to have slowed down, not as insistent as the music of a wild cricket. She wondered if it could become tame in so short a time, or if crickets ever did become tame, or whether it was sad to be taken from its grassy world into this stale, dim, sterile environment. She couldn't help but think the cricket might resent its captivity, missing its mates and adversaries and free access to the dangerous field that was its universe. Animals, caught in a trap, had been known to gnaw off their limbs to escape. Only human beings could imagine that safety was better than freedom.

It struck her that while she was out in the field looking for the cricket, she could have melted away into the woods along the railway track, or in the opposite direction toward the refinery, and no one would have stopped her. But she had been thinking about another person's comfort and well-being instead of her own—Jeff, and his unfathomable fear of the coming storm. Was it a trap, to be thinking of another person's welfare, if it prevented her from making a break toward freedom herself?

Adriana felt exhausted thinking about it. She lay in her hospital bed, splayed out like a starfish at the bottom of a tidal pool. She'd been here a month, gone from a voluntary patient to an involuntary one, from depressed to psychotic. What would happen to her, in the end? She couldn't see her way clear of this place. That was the knot in her stomach that kept her weak. But there was something, an insistent creaking like the voice of a cricket, that called out from the depths of her.

CHAPTER 25

At supper the nurse offered Adriana a tray of sweet and sour meatballs and rice, and she polished them off, wishing for the first time there were more. It didn't occur to her till after she finished that she had forgotten to wonder whether or not they were poisoned.

There was something else kindling inside her. She felt stronger, somehow. It wasn't anything she had done or any decision she had made, so she figured it must be the medication. Everything was the same, but now she had something holding her upright, a feeling familiar from her past that she was in control, and a sense that somehow, things were okay. She couldn't describe it any better than that.

Marlene was looking sidelong at her from the table by the window, where Redgie was finishing his meatballs. She smiled when Adriana caught her gaze. "You'll be alright, dearie," she said. "You'll be just fine." Adriana nodded and looked down—she believed her. And she saw in a flash that all of them here in the hospital were creeping gradually toward health. Adriana stood up, smiling, and put her tray on the counter.

Elspeth who had come by to relieve the other nurse of

kitchen duty, beamed. "How was supper?" she asked.

Adriana shrugged. "Good," she said.

"Want more? Jeff said he's not eating supper tonight." Adriana thought about it but shook her head no. She wanted to be careful. Meanwhile Redgie thrust his hand in the air, declaring, "I'll have more!" Elspeth let Adriana go with an affectionate tap on the hand.

Adriana wandered down the hall in the direction of her bedroom. Across the hall, she thought she heard Jeff moan in his sleep. She peeked through the open door, hoping he wasn't having a nightmare about the approaching hurricane. The curtain was drawn around his bed.

Adriana fell asleep and dreamed she heard a cricket somewhere in her room. She looked up and down for it but couldn't find it. She tore apart her bed, even ripped open the mattress but it was nowhere to be seen. Adriana stood with mattress stuffing in her hands, wondering what her mother would do when she found her.

She awoke to the sound of a commotion. When she opened her door to peer into the hallway, a nurse motioned to her to close it right away. But before she did, she couldn't help but see the blood, spattered on the hall floor and the door frame of the room across from hers.

She knew it was Jeff. Adriana sat on her bed and shivered. What had he done? She pulled her knees up to her chin and wished herself sightless and mindless, but the smell of blood crept under her door.

The sounds in the hall were calming down, but Adriana didn't attempt to leave her room. She would rather wait until all signs of trauma had been erased, because she was afraid that if she saw Jeff's blood on the floor, she would truly go mad. This place, this terrible place—it was supposed to be somewhere to heal, but it had sucked them all into itself like a vortex.

Adriana knew she had to imagine her way out of here It would be like unravelling something— herself—and knitting the yarn of her into something new. She could do that. She was full of fear, that she somehow belonged to this place—but if it was fear that could carry her forward and out into the world, she would hold on to its fiery mane with all her strength.

After a short while, she heard the cleaning staff come with their mops and buckets to begin to tackle the mess. They were more subdued than usual and clearly did not relish their duties. Adriana imagined the water in the buckets turning pink and the cleaner's uniform spattered red.

When the cleaners left, Adriana opened the door to peek outside. There were two pylons with a plastic sign, that said "Caution–WET" and the floor shone. There was no blood that Adriana could see anywhere. She stepped out into the hall, carefully, and glided silently toward the nursing station.

Elspeth and Jeff's nurse, a short heavy woman with spiky hair, were speaking in low tones. They looked up when Adriana approached them. Elspeth smiled wearily. Adriana asked, in a small voice, "What happened to Jeff?"

Elspeth glanced at Jeff's nurse, who excused herself. Elspeth said, "Let's go have a chat." Elspeth led Adriana to an interview room, where the cloudy sky let in a light that was almost incandescent. Adriana sat down. She had already lost hope.

But Elspeth began with the good news. "Jeff will be alright," she said. Adriana felt her cheeks begin to burn. "He hurt himself badly but we found him in time. I'm not supposed to talk about other patients with you but I wanted to reassure you he will be fine." Adriana's heart beat in her throat.

"Somehow," Elspeth said, almost to herself, "He got hold of a glass jar." Adriana stopped breathing. "He smashed it and used it to try to cut himself." Adriana made a strangled cry. She covered her face with her hands.

Elspeth put a hand on Adriana's shoulder. "It's alright," she said in a troubled voice. "He'll be fine." Adriana tried to stifle her sobs and tell Elspeth the truth.

"It was... my fault," she managed to squeeze out.

Elspeth looked confused. "Why Adriana, of course it wasn't—"

"I gave him the jar," Adriana wept bitterly. "It had a cricket in it."

Elspeth sat down on the sofa beside Adriana and put her arm around her shoulders. "Oh no," she said. "Adriana." She buried her face in Elspeth's shoulder. "My dear girl," she murmured, stroking Adriana's hair, plastered to either side of her tear-stained face. Adriana was filled with such regret that she could barely move, except to cover her eyes with her hands. "We tell people not to bring glass into the unit but sometimes we forget. It's quite likely I didn't remember to tell you," she said, her voice strained.

Adriana looked up. Elspeth's brow was knit together and her mouth was pinched. "No, no, no," Adriana said softly. "I knew the rule. I just didn't think it mattered."

"My dear girl," said Elspeth, stroking Adriana's hair. "You didn't mean any harm. Don't blame yourself."

Adriana quaked inside, but she had to ask, "Where did they take him?" At least she knew it wasn't to the morgue. Elspeth shook her head. So she had decided to follow the rules. Adriana imagined the ambulance had driven just up the road to the Dartmouth General, that they'd taken Jeff in right away to the emergency department and bandaged him up. "Will he be coming back?" she asked. Elspeth stood up regretfully, opening her hands. She didn't know, or wouldn't tell.

Adriana left the interview room ahead of Elspeth, who headed for the nursing station. Adriana saw that, though the common room was empty, the TV was on, blaring the Weather Channel. She sat down and watched Hurricane Juan's massive footprint make its way up the eastern seaboard. No wonder Jeff was frightened—it was likely the biggest storm he'd had to face in his life. The announcer, a young woman in a burgundy skirt and white blouse who looked barely old enough to be out of school, swept her arm up the Atlantic coast of the United States. "It's going to be a big one," she said ominously, smiling all the while.

Adriana went back to her room. Samantha was there, and turned her head in greeting, but didn't say a word. She seemed almost blissful, Adriana thought. "How was your date?" she remembered to ask. Samantha rolled on to her side to face Adriana.

"It was brilliant," she said. "Tony was every bit a gentleman and the choir music was so...." She stretched her 6-foot frame luxuriously. "So... spiritual. We had a good time. Afterwards Tony took me to Tim Hortons." Adriana's eyes opened wide in surprise. That didn't sound like something Tony would do. There were rules, after all. But then she thought, perhaps as a move to keep the patients off the unit while Jeff was taken to hospital, the chapelgoers had been allowed a small field trip. "And then we went for a drive in his car. A perfect night," she sighed. Adriana nodded warily. It sounded like wishful thinking to her, but she didn't really know, and didn't want to extinguish Samantha's happiness.

Samantha rolled on to her side. "That poor boy," she said pityingly. "The one who cut his throat earlier today." Adriana stiffened. "Have you heard how he is? Redgie told me they took him up the road to the Dartmouth General."

Adriana shook her head, feeling slightly dizzy. Samantha, her ebullience undampened continued to babble on about her "date," punctuating her monologue with bursts of giddy laughter. Adriana got into bed and pulled the covers over her, trying to escape. It would be better to counter Samantha's patter with a firm statement, like she was tired and wanted to go to sleep, but she didn't have the where-withal to utter a sound.

Adriana slept through the night, and late into the next morning. She awoke with a start at 10 a.m. Jazz would have gone to the hospital already. She might even be home now. Adriana wanted to call, but felt too weak to get out of bed. She thought of Jazz, lying in a bed similar to the one she occupied, recovering. What did that mean exactly? Recovering from blood loss, from bodily pain, from heart break? She put her hands over her eyes. She didn't want to picture Jazz there at all, but she made herself. Jazz lying in the hospital bed, her lips pale against her bloodless face. Would she be thinking of the future or the past?

Adriana knew Jazz would survive, no matter what she was feeling or thinking. That was the difference between them—Jazz was the unstoppable one, who could push through anything. But would she be strong enough, physically, to stand up and walk back out through the hospital door? Adriana pictured her clutching her abdomen. But she knew Jazz's mouth would be a tight line, and no matter what, Jazz would say to herself, "It's over, I've done my job, now I will go home."

Adriana hoped Jazz would forgive her for not being with her, but somehow she knew she would, just as she forgave Jazz for not visiting her in the hospital. Their friendship was not something flimsy or disposable. It was as though they had made a pact with one another—Jazz would always be there, ready to nudge her forward, and Adriana would always be ready to believe in Jazz, in a way no one else had. Their lives had veered off course for awhile but they would always eventually, intertwine again.

CHAPTER 26

Adriana finally got out of bed at lunch time. Samantha had left the room, her bed a mess of rumpled covers. Adriana stood looking at it for a moment. She made a decision, and stepped away from her own bed without making it. She escaped into the hall before she could change her mind.

Adriana went to the kitchen to call Jazz. She sat at the counter, dialed the number. Someone picked up the phone on the other end. "Jazz?" she asked.

Jazz's mother drew a sharp breath. "Adriana," she said, and Adriana could hear the displeasure in her voice.

Adriana swallowed. "Is Jazz there?" she asked.

Mrs. O'Connell replied, short and sharp, "No, she isn't. She's in the hospital. You should have told me, Adriana," she said in an accusatory tone.

Adriana gripped the phone. "Is she alright?" she asked.

Exasperated, Mrs. O'Connell said, "No, she's not. But she will be. She's able to have visitors. Dartmouth General. Now if you'll excuse me," she said and the phone clicked off.

What could have gone wrong? A hundred things, Adriana thought. Perhaps not all of them life-threatening, but enough of them were serious that it was easy to see why

Jazz's mother was upset with her. She could have lost her daughter, without even knowing she was in trouble, without knowing that she was going to make the biggest decision of her life. She felt as though all her blood was draining out of her, leaving her even paler and weaker than before, but of course that was her imagination. It was Jazz who had bled, and Jazz who lay in a hospital bed now with her mother's knowledge upon her.

Adriana felt a shiver down her spine. She could barely think. Teeth chattering, she put on her jeans and sweater, and went to find Elspeth. She was in the office behind the nursing station. Adriana could see she was deep in thought. When she saw Adriana standing there, Elspeth's face changed, like a cloud had passed over it. Adriana wrapped her arms around herself and waited. Elspeth spoke in a low voice. "You look like you just ran into an iceberg," Adriana nodded. Elspeth, slightly confused, asked her "What can I do for you, my dear?"

"My friend is in the hospital," Adriana stammered. "Something went wrong. Can I go visit her?"

Elspeth's brow furrowed. "I'm sorry to hear it. I'll talk to Dr. Burke to see if he'll be willing to give you back level six privileges. Don't get your hopes up though. I'll let you know if the doctor will see you before he leaves this afternoon."

Shaking inside, Adriana returned to her room. She took out the knitting needles and yarn that she'd scrounged in the OT room and began to knit a scarf, but her fingers trembled and made it impossible to work. She put the knitting aside, stood up and made her bed, automatically it seemed, but it still helped calm her nerves.

After lunch, Adriana sat down in the common area. Someone had started doing a puzzle of some llamas standing in a field. They had managed to finish the llamas but the grass around them, the more difficult part of the puzzle, was still in pieces. To distract herself, Adriana began to work on those areas, and soon lost herself in the activity. It felt good to be absorbed by something, even something as inconsequential as a puzzle.

Marlene sat on the other side of the room, watching her. Adriana hadn't noticed her come in. Suddenly the elevator opened and a woman in a hair net pushed a trolley of supper trays into the hall. "Trays are up," Marlene crowed, and Adriana looked at her, startled. Could it be supper time already? That meant she'd been sitting there for at least four hours. Marlene cackled as though she'd played an enormous joked. Adriana wondered where Redgie was. It wasn't like Marlene to be without him.

Adriana waited twenty minutes before she went for supper. She didn't like to sit there amid the silent, shaky-handed, old people, some of whom had been waiting for their meal for half an hour. She preferred to go as they were leaving, and eat alone. She knew it was because she didn't want to be reminded of what awaited her, fifty years from now. It was unfair and ungenerous of her, she knew, but being among these debilitated older folks tightened the knot in her stomach, and she felt she had no control over it.

As she sat down to eat, something told her that she wouldn't be seeing the doctor this afternoon. Her stomach swooped. She ate her baked chicken leg slowly, with dry eyes. She felt like a desert. Jazz would be lying in her hospital bed, pale as sand, with her mother beside her.

Elspeth peeked her head in the door. She came to sit down across the table from Adriana. "Dr. Burke didn't have time to see you today," she said regretfully. "But he'll see you first thing in the morning tomorrow. I'm sorry," she said and shook her head. "There are just so many things going on, with the hurricane coming tonight."

Adriana had forgotten about the hurricane. How was it possible, she wondered, for the mind to have so many compartments? She had been feeling anxious about the storm and then she put it completely away in a drawer, so she could worry about Jeff, and then Jazz. It seemed incredible that the mind allowed for such forgetfulness. Was it the hippocampus, floating around in the slosh of her brain, that had lost its power?

Adriana returned to the llama puzzle but she didn't have the heart for it anymore. Instead she sat beside Marlene and some of the other patients, watching the storm track north on the television weather map. Marlene rocked silently, not really watching the TV. "Where's Redgie?" Adriana asked. Marlene cackled and put her finger to her lips and hushed her loudly.

Someone changed the channel to an old sitcom Adriana had never seen before. It was stupid. She got up to leave, pushing the table with the puzzle away from her. The puzzle slid off, onto the floor. Everyone in the room turned to look, and Adriana began to cry. She started to pick up the pieces and to put them back together but nothing fit. Other patients tried to help. The depressed woman that Adriana had seen combing her fine brown hair as she walked down the hall bent down and picked up a few pieces and an old man shuffled some pieces into a pile with his feet. Marlene sat impassively and rocked.

Adriana escaped as soon as she could, returning to her room. She climbed into bed. Really, she didn't care about the puzzle or the hurricane or anything else. She was aching for Jazz, and for Jeff, both lying in beds in the hospital just up the street. She hoped the evening would bring them peace. She wished she could shake the sense of dread that gripped her.

CHAPTER 27

Adriana lay awake until a nurse called, "Medication time." She went to stand in line with the other patients from the unit. The woman who combed her hair was there, but Jeff was missing of course. So was Redgie.

Redgie's nurse Tony, the one that Samantha was smitten with, examined the sign-out book. When he straightened up, his smile was gone, and he quickly walked toward the nursing station. Adriana overheard him on the phone, talking to security. "He's been gone for hours," he said, pulling his hand over his face. "No, I didn't notice. The sign-out book says he's going to stop the hurricane."

Adriana, standing at the window in the common room, watched security combing the grass below the hospital and disappear over the bank down to the railway track. The police had been alerted, and were checking the bridges. Adriana wondered if they thought Redgie would try to make a human sacrifice of himself. Elspeth was long gone for the day and Adriana didn't feel there was anyone else she wanted to talk to. She went to her room and sat on her bed. *Please let them find Redgie*, she prayed. *Please let Jazz be okay. Let Jeff be fine.*

Adriana felt she had done all she could. She lay down on her unmade bed, exhausted, and slipped into unconsciousness.

At midnight she was awakened by the enormous sound of the wind and rain lashing the windows. It was a wild and unholy sound, as though the hospital were being attacked by ravenous animals

Adriana, quaking, got up to go to the toilet. In the nursing station, Tony was on the phone, his face taut with anxiety. The other nurses were speaking to one another in hushed tones that she couldn't hear through the glass that encased the nursing station offices. Adriana had never heard such wind before. The wind often moaned around the building, like a pack of ghost wolves. Now it was the booming, hysterically angry voice of her mother writ large. It had been weeks since her mother had bothered her and now here she was, circling the hospital and shrieking accusations. Adriana sat on the toilet, her hands over her ears.

When she came out of the washroom, she saw Marlene sitting in a chair by the common room window. Adriana thought she watched out the window the way women have for centuries when their men went to sea. Was Redgie out there somewhere, battling the elements? She imagined him standing on the stony finger of land on which the McNab's Island lighthouse was built, arms upraised shouting into the hurricane to stop, be calm, to return whence it came. And the hurricane, like a dragon, encircling him.

Back in her bedroom, Samantha was pacing between the bedroom door and window. She barely acknowledged Adriana's return, except to shorten her path on the way to the door. She was keyed up, ready to explode. Adriana slipped under her covers, and closed her eyes tight, hands over her ears.

There was a sudden flash of light and the sound of sparks like an old-fashioned camera bulb going off. One of the outdoor lights had blown and the room grew darker. Samantha stopped in her tracks like a deer in the headlights, and then she began to howl. "Make it stop!" she cried, as though in agony, then moaned as she collapsed to the floor. Adriana threw the covers off the bed and stood up. But what could she do? Samantha was too big to lift.

Adriana knelt down beside Samantha and stroked her hair with a trembling hand. She began to hum a lullaby, whose words she knew, but didn't understand. It was a Slovak song her mother used to sing to her. Adriana's voice jerked when she jumped at the sound of tree branches cracking and power lines come loose and sparking. Samantha muttered and blubbered till her sobs grew quiet, and her breathing slowed. Adriana, calmer now herself, followed the lullaby with another mournful tune about the Slovak countryside and then with "Let it Be" and "You Are My Sunshine." Samantha lay quietly, her enormous knees pulled up to her chest. Adriana took the blanket from Samantha's bed and covered her with it, leaving her asleep on the floor, then crawled back into bed herself.

But Adriana stayed awake, eyes dark and fearful. The violence of the storm—overwhelming, unrelenting—had driven patients out of their beds. She heard them moaning in the hallway and the nurses trying to soothe them in low tones. Someone, perhaps the brown haired woman, sounded inconsolable. Eventually Adriana managed to tumble unconscious, as though into a lightless passage. Sleep had always been her refuge, and it remained so, even in the face of a hurricane.

Adriana woke up slowly when the sky began to lighten, afraid almost to open her eyes. Outside, the sun was burning its way through the cloud. She sat up slowly, pulling her blanket around her. The trees had been partially stripped of their leaves , which were strewn all over the ground or plastered to the windows. Branches had come down, some of them blown across the parking lot. Everything looked new, freshly washed, chaotic. Adriana felt a surge of feeling in her throat that she couldn't recognize.

Her watch ticked loudly, as though it were the only thing that had survived the storm. It was almost 7 a.m. and Samantha was gone. Eventually, Adriana made her way to the kitchen, past a few people in the common room, stunned and dishevelled as refugees. As they waited for breakfast in the kitchen, patients looked out the window and shook their heads, exclaiming, in voices thick with medication and dulled by illness. Marlene was on the phone. "They didn't find him. No," she said, blowing her nose, her voice loud and teary, ending in a howl. "I thought he'd be back by now."

Adriana realized she hadn't called her father and that he hadn't called her. After Marlene finished, she dialed her home number on the kitchen phone. It rang and rang, but her father didn't pick up.

She tried to reassure herself. The battery charger for the phone at home was plugged into the wall and it was unlikely it was working. Her father had Beth to occupy his thoughts and it was likely they were busy surveying the storm damage and cleaning up the yard. She pictured her father shaking his head at the downed trees and power lines. That's about as upset as her father would get about a situation like this. It was only if the people he loved were in danger that he would worry, and he would know she was in a safe place. At least it was as safe as the patients it sheltered. She shivered, realizing he had not yet heard what happened to Jeff.

Adriana made an instant decaf, then toast slathered with Cheez Whiz. From the kitchen window, she watched a handful of security guards survey the damage to the trees, cars and buildings. A few nurses also stood in a group, including Elspeth, who was just coming on shift, and Tony, whose shift just finished. They spoke together in what looked to be low and urgent tones. Elspeth put her hand on Tony's arm and he wiped his eyes with the palm of his other hand.

Adriana wondered if they had found Redgie. Maybe that's why Tony was crying—maybe they'd found him. Maybe he had washed up under the bridge. Maybe he was pinned under a tree. But maybe they hadn't found him and they didn't know where else to look.

Marlene had hung up and was making herself two cups of coffee. She wore her parka as usual, but now completely zipped with the hood up. Her hands shook, and coffee sloshed onto her fingers and the floor. She carried the two styrofoam cups to the table where Adriana stood, and sat down across from her. Marlene didn't say a word to her but drank the coffee in small, regular slurps. Then she drank the next cup, more quickly, since it had cooled, but with the same mechanical motion. After she was finished she threw the Styrofoam cups in the garbage and stalked from the kitchen. As she left, she let out a tremulous wail, which continued down the hall. The sound sent ice through Adriana's blood.

Adriana made her way to the common room. Everyone at the nursing station was discussing the storm. "They're telling people to stay off the roads," one woman said.

Another snorted and said in a loud whisper, "No way I'm staying here all day! I'll end up crazy like the rest of them."

Adriana straightened up as she walked by them, glancing disdainfully at them, her head in the air like a queen. She hoped they felt ashamed of themselves.

On television there was news that a paramedic had been killed when a tree fell on his vehicle. Adriana couldn't imagine what that would be like, to be crushed to death in the back of an ambulance. She wondered, aimlessly, whether there had been a patient with him. What if Redgie had been in that ambulance?

Adriana's brain jangled. What were things like at the Dartmouth General, she wondered. There were no trees to come crashing down on an ambulance or pierce a window. Surely they had generators to keep the place going. She imagined Jazz, a small bump under the covers of her hospital bed, pale and exhausted. And Jeff, taut and fearful after being awake all night, gradually loosening his grip on consciousness, now that the wind and rain were over.

Adriana made herself have a shower and put on a clean pair of jeans and a T-shirt, with a johnny shirt around her shoulders. She combed her hair, which was growing out but still lopsided, and gathered it into a ponytail. She felt as ragged as a leaf torn from a tree. This year, she would turn 20 and her father was already 50. She had noticed the wrinkles around his eyes, and saw the same crow's feet beginning at the corners of her own. How was it possible that she had grown up, and her father had grown old? It seemed like her mother's funeral happened yesterday. But that was what everyone said, about the passage of time. It must have some mysterious property, which allowed the seconds to contract, until they barely seemed to mark time at all. Like a thread pulled tight, bunching fabric into a series of pleats.

Elspeth was in the nursing station when she finished. It

was a quarter after 11, almost lunch time. Adriana realized that she like everyone else had begun to mark time by hospital meals. Elspeth looked determined and purposeful, Adriana thought; maybe even grim. But her face softened when she spotted Adriana hanging forlornly by the nurses' station. "How did you sleep in the hurricane?" she asked. Adriana realized, with wonder, that she'd had remarkably undisturbed sleep. "It was fine," she said, eyes wide. Elspeth laughed. "Maybe you are one of those people who could sleep through a train crash," she said. "And that's not such a bad thing." Adriana nodded. It had saved her the trauma of seeing the physical world thrown about like a rag doll in the mouth of a dog.

"Can I talk to the doctor today about my privileges?" she asked, her voice wavering slightly. What if Elspeth said no.

But to Adriana's relief, she answered, "Of course. I'll ask him if he can see you this morning."

Samantha drifted on to the unit in a daze, her arms full of bags of ketchup chips and a can of diet Coke in each fist. Adriana felt something like relief leap in her chest, but Samantha didn't acknowledge her. She flopped down in a chair in the common room, and stared at the wall. Adriana tried to catch her gaze but Samantha, in her trance, did not respond. Adriana wondered if she had slept, or if she'd gotten up and paced the hall all night. Samantha looked old too, Adriana thought. Her face sagged, and the light had gone out of her eyes.

Marlene walked into the common room and turned on the television. Samantha seemed to wake up enough to put her hands over her ears, and begin to rock. Adriana sensed her distress, and after taking a moment to find her courage, she motioned to Marlene to turn the sound down. "Please," she said, gesturing to Samantha.

Marlene stood up and began to throw whatever she could get her hands on, screaming "This is my hospital and I want to watch TV." Samantha cowered and moaned, while Adriana, shocked, tried to protect herself from the books and magazines and board games that Marlene was launching into the air. "You can kiss my ass," she screeched, dancing around in her red parka. Elspeth in the nursing station picked up the phone to call security. Marlene at the height of her anger, shrieked, "You're not even a real woman! You're a disgusting, a.... a stupid freak!" Then, having exhausted her anger, sat down in a rocker and began to watch the television. The hurricane was all over the news. Pictures flashed across the screen—trees down, cars smashed, and rocks as big as shopping carts tossed from the harbour onto the shore.

Marlene began to cry, a loud, blubbering sound. When security arrived, with a stretcher, Elspeth motioned for them to stand back so she could talk to Marlene. They stood back and, while Elspeth crouched beside her and spoke quietly, patting her hand; patients stopped in the hall to see what was going on. The security guards waved them on, as though directing traffic. Samantha's eyes closed as she tried to shut out the noise and sights around her. The payphone began to ring, but no one answered it.

Surrounded by magazines that lay where they landed, Adriana, traumatized, sat rooted to her spot on the couch. Samantha, whose moans had died to a mutter, seemed almost amphibian to Adriana—barely human, her features thick, smooth, and damp like the limbs of a salamander. It was hard to imagine only yesterday she was coquetting with Tony, excited as a school girl on her first date.

Elspeth knelt beside Marlene, whispering to her when

the hospital chaplain, a young, clean-shaven man dressed casually in a short sleeved shirt and cargo pants, appeared at her shoulder. Elspeth got up off her knees, heavily, with the chaplain supporting her elbow. Marlene's face, blurry and smudged, looked up at him, beseeching. "Is he gone? Is Redgie gone to Heaven?" she asked in a voice thick with grief.

The chaplain spoke quietly. "We don't know where Redgie is," he said, truthfully. "Maybe we can say a prayer for his safe return." Marlene clutched his hand in both of hers, and closed her eyes, tears still streaming down her cheeks. "Father, you say a prayer for him... I can't." The chaplain smiled and nodded, and in a low voice which Adriana could barely hear, began to intone the Lord is My Shepherd. The security guards drifted away and Elspeth turned her attention to Samantha .

Adriana could only half hear what Elspeth was saying to Samantha, who held a pillow to her cheek and sucked her thumb. From what she could gather, Elspeth was trying to reassure Samantha that Marlene was distraught over Redgie, that she lashed out without thinking, that Samantha could disregard Marlene's words as those of a woman who was ill and in great emotional pain. Adriana could see that Samantha, glassy eyed and unseeing, was in a world of her own, driven there by the hurricane and Marlene's fury. Elspeth encouraged her to get to her feet and led her to the bedroom. Adriana hoped sleep would help Samantha find her way back to this world, as bleak as it was.

Adriana found her way to the kitchen phone. After a few rings her father answered with a breathless hello. Adriana felt a rush of happiness. "Hi Dad," she said.

"Adriana, thank God! I couldn't ring you till the power came back on." He told her that the neighbour's tree had fallen in front of his car and some smaller trees had blown sideways to rest against the roof, doing some damage to the eavestrough. "But we're okay," he said. He lowered his voice. "Though Beth is a little traumatized. We won't come to visit you yet, not until the roads are cleared. They've called in the army," he said incredulously. Adriana pictured him shaking his head.

"Give Beth a hug from me," she said, before she hung up.

Her Dad would be fine, but she wondered about her sister. She imagined Beth huddled in a chair with a blanket around her. The similarity with Samantha's state disturbed her. Beth was so vulnerable, so fragile and Adriana feared that if anything upset her, Beth would lose her mind. Their father was not equipped to look after her by himself. Adriana wanted to go home.

CHAPTER 28

Lunch came and went. Adriana felt antsy, waiting to talk to Elspeth and the doctor about leaving the hospital grounds to see Jazz. Elspeth seemed to have disappeared. Perhaps she was with Samantha, who had also vanished. Adriana saw Dr. Burke a few times, striding purposefully down the hall, always hurrying somewhere else. She tried to ask when he would see her, but he put his hand up and said, "I'll talk to you soon, Adriana. Just hang tight."

As the afternoon wore on, Adriana felt more and more stressed. It seems that the nurses and doctors were rushing around putting out emotional fires, talking to everyone except her. There was nothing for her to do except to look out the window, and survey the damage. Desperate for a distraction, she went to her bedroom to knit.

The sound of the needles clicking always calmed her. She turned on the small radio her father had brought her. She tuned it to a station that played bland and tinny pop tunes, avoiding any news of the hurricane. Adriana was surprised at how absorbed she was in her task—an hour had passed and she had barely noticed. Strangely though, she felt like she was on display, being watched by an audience that was holding its breath. She wished Samantha was there to distract her.

There was a knock and Dr. Burke stuck his head in the bedroom door. "Adriana, I can talk to you now." He smiled, tipping his head toward her. "Knitting are you?" Adriana nodded. She felt awkward. Usually Elspeth would be there to act as a buffer. As though reading her thoughts, Dr. Burke said, "Elspeth isn't able to join us as she got called away because of an emergency," he said. Adriana wondered whether her daughter, in bed with depression, had needed her to look after the baby. "But Fiona will sit in for her," Dr. Burke nodded. Fiona, Adriana thought, startled. It hadn't occurred to her that Fiona might work anywhere but on Short Stay.

Dr. Burke held the bedroom door open for Adriana and they walked a few metres down the hall to the interview room where Fiona was sitting. She was more noticeably pregnant and looked tired, with dark circles under her eyes. She smiled at Adriana and said, "Hello, my love. I've been called in to fill in for Elspeth. Hope you don't mind." Adriana smiled and shook her head. "I'm hardly fit to be seen, but I know you'll forgive me," Fiona said with a wink.

Dr. Burke, as usual, got right down to business. "How have you been feeling over the last 24 hours?" he asked. Adriana thought about it. It seemed she had been on edge ever since she heard about Jazz's plans. She wasn't sure what answer Dr. Burke wanted, so she told the truth. "I've been worried about my friend. She's in the Dartmouth General because something went wrong with her abortion. And I'm worried about Jeff. And also my little sister." Adriana put her hand to her forehead. She knew she had almost no hope of being granted a pass, after absconding to Jazz's house the other day.

Dr. Burke nodded, pleased, she thought, with her straightforward answer. "I understand you want privileges to go visit your friend in the hospital," he said. Adriana looked down. Why did she feel like she was asking for a big favour? Dr. Burke, bent sideways to catch her gaze. "Is that right?" Adriana nodded.

"Generally, we would be hesitant to let you go, after the events of the last few days, but these are unusual circumstances. If we let you go, will you go only to the hospital to visit your friend, and then come back here immediately afterward? I'm afraid we can't let you go see your family yet. You'd have to walk there, because the roads aren't clear." Adriana gawked, surprised. She nodded vigorously.

Dr. Burke continued, "If you agree to be back here in an hour, you can go. Be careful on the streets though because a number of trees are down and there are crews trying to clean things up." Adriana, face red with emotion, nodded. Dr. Burke was taking a chance on her. His face looked kinder than she remembered, softer around the edges.

"Let's see how your pass to visit your friend goes. If everything's okay we'll talk about a weekend pass for you to see your family." Adriana felt a rush of relief. Finally, something was changing, moving. She needed to feel the air flowing past her, so she'd know it was real.

Adriana put on her sneakers and a jacket, and made her way to the entrance. The air that greeted her was moist and fresh, and the sun was trying to materialize from behind the clouds. Adriana's mouth hung open at the sight of branches and trash scattered over the lawns and the street, empty of cars but covered with leaves. She felt a bubbling of gratitude that the hospital hadn't crumbled under the enormous hand of the storm. She wasn't the only one surveying the damage—everyone looked slightly dazed, as though they had wandered out of a bomb shelter. She couldn't tell whether they were patients or people living in the neighbourhood, since the hurricane had reduced all of them to astonishment.

The Dartmouth General was just a few minutes' walk up the street. Adriana could see its ugly bulk on the next hill. She had one hour.

Adriana asked at the information desk for Jazz's room. She took the elevator up to Jazz's floor, which seemed unusually quiet. Jazz was lying in bed asleep, her mother beside her. Mrs. O'Connell nodded to Adriana with a tight-lipped smile. "She just drifted off," Mrs. O'Connell said. "She wondered if you'd come." Adriana looked at Jazz's pale face. She looked about 13 years old.

Mrs. O'Connell was rubbing Jazz's hand gently and soothingly. Adriana was seized with sadness. How hard for a mother to see her child in pain and distress. "Is she going to be okay?" Mrs. O'Connell's gaze was soft, not judgmental. She nodded at Adriana, her smile flickering like a television screen. It was not the prim, humourless Mrs. O'Connell that Adriana was familiar with who patted the seat beside her, inviting her to sit.

Jazz had an IV in her arm and wore a blue johnny shirt, under the white blanket. Her eyelids fluttered and she turned her head, moaning softly. Mrs. O'Connell's mouth trembled, as she put a hand to her daughter's forehead. Jazz's eyes opened slightly, but she didn't seem to see Adriana, though she was looking in her direction. Mrs. O'Connell stroked her cheek, and her eyes closed again.

Adriana understood why Jazz hated the hospital. She

was reduced, here, to a level of helplessness that was so out of character for her that she was barely recognizable. Adriana smiled shakily, telling Mrs. O'Connell, "I can't stay," without explaining the hour-long pass, and the fact that she couldn't bear to sit with Jazz's mother, wavering on the edge of tears. Mrs. O'Connell nodded and gazed at Jazz. "Please tell her I came by," Adriana whispered.

On the way to the elevator, Adriana caught sight of Elspeth, sitting in a hospital room at the end of a bed. She stopped short, anxious. Was Samantha in that hospital bed? She stood and waved at Elspeth, as if to a stranger whose attention you wanted to catch. Elspeth smiled and waved back. When Adriana reached the door to the room, she saw it was Jeff, not Samantha, in the bed. Jeff was watching television, his neck covered in a clean white bandage. There was no more fear in his eyes. In fact he looked quite cheerful.

Elspeth patted the chair next to her. Adriana sat down, because she didn't know what else to do. Jeff lifted a hand in greeting, not very high because it obviously hurt his neck. "I'll be coming back to the NS tomorrow," he said, without any preamble. Adriana nodded, shakily. Elspeth looked more at ease here than Adriana could remember. Jeff pointed the remote at the TV to change the channel, and turned to Adriana, his eyes large and dark. "Did you walk here? What's it like outside?"

Adriana trembled with relief. He didn't blame her for the jar. "The sun's trying to come out," she said in a tremulous voice. "There are leaves and branches everywhere…" her voice trailed off.

Jeff nodded, satisfied. "It's just like on TV," he said, and turned back to watch the coverage of the hurricane. For a moment, Adriana felt confused, but then realized he was right. It *was* just like on TV.

Elspeth looked at home here. Adriana wondered what it was that made her relax, compared to at the NS. Maybe the mental hospital reminded her too much of her daughter. Elspeth had never told Adriana anything about her except for that first confidence, and she hadn't admitted that it wasn't a friend she was speaking about, but herself.

Adriana was almost afraid to ask Elspeth anything. But when Jeff's attention was riveted by the TV, she turned to Elspeth, and in a low voice, ventured, "and Samantha?"

Elspeth shook her head. "I can't tell you anything, Adriana, you know that." But she was smiling and Adriana knew she wouldn't be if something terrible had happened.

Adriana's body slowly relaxed, overcome by exhaustion. She leaned back in her chair and gazed up at the ceiling, wishing she was a little child and could sit on Elspeth's lap, nestle against her bosom and sleep. Elspeth stood at the window, surveying the hurricane damage. From the back, Elspeth looked substantial, her shoulders broad and solid— but Adriana noticed she stooped slightly and that there was more grey in her hair than she'd noticed before. Adriana felt a twinge of sadness. Elspeth was like a mountain peak, always strong and always there. It was frightening to think that Elspeth would fade into old age, like everyone else.

Adriana knew her hour was almost up and it was time to return to the mental hospital. She stood up, and Elspeth turned around, smiling regretfully. "You're going back?" she asked. Adriana nodded. She'd escaped twice and returned once on her own. This time she would go back to keep her promise to the doctor. And Fiona.

Elspeth sat down heavily in her chair. "Mental hospitals

are going the way of the dinosaur," she said. Adriana wasn't sure if Elspeth was speaking to her, or to herself. "There's got to be a better way of treating people," Elspeth continued, shaking her head. "I never want my children or their children to have to come to a place like the NS," she said.

Adriana stood with her mouth open. She'd never heard Elspeth talk about the mental hospital that way before. In fact, Elspeth had once told Adriana that she's made the right choice by admitting herself, but maybe it was because it was the only choice.

Usually Elspeth was the one who listened, her head cocked to one side. She smiled at Adriana, slightly embarrassed. "Now you've heard my rant," she said. "I know you need to go back. Just don't stay there long," she said. "Don't let it grow on you."

As she walked up the street to the NS, Adriana thought about what Elspeth had said. She wondered if Elspeth was really afraid that she'd get used to the hospital and not want to leave. There were some people, she knew, who lived in the hospital for years, and others that returned as regular as clockwork, their lives so dreary or their illness so severe they couldn't stay away from the place.

Adriana stepped over branches on the sidewalk She realized she was between worlds—ill enough to be hospitalized and healthy enough to traverse a street turned upsidedown by a hurricane, in order to comfort a friend and to keep a promise. Who was she, besides a mental patient? A daughter, a sister, a friend. She considered herself to be loyal, discreet and by nature an extrovert, though since puberty she hadn't given any indication of that side of herself. She liked depressing music, hated crowds, and had a penchant for fading into the background. She enjoyed being alone and didn't mind the dark, could speak English and a smattering of French, liked Chinese food and road trips. She remembered fishing with her dad at the lake at dawn, how it felt to sit beside him on the rocks at the shore and breathe in the smell of the still water, and feel her forehead relax and her whole body loosen. That was who she was, under all the layers of worry and illness.

Adriana checked her watch. She had five minutes to spare, so she sat down on a bench under a maple in front of the Purdy building. Some of the branches had been stripped of leaves, but for the most part the tree was lush and intact. Adriana looked up into the crown of the tree, which reminded her of a brain on its stem, the branches and twigs like a network of neurons. It was so mysterious, this green world, inhabited by birds and caterpillars, like a secret planet unto itself.

It was time. Adriana walked into the Purdy building, as she'd agreed. It didn't feel so much like a prison now, but a temporary resting place, from which she would soon be released. It surprised her to feel whole and hopeful, as though she'd misplaced herself somewhere and had just now found herself again.

CHAPTER 29

Adriana Song signed her name in the book at the door to Mayflower. Usually she simply scribbled her signature to get it over with but today she lingered, staring at the plump cursive. That was her, Adriana Song, whom Elspeth said had a beautiful name.

The halls were quiet for once. She savoured the silence but realized it might not bode well, after all. Where was Marlene? Had Redgie come back? And what about Samantha? She felt herself begin to vibrate with anxiety, but she wanted to preserve her calm, so she took a deep breath in and out.

She sat down in the kitchen, where the stainless steel countertop and the tile floor gleamed. Adriana was glad to be alone here, even if she realized that it wouldn't last. It occurred to her that since her mother had died she'd always been most happy when she was alone with her thoughts. Even Jazz hadn't been able to enter the door that lead to her private mind, and that was the way Adriana wanted it to be—her memories tucked away inside the sea horse's pouch. She had too many shameful, dark and selfish thoughts that she didn't want to share with anyone.

Adriana proceeded to her room and saw the staff in the back office in a sombre meeting of some kind. Colin, the student doctor stood in the hallway looking shattered, his hands over his face. Marlene was rocking in a chair in the common room, as though it were serious business, as if she could rock herself to some distant location. The hurricane had gripped and shaken this place, and she had come loose from it, like a leaf from a tree. It was time for her to go.

Samantha's bed had been made neatly. There was no sign of her belongings or her comforting messiness. Adriana stood in the door of the room without going in, until she saw the note on her bed. She picked up the onion skin paper and unfolded it. Samantha had written something in a blue fountain pen. *Dear Adriana*, it began. *They're moving me to Laurel unit. I hope you will visit me.*

Adriana sat down on the bed. It was as if Samantha had never been there. If Adriana chose to ignore this note, she could pretend she and Samantha had never crossed paths, that Samantha didn't even exist. When she left the hospital, she could leave it—all of it—behind. But she thought of Samantha's sad eyes, her big helpless hands. Samantha, who had no one. She couldn't just let go of her, even though that would be the easiest thing to do. A visit was in order.

Adriana went downstairs to the vending machines to buy ketchup chips for Samantha. On her way back up in the elevator, she found herself humming one of her mother's Slovak songs. Because her mother only sang it when she was sad, Adriana thought of it as a sad song. But within the sadness was a seed of happiness, a persistent grain of sand in the oyster of her depression.

Laurel unit was only across the hall from Mayflower, but to Adriana it felt like she had landed on a strange planet.

The rooms were laid out in a mirror image to the rooms on Mayflower, and much was the same—the blaring television set, the listless people waiting in the kitchen for the next meal, the slamming of doors, and the clipped footsteps of nurses. But there was something in the air, maybe a brute reality, which was different from Mayflower. It may simply have been because Laurel was on the north side of the building and didn't see as much sunlight as the south side, but Adriana felt entombed as she made her way through Laurel, looking for Samantha's room.

Adriana located her across from the laundry room, from which could hear the muffled sound of someone's washing tumbling in the dryer. There were three other names on the door, which Adriana paid no attention to. Samantha lay stretched out on her side on her bed, her panty-hosed feet twitching. She had a melancholic look, but when she saw Adriana, she brightened. Adriana felt ashamed of herself for even considering forgetting about Samantha.

"Well, hello!" Samantha called out and struggled to sit up. Though she sounded cheerful, there was something bleak about her eyes. Adriana stood in the doorway, exposed and awkward. Samantha waved her in and reached out a hand for the ketchup chips. "My favourites!" she squealed. The bump under the bedcovers in the opposite corner of the room snored and rustled. Samantha covered her mouth with her hand and lowered her voice to a whisper. "You do know me!" Adriana resisted the impulse to roll her eyes. Everyone knew Samantha liked ketchup chips.

Everything was about the same here as in Mayflower; same chair, bed covers, locker. The same smell, not antiseptic, but as if someone had cleaned half-heartedly and tried to cover up the scent of decay. Samantha looked stranded here, whereas she had seemed quite at home on Mayflower.

"They didn't want me around Tony," Samantha said softly. "They thought I was too attached. They don't know anything about love." Adriana nodded warily. She didn't understand the way these decisions were made, or by whom, but she thought it very likely that Tony had had some say in it.

Samantha lay back on her bed, and breathed. "Will you read to me?" she asked, turning her massive head toward Adriana, who nodded and looked around but didn't see a book. Samantha gestured toward the bedside table. "It's in there," she said. Adriana opened the drawer and shuffled a couple magazines aside. There was only a small hard cover notebook, which looked quite old, and a cookbook. She picked up the cookbook and stared at the cover, which was decorated with a photo of red and yellow apples. "Not that one," Samantha said, closing her eyes.

Adriana pulled out the notebook, its yellowing pages rasping at her touch. She opened it to a handwritten page with a faded newspaper article taped opposite it. There was a photo of a young man, a teenage boy, striding through a ribbon at a finish line. The caption said, "Samuel Johns Wins the Race Walking Competition in Brighton Saturday Past." Adriana stared at the photo. There was Samantha's nose and eyes and puffy hair. Could this be her brother?

Samantha closed her eyes and smiled. "My finest hour," she said. Adriana stared at the book in her hands, afraid to look up.

"Adriana," Samantha said, startling her. She glanced up into Samantha's sad eyes. "I have been a woman for more of my life than I was a man." Samantha sat up, put her legs over the side of the bed, with her back to Adriana and began to unroll her knee highs. Adriana's face felt hot. She realized she was flushed with anger.

"I didn't tell you, because it didn't seem important. To our friendship," Samantha continued, "which I treasure." She looked shyly over her shoulder at Adriana. "You are my first friend in a long time."

Adriana took a breath. She was surprised to realize that Samantha was her first friend too, in years. Besides Jazz, her father, and now maybe her sister, she didn't really have anyone else. Samantha swung her legs back onto the bed again. Adriana noticed the scars for the first time. "My father used to beat me, with a broom handle," Samantha said, "When he caught me dressing in my mother's clothes. He was so afraid," she laughed softly, "that I'd grow up to be a pouf. It was almost a relief to him I think that I became a woman."

Adriana was speechless. Samantha looked at her kindly. "It's a shock to you? Some people know right away that I wasn't born a girl. It takes them a while to adjust to me. But you," she smiled, "You were too wrapped up in your own thoughts to notice." Samantha lay back in her bed, eyes closed. Adriana noted her big hands, her coarse features. How had it never occurred to her that Samantha had been a man? It seemed so obvious now. Adriana experienced a shudder of revulsion, an involuntary, visceral reaction— and then a flash of shame, like the sting of a jellyfish.

"I know it must seem strange to you," Samantha said, "But I wish everyone could design their own bodies. That way you'd get exactly what you want."

Adriana thought about it. If she were to design her own body what would it look like? She imagined herself with wavy auburn hair, pale skin and startling, turquoise eyes. She would still be a woman but a striking one, one that people would notice when she walked down the street. One that Peter would notice, if the truth be known. Adriana turned that idea over in her mind. She had been trying to fade into the background for such a long time. Did she really, secretly, want to be noticed?

Samantha's eyes were open, shining with tenderness, tinged with sadness. What kind of life must she have led? Adriana wondered. To be in a body that you feel doesn't belong to you. It would be a nightmare of a kind, a terrible, unending solitary confinement. Like being locked in TQ every day of your life.

Neither of them spoke, as the light shrank between them in the fading afternoon. Something made sense, finally, to Adriana. She realized that in this one life every moment counts; not a second is without meaning or import. The time she spent in anguish or boredom, meant something, was part of the path she was following. She had always thought the secret of this life was to be happy and that she was failing miserably—but the idea that her suffering had meaning gave her a sense of hope.

Samantha's eyes closed again and she looked perfectly at rest. Adriana closed her eyes too. She was nowhere, nothing, a dust mote. She pulled her knees up to her chest, shivering with cold.

Samantha began to snore, and Adriana watched her as she slept, her leonine head propped up on the pillow, her huge hand dangling. Adriana wondered if she ever regretted becoming a woman, whether she'd ever thought she'd made a mistake. It was unthinkable to Adriana that a person could be so sure that a decision was the right one as to forever alter who they were. But given the chance to design her own body, wouldn't she have done the same thing?

Adriana's mother stood there, arms crossed. She had a

bemused smile on her face. For the first time it seemed her mother wasn't sitting in judgement on her. Adriana felt relieved, elated even.

Samantha smiled in her sleep, a bubble forming at her lips, like a newborn baby.

CHAPTER 30

They found Redgie's body washed up on the shore by the Dartmouth ferry terminal. Adriana didn't hear about it until his son, whom Adriana had never seen visiting him, came to pick up his belongings. The man looked tired and haggard, though he couldn't have been more than 40. Marlene sat and rocked in the common room, moaning softly to herself. Marlene's nurse that day, a woman with dyed black hair and a beauty mark on her cheek, spoke to Redgie's son in low tones. He approached Marlene with a plastic grocery bag in one hand. "I understand you were a good friend of Redgie's," he said. Marlene paid no attention, continuing her rocking. Redgie's son hung the grocery bag from its handles on the back of the rocker. "Something to remember him by," he offered helplessly. He turned and walked out, his shoulders bowed.

Marlene kept rocking. Her nurse, walked over and took the bag off the back of the chair and put it in Marlene's hands. Adriana could see it contained Redgie's fur hat—his prized possession—and a well-worn Bible, the gold gleaming on the edges of the pages. Marlene stopped rocking and looked at the objects on her lap for a long time, before she touched them, tentatively. She opened the Bible to one of the dog-eared pages to examine it. A slip of paper fell out.

Adriana knew Marlene would have a hard time bending over the pick it up so she slipped over, scooped it up and handed it to Marlene. Marlene held it in her hand a long time, and Adriana couldn't help but read it. In large, ragged handwriting it said: "Jesus says; brush your teeth three times day, for the Father, the Son and the Holy Ghost."

Marlene handed the paper to Adriana. "I can't read," she said quietly. "Can you tell me what it says?"

Adriana read the words on the paper, shakily. Marlene nodded sagely, and opened the Bible to another slip of paper. Adriana read, "Pray every day and wear clean pants."

Marlene began to cry. "Redgie only wanted the best for people," she sobbed. She closed the Bible on her lap and put the fur hat on her head. Wiping her nose with the back of her hand, she stood up and knocked on the door to the nursing station. The student doctor, Colin, was in the back, working away on a computer, but he looked up when he heard Marlene calling to him. His shoulders sagged slightly, his chest was thin and a long tie dripped from his collar. Adriana thought she knew what he'd look like when he was middle-aged and balding.

Marlene handed him the Bible. "This was Redgie's," she said. "He'd have wanted you to have it," she said. "I can't read it." The student stood with the Bible in his hand. Adriana could see he didn't want it or anything that reminded him of Redgie, but as painful as it was, he accepted it from Marlene.

Adriana pictured Redgie standing at the edge of the harbour, the hurricane roaring around him. In his hands were strips of paper—his messages—that he wanted to float free in the water, to be carried away to those in need. But the wind grabbed them from his hands and blew them over his shoulder. Redgie bent down to release the papers into the water but like a giant hand, the surf came up and grabbed him, pulling him into itself. For a moment he flailed, then was sucked under. Adriana was pretty sure the student doctor pictured it that way too. His eyes glistened, dark and painful.

Adriana felt frozen in place. Marlene, wearing Redgie's fur hat, stood proudly before making her way to the kitchen. She was full, Adriana thought, leaving her sorrow behind her like a rag. No one could take away the fact that she had loved a man who had gone out to stop the hurricane and died trying.

That afternoon, Adriana dreamed of Redgie surrounded by the hurricane like a vine that curled around him. He was struggling to speak but only garbled words came out. Jeff began to cut away the vine with a machete but he kept cutting himself, so that by the end, they were both covered with blood.

Adriana cried out in her sleep and woke herself up. The room was grey and cold. She felt weak from the dream but from out of nowhere a surge of determination not to remain there coursed through her. Adriana got out of bed and went out into the hall, looking for someone to talk to. There was no one in the common room, except for an old woman who had fallen asleep on the couch.

Colin was sitting in the nursing station reading and looking like he needed a nap. Adriana saw the book in his hands was Redgie's Bible. It reminded her of her mother's Bible which sat unopened on the bookshelf in her bedroom, dog-eared and worn. Adriana knocked on the half door to the nursing station and smiled when he jumped, his hair dishevelled as though he'd been sleeping.

"Hi Adriana," Colin said.

"Hey," Adriana said, lifting her hand in greeting. "Could I talk to you?"

Colin looked surprised. He put Redgie's Bible to one side. "Sure," he said. "Let me get a nurse."

Adriana shook her head. "Can we just talk in the common room?"

He nodded. "Sure."

Adriana sat down on the couch facing the window and turned off the TV with the remote. Colin straightened his tie, crossing his long legs at the ankle in front of him. He looked more serious than usual. Not surprising, given the circumstances. Adriana wasn't sure what to say. She almost would have preferred to sit there silently with him, but she didn't think he was the type to be comfortable with silences.

"How are you feeling today?" Colin asked. It was the lamest of the lame questions in the doctor's arsenal. But Adriana took it at face value. How was she?

"Terrible," she said. She began to talk about the things that had been on her mind—Jazz and the abortion, Jeff's suicide attempt, Redgie, and the fact that she was afraid of what the future would hold for her, if she had a future. The student doctor, who had at first looked miserable and preoccupied, listened intently, nodding here and there but not interrupting. Eventually Adriana felt emptied, at peace. The student doctor looked full, almost round.

Maybe, Adriana thought. Maybe she had misjudged him and he was okay with silence. Maybe she was the one who couldn't bear the air waves flat-lining between her and another person. But soon the student doctor, uncrossed his legs and leaned forward, obviously excited. "You've shared a lot, Adriana," he said. "You've had a lot on your mind." Adriana thought that was stating the obvious, but she nodded.

"I think the key is to take it one day at a time, one small step at a time." Adriana resisted the urge to roll her eyes. Colin said, "I mean, everyone has their fears and their hopes. Everyone, no matter who they are. But if you let yourself just focus on what you can do today—instead of what you did or didn't do yesterday, instead of what you should do tomorrow—it gets easier." Adriana didn't follow the logic. "I mean," said the student, earnestly, "We only have this moment. Yesterday is lost to us and tomorrow is unknowable. What's the point of pulling our hair out about it?"

Adriana was usually resistant to such platitudes, but something made her stop and consider the implications of what the student had said. She had thought about it on her own—her one life was all she had. She could imagine what it would be like to float free from time, but that was not what life was really like, and not what Colin meant. He was talking about being fully present in the moment, fearless, absorbed, engaged. For some reason the idea terrified her.

Colin could see Adriana was anxious about something. "Does what I said make sense to you?" he asked. She nodded, then shook her head. She started to weep, and put her hands in front of her face. Everything seemed too much... especially the task of walking, one foot in front of the other, into the future, when the responsibility for those steps laid squarely on her own shoulders.

"Adriana." Colin said, touching her hand. "It's okay. We're all just doing the best we can." He looked ashamed that he had upset her.

She tried to tell him it wasn't his fault. She knew what

he was saying was right and it was supposed to be comforting, but she couldn't shake the idea that, for her, the path through life was a battle against rust and weeds.

Colin looked like he was going to cry too. He was not much older than Adriana really, and he had had to deal with the death of a patient. It might have been his first death. The first of many in the career of a doctor. How weighty a burden that was. She thought she could imagine how it felt. Adriana wiped her nose and tried to smile, which was the most comforting thing she knew how to do. Relieved, he smiled back "Are you okay now?" he asked. Adriana nodded, even though it felt to her as if she were trying to climb a waterfall.

Colin stood up. He was rumpled from head to foot, as though he'd gone to bed in his clothes and was just now waking up. "I guess I better get back to work... I mean, to the thing I was doing on the computer," he said, flustered. Adriana smiled for real when he turned and she saw the back of his shirt flapping behind him. If talking to her wasn't work, she supposed she could take it as a compliment.

Adriana stood up. She wore her street clothes, with a johnny shirt like a bathrobe on her back. She was half patient, half civilian. Did she need to choose? She walked to her room, where Marlene was sleeping soundly, her snores like the roar of a lion. Adriana sat on her bed and watched. It was normal here, to find someone new in your room, without consultation or warning. She'd wondered how long it would be before someone took Samantha's place for good, wiping away every trace of her.

Adriana knew Marlene was living with a hurt so deep it must burn inside her. She knew what it was like, to be so full of pain that the only relief is sleep. There was something healing about it and about the dreams that persisted in some pocket of the brain while the world kept turning, relentless and unforgiving.

Adriana thought about her hippocampus, how it had seemed to float free in the slosh of her brain. Somehow, she had given up the delusion that her brain had liquefied, that her memories were in danger because the hippocampus had escaped its moorings. Such a strange preoccupation, she thought. Where do these ideas come from, these odd, outlandish notions that populated the minds of the mentally ill? She realized that for a long time she had been preoccupied with the past, and that the fear of losing it could well have sparked the fiction that something had gone haywire with her brain. She was almost nostalgic for the time when the weirdness made sense, when everything seemed to be part of a pattern that had its own logic.

She looked up at the ceiling. It was just a ceiling, with blank tiles and nothing gleaming from their holes. Without the cameras behind them, and without her mother glaring at her, Adriana felt alone. For the first time in a long while, she experienced melancholy—not the grinding depression she'd been under for months but a kind of beautiful hopeless longing. It was actually the other side of happiness.

CHAPTER 31

Jazz called in the late afternoon. Adriana hung on to the phone with both hands. "Thanks for coming to see me," Jazz said in a small, flat voice.

Quickly Adriana said, "Your mum told me." Jazz didn't have to explain anything. Adriana could tell she didn't want to say a lot in front of her mother. "Jazzabel, don't worry," Adriana said, "About anything. Everything is okay."

Jazz let out a breath. For once Adriana was the parental one.

"Okay," Jazz whispered. Adriana wished Mrs. O'Connell would go get herself a coffee, so they could talk. She heard Jazz's mother rustling and speaking in a low voice to her daughter.

"I have to go," Jazz said.

In her best grown up voice, Adriana replied, "Girl, you eat your applesauce. I'll call tomorrow."

When Jazz hung up, it felt to Adriana as though a book had closed. They had come to the end of something, and while it was sad, it was also a relief of a sort. Adriana thought of her sister, and the limbo she occupied. She needed an ending too.

Adriana returned to her room, and settled into her knitting. Getting lost in knitting was not like getting lost in psychosis—there was a rhythm, a pattern, and a kind of humble necessity to it. Psychosis felt larger than life, out of control, and in some way, wasteful—of energy, health and time. It was a diversion on the path of life, one which weakened a person.

There was a knock on the door. Adriana looked up, slightly disoriented. Beth entered first, soundlessly and their father, with his arms full of bags and wrapping paper, followed. "Hi, darling," he said, ebullient but nervous, almost shy. It had only been a few days since they'd seen her but the hurricane had intervened, like a huge semicolon, and none of them were sure of what came next.

Beth stood at the end of Adriana's bed and stared at nothing in particular, while Mr. Song, set the packages down. "We're so happy to see you," her father said, hugging her head to him. After a long while he let go, and Adriana almost felt displaced, as though she'd been taken by a wave and dropped on a foreign shore. Beth looked adrift too, and Adriana felt a kinship to her that was more than blood.

"It's Beth's birthday!" Mr. Song said, too loudly. Adriana gaped. Of course it was. She had totally forgotten.

Adriana stretched out her arms to her, saying, "Beth, honey. Happy birthday."

Beth moved to the head of Adriana's bed. Adriana wrapped her in a bear hug, and squeezed her shoulders. Beth made no move to let her go, and in fact seemed to have wilted into her arms, so Adriana kept hugging her, until Mr. Song, beaming his approval, thrust a gift in Beth's direction. Adriana patted the bed, indicated Beth should seat herself there, which she did, but then seemed not to know what to do next. Mr. Song thrust a clumsily wrapped present toward her. "This one's from Adriana," he said

It was a strange shape for a present. In fact it looked suspiciously like a football, but as helpless as her father was at coming up with appropriate gifts, she didn't think he'd go that far wrong. It was in fact a football-shaped bowl on legs, glazed a beautiful blue, with a chopstick holder and a pair of wooden chop sticks. Adriana thought he must have bought it at the Japanese store. Was it as close to a Chinese present as he could get?

Mr. Song handed Beth a mesh bag full of gold foil covered chocolate coins. Adriana felt a pang of something. Those were her favourite birthday present. Had her father forgotten? But Mr. Song patted Adriana's arm. "Some for you too, big sister," he said. Adriana smiled, a real smile that made her eyes crinkle and her cheeks round. Beth sat with a chocolate coin in her mouth, watching them both.

Adriana never enjoyed her own birthday, because she hated everyone looking at her as she opened her presents. Beth didn't seem to mind—she ploughed through unwrapping the gifts with very little comment. Her eyes looked tired and sad, Adriana thought. She wondered what Aunt Penny would have done for Beth on her birthday. Maybe there was a special ritual of some kind.

Afterward, Beth seemed defeated by the mound of presents on the bed. In the face of her resignation, Mr. Song nodded to Adriana surreptitiously. Adriana picked up a book of fairy tales that her father had wrapped for Beth and began to read. Fairy tales were full of wicked stepmothers and magic, but Adriana was a sucker for the fight between good and evil. Beth's eyes took on a faraway look. It scarcely seemed possible that she would be a teenager this time next year, Adriana thought.

Snow White had a wicked queen of a stepmother to tor-
ment her. Sometimes, Adriana remembered, she had pretended her own mother was that wicked witch and that her
"real" mother had somehow sacrificed her life to protect
Adriana from evil. When Viera died, Adriana felt a terrible
gnawing guilt, as though her fantasies had engulfed them
both. Since then, she made a point of regarding her mother
with an even detachment, which had led to a kind of truce,
though an uneasy one. Viera had stood in constant judgement of her, until just recently. Now Adriana was uncertain
of what to expect from Viera, whose smile had faded, along
with her wickedness.

Mr. Song excused himself to go to the washroom. It
seemed, he thought, that the mental hospital always made
him want to pee. Was it the gloom of the place, despite all
the large prints of cheerful paintings, and the rustic touches,
like the hand-painted border around the nursing station?
Mr. Song wished there was a two-way mirror so he could
see what his daughters were up to without them knowing
he was watching. But first he needed to empty his bladder.

Adriana read Beth the miraculous ending to the story of
Snow White. Beth took the book in her hands and silently
examined the illustrations, detailed line drawings in black
and white. Without looking up, she asked Adriana, "Do
you think we'll ever have a stepmother?"

Adriana's eyes widened. She hadn't considered the possibility for a long time. She shrugged, her hands open. Beth
seemed to be waiting for something. "Dad's not dating
anyone right now," Adriana said. "He's only had one date
since Mom died." That was the first summer he was alone
and the secretary of the engineering firm he worked for,

Doris, had her eye on him. But her father didn't know how to woo a woman. He invited Doris to supper with himself and Adriana. Maybe she was expecting something fancy from an engineer but he served spaghetti, garlic bread and grape juice. There was one rose in a glass vase in the centre of the table. Doris, looking for something to say, commented, "My favourite flower!", which Adriana thought was lame, because the rose was just about everyone's favourite flower. Mr. Song proceeded to tell her how he always had a flower on the table because his wife had loved them. Doris's smile withered and she sat rigid in her chair for the duration of the meal. When they were finished, they all sat awkwardly on the living room couch and played the board game Sorry, which Adriana now thought quite appropriate. It hadn't occurred to Mr. Song that including his daughter on his date with Doris would be a problem, but clearly it was. They never repeated the occasion and Mr. Song never even mentioned dating Doris again. It was to Adriana as if the evening had never happened, or even stranger, as if it had never registered on Mr. Song's radar as an event of any note.

Beth gazed at Adriana as though she were trying to make up her mind about something. Adriana squeezed her hand. "It's okay, Beth. I know you worry, but things will work themselves out." Adriana didn't know for sure if that were true but it was the kind of thing her Dad would say, trusting and ever-hopeful.

Beth looked a lot like their mother, Adriana thought, but she didn't have that hardness at the core—she was just a traumatized little girl. If Viera had been alive, she might have sat Beth down and given her a stern talking to, but Adriana just held her sister's hand. She had a strange mixture of emotions mingling inside her—pity and anger, judgement and compassion, and misery. Adriana knew that she wouldn't choose to be the grudging older sister when she got out of the hospital, but she was fearful of what the relationship with her sister would demand of her. Would Beth want her attention all the time, or her approval?

Adriana was still holding Beth's hand when Mr. Song came back into the room. He sat down in the chair by the bed and sighed happily. He looked like he might be settled in for the afternoon, but Adriana suddenly felt like she needed to be alone, to sort things out in her head. She gave Beth's hand a squeeze and let go. "Thank you for coming," Adriana said, smiling at them both. She wasn't sure how to tell them she wanted them to leave, but Beth stood up, her grey eyes rimmed red. She was ready to go home for a nap, or a little television therapy, Adriana thought. Mr. Song, slightly disappointed, got to his feet. Adriana held out her hand to her father. "I'm a bit tired, Dad," she said by way of an excuse. It was the first time she'd ever explained herself to him. Mr. Song nodded eagerly, sensing something had changed though he was not able to put his finger on what or how.

"You rest then," he said, steering Beth toward the door. Beth looked back at Adriana, who waved at her from the bed. She felt as though she were sending her younger sister off on a long voyage, a voyage she too had navigated through storms and gales, without a map. She hoped the Song family constellation, small as it was, would be enough to guide her sister to a safer path than the one she found herself on.

CHAPTER 32

At supper, there was an extra tray with a roast beef dinner on it. Adriana didn't think twice about forgoing her plastic-wrapped sandwich. A hot meal was still like a revelation to her, after so many meals of hard boiled eggs and cereal. Then she returned to her room, eager to take up the knitting again. She was careful though, aware that this hobby of hers could become an obsession, that it was bordering on one already. When there was a knock on the door, Adriana let the knitting fall in her lap.

Fiona poked her head into the crack of the open door. She looked very tired. "Hi, Adriana," she said. "Elspeth will be coming back soon. I'm off shift now and won't be coming back to this unit, but I wanted to tell you that Dr. Burke discontinued your sleeping pill. He thinks you'll do do okay without it," Fiona said, smiling encouragingly and smoothing a place to sit on Adriana's bed with her tanned hand. Adriana realized that was considered progress, here in the mental hospital. Every little movement toward passing through those stone gates was something to celebrate. And actually, strangely, Adriana felt a puff of pride. "So I wanted to say goodbye." Fiona admitted. Adriana looked at her, regretfully. "Actually I'm going on maternity leave, so I won't see you before you leave the hospital."

There were lines on Fiona's face that Adriana hadn't noticed before. Crow's feet at the corners of her eyes, and deep laugh lines around her mouth. Also, little wrinkle lines in the middle of her forehead, from worry. Fiona took Adriana's hand. "I have a daughter your age," she said, smiling. "And a granddaughter." Adriana's eyes widened. "My daughter is a smart girl, like you, but she followed too closely in my footsteps. She had her daughter when she was 18. And my daughter is depressed, too sick to take care of her child. So that's my job." Fiona didn't look bitter but she did look worried. "I decided to have this baby before it was too late, and so that my granddaughter would have someone to grow up with. I don't know whether it's the right decision, but then, no one ever really knows that, do they?" She smiled, sadly, Adriana thought. So it wasn't Elspeth at all. It was Fiona.

Adriana leaned back against her pillows. Fiona was a grandmother, not the golden girl she had thought. Adriana shook her head. It wasn't possible. Fiona smiled and patted her hand. "My first daughter was an accident," she said smiling. "A happy accident. But my second is definitely part of a plan. The father knows about the plan, but doesn't intend to be a part of this child's life," she said rubbing her belly thoughtfully. "That's his choice. I'm just grateful he did me this one little favour before we parted company."

"Congratulations, Fiona. I think you must be a great mom," she said quietly. Her head ached. She closed her eyes. The sound of her voice, saying something so unremarkable, nevertheless felt strange and new.

Fiona got up from the bed and waddled toward the door.

"Adriana, my sweet," she said. "You don't need to know it, but my first daughter doesn't want to be admitted to the NS, even though she has been depressed a long time, even though she needs to be here. I don't blame her. I'm trying to take care of her at home but it's not easy. You did a brave thing to come here, and I hope you'll be just as brave when you leave. I'll have to say goodbye now, but I hope you keep making good choices. Go be happy and healthy and skedaddle out of this place soon," Fiona smiled, and closed the door behind her.

Fiona was like a beacon, a shining light on the shores of happiness. Even now that she knew Fiona's story, there was something about her that was like gold. Adriana knew it wasn't courage that brought her to hospital, but the opposite. She had been at the end of her rope, frantic and afraid. And hopeless. That was the worst of it. And there was Fiona, choosing a life for herself that would have caused Adriana to despair. But she chose it for a reason and she was clear about what she wanted. Adriana felt like she was still groping in the darkness, not able to see beyond her fingertips.

She looked down at the knitting in her lap. What was it that drove her? Making scarves didn't indicate any kind of plan. The opposite in fact. She was still trying to keep reality at bay. Jazz had once told her, "Put your knitting needles away, grandma, and come play." Jazz, who wanted to be a doctor (when she didn't want to be a chemist or a kinesiologist). She took the right courses at school, even though she struggled with the sciences. She was always planning something.

Adriana didn't know what it was that held her back. She had guessed by now that most people didn't have a long-dead mother sitting in the back of their head, waiting and watching. The medication seemed to keep her at bay, but she was aware of her mother's eyes on her just the same. It occurred to her that she had spent more time trying to placate or avoid her mother than she had thinking about her future. And her relationship with Peter was just one more attempt to be someone, in that case a girlfriend, instead of herself. And it had been a failed attempt.

It felt like something had shifted in Adriana's head. She realized that her brain no longer felt like a murky slosh, but more like a darkened room, where someone was moving furniture around. There was a ray of light, illuminating dust motes that floated like tiny sea creatures in the dense shadow of her mind.

She got out of bed wrapping her latest scarf around her neck. It was fuchsia and orange, too bright for a depressed person. Adriana guessed she would have to choose between her scarf and her diagnosis. She decided on the scarf.

CHAPTER 33

The hallway was deserted and there were just a couple people in the common room. One was a sleeping man. He looked somehow familiar, although she was certain she hadn't seen him on the unit before. The other was Samantha, her massive frame squeezed into the rocker, her legs stretched out in front of her. She beamed at Adriana.

"I came to see you," she said. Her mouth crumpled a little. "Tony is off shift so they let me visit." Adriana sat down cross-legged on the couch across from her. Samantha looked just the same, but her face was tastefully made up. "They said you were sleeping so I waited out here for you."

Adriana smiled, and Samantha let out a loud guffaw, which she stifled immediately with her large hand. The orderly looked at her with disapproval, and the sleeping man on the couch, opened his eye blearily and rolled over, his back to the room.

Samantha leaned toward her, confidentially. "Things are better over on Laurel," she said, with a sidelong glance at the orderly, who glared at her. Samantha smiled back sweetly, and whispered aloud. "They don't treat you like a criminal for expressing yourself over there," she said. The orderly stood up and went into the back room of the nursing station, clearly miffed. Samantha laughed, a lovely peal that overflowed itself, and the man on the couch stirred slightly. She clapped a hand over her mouth again. "Don't want to wake up the poor soul," she said. "He looks like he needs all the sleep he can get."

Adriana played with the scarf around her neck. There was something she wanted to ask. "Samantha," she said.

"Yes, my pet?" she asked.

Adriana took a breath. "When you were my age, did you know you wanted to be a woman?"

Samantha smiled and nodded, her eyes bright. "I knew since I was a little boy," she said. "Since I was two years old."

Adriana let that information sink in. She didn't remember anything from that young age. She suspected Samantha might be imagining it. "Did you ever wonder whether you were making the right decision, when you became a woman?" There, she'd said it. Did Samantha have doubts? Regrets?

Samantha reached over and took Adriana's hands. "I never doubted myself. Not for a single minute."

What would that feel like, Adriana wondered. To know something with such clarity, and something so huge, so life-changing. She had never felt that sure about anything. And then to wake up, in the body of your choice. Would it be like dying and going to heaven, Adriana wondered? To finally be in the body you craved, would that be as freeing as having no body at all? It was something Adriana couldn't imagine. She had spent so much time trying to fade into the background, that to launch something as spectacular as a war on her own body seemed unthinkable. But then there were her haircuts, lopsided, striking in their unconventionality. She had allowed Jazz to do many experiments with her hair, without a word of protest. She may have been trying to blend in but a part of her obviously wanted to stand out.

Samantha leaned back in her rocker and closed her eyes. She seemed happy, Adriana thought. Despite the whole thing with Tony and the shock of the hurricane, she was smiling. Adriana felt ashamed of herself. "Sam, do you want to go downstairs and sit out back?" Adriana asked. Samantha's eyes popped open. Adriana realized she had never called her Sam before, and had never asked to do anything that took them away from the unit. Samantha grinned, and Adriana noticed how small her teeth were.

"Why I would be delighted!" Samantha said, in her best southern belle drawl. "Just let me go get my jacket." She heaved herself out of the rocker and went off toward Laurel.

Adriana stood by the pay phone. She wanted to call Jazz but something told her to give it a little more time. Adriana wasn't used to heeding her own instincts, but she figured that it might be time to start.

The phone rang and she jumped, then collected herself enough to answer it. "Mayflower Unit," she said. There was a pause and then a rather prim female voice asked, "Could I speak to Bartholomew?" Adriana tried to think. Was there a Bartholomew on the unit? She didn't think so. "He's rather new," the voice on the phone said. Adriana stepped around the corner where the man lay on the couch facing the wall. His eyes were open. "Are you Bartholomew?" she asked. He turned to look at her, and in his eyes there was a faraway light. It was him—Bartholomew Banks, the spiritualist that Jazz had taken her to see, a whole other life ago.

"That's me," he said, his voice gravelly from sleep. He slowly pushed himself to a sitting position. The phone wouldn't reach him.

"There's a chair here by the phone," Adriana said and he rose stiffly, but almost majestically, she thought. She handed over the receiver. He wasn't wearing a buckskin like that night at the Westin, she noticed, but a neat buttoned down shirt and jeans with the same cowboy boots.

Samantha buzzed in and walked toward Adriana, but was clearly intrigued by Bartholomew, now that she saw him upright. Adriana had to admit he was quite a striking figure with his shaggy head and neat cowboy attire. She pulled the johnny shirt around her. She doubted it was cold outside but it was October now. She realized suddenly that it was her father's birthday, the day after China celebrated its national holiday. Her father hadn't mentioned it when he came to visit and Beth probably didn't even know. Adriana felt a pang of sadness. Her dad always remembered her birthday. Damn brain.

Samantha leaned toward her. "Who is that charming fellow?" she whispered.

"Bartholomew Banks" Adriana answered, apprehensive. He looked up from his conversation, his eyes glowing with an unearthly light. Samantha smiled, hungrily. Adriana took Samantha's elbow and steered her toward the exit. "He's a spiritualist," she offered.

" A... what's that?" Samantha asked.

Adriana sighed. It felt like too much to explain. "He talks to dead people," she said, heading for the stairs. "Let's go outside." Samantha was clearly perturbed by the appearance of the handsome stranger, and the fact that Adriana knew him. She even forgot to buy herself a bag of chips and a pop from the machine in the basement when they passed it.

"How do you know about all this?" she asked. Adriana shrugged.

"Jazz took me to see his show before I ended up in hospital" she said.

Samantha was awestruck. "He does shows? Where he talks to the dead?"

Adriana shrugged again. "He *says* he talks to the dead, anyway," she allowed, pushing open the door to the back of the hospital. Samantha, lost in thought, sat down under the overhang on the first low plastic bench she came to. It looked like it had sat there since the 1970s.

The harbour was calm and grey, reflecting the clouds overhead. There were crickets in the grass, calling to one another from between the goldenrod and aster. Adriana thought about Jeff, and wondered what had happened to the cricket when he broke the jar that was its home. She imagined it crawling under the bed, away from all the blood, and she shivered.

Samantha seemed to forget about Bartholomew Banks. "Are you cold?" she asked, concerned. Adriana realized she was. Samantha stood up. "You should have brought a sweater." Adriana shrank. It was something her mother would have said. But Samantha wasn't criticizing her. She put her enormous arm around Adriana's shoulders and laughed. "You are such a young person. Young people never think about things like whether they'll be too cold. It's only old ladies like me that dress for the weather," she said and gave Adriana's shoulders a gentle squeeze.

They sat side by side on the plastic bench until a wind swept from the harbour across the sewage pond. Samantha held her nose and Adriana stood up. "Let's go back inside," she said. Samantha got to her feet and stretched upward, grasping her hands high above her head. "It's been ages since I did yoga," she said. "I'm all tied in knots." Adriana looked shocked. She couldn't imagine Samantha doing yoga. Samantha glanced at her, sideways and shy. "Yoga is for everyone," she said, "even old ladies like me."

Adriana realized her head was full of knots. She had so many preconceived notions and thoughts that led nowhere but tied themselves up in a tangled mass. Somehow they had to be isolated and eased open. Was there a medication that could do that?

Samantha was humming a tune that Adriana recognized but couldn't place. They walked toward the elevator and, with a flourish, Samantha pulled some coins out of her pocket, and halted in front of the vending machine. So she hadn't forgotten. It occurred to Adriana that our habits are as much a part of us as the limbs of our body. She watched Samantha delicately fishing one chip at a time out of the bag that looked so small in her hand.

As they ascended to the third floor, Adriana realized she wasn't even sure what her own habits were. She knew that she slept when confronted with emotionally thorny problems, and let Jazz take the lead in everything—that was a kind of habit. Was her mother's presence in her mind just another habit? Adriana was struck with the idea that if we were able to shed our habits, it would mean freedom. But then, who would we be? Maybe, like Samantha, who shed her body's habitual form, we would become the people we always wanted to be. But maybe, instead, we'd be lost at sea without a life raft.

Adriana exited the elevator, Samantha trailing behind her. When Samantha put her hand on her arm, she noticed for the first time that the older woman had a slight tremor. It could be a side effect of medication but it could be something else. How had she not noticed it before?

Adriana shook her head, as though trying to shake off her self-absorption.

The kitchen was crowded with patients. Adriana could see from the doorway that Bartholomew Banks was no longer on the phone. As she and Samantha were buzzed in, they spotted him in the kitchen, sitting at one of the tables with a Styrofoam cup in his hands. Samantha patted Adriana on the shoulder by way of goodbye and went to sit down at the table opposite Bartholomew. He looked up, his eyes glowing with that strange light, and nodded at Samantha, who put a hand in front of her mouth and tittered, like a school girl.

Adriana continued down the hall to her room. Marlene was sitting on the edge of her bed, legs shuffling back and forth in pink fuzzy slippers. Adriana could see she'd been crying. She sat on her own bed and hugged her knees, against the contagion of Marlene's misery. "Is it suppertime yet?" Marlene asked in a voice thick with snot and tears. Adriana looked at her wrist. It was already 4 p.m.

"Soon," she told Marlene, who lifted her legs onto the bed and curled up, her thumb in her mouth.

Adriana straightened the things on her bedside table—a travel clock, a Styrofoam cup, a newspaper. She made her bed, then lay down on it, but she couldn't sleep. She thought about knitting, but for the moment it had lost its appeal. Adriana finally accepted defeat and got up and wandered to the kitchen

Samantha was now sitting at the same table as Bartholomew Banks, and was seemingly in deep conversation with him—at least, she was leaning toward him, earnest and confidential, and he was nodding. Adriana sat at another table, as far from them as she could get. Not that she wasn't curious, but she knew Samantha would prefer it that way. She would have to return to Laurel for her own supper, and Adriana knew Samantha was trying to hang on a few seconds more, until the nurse at the counter asked her to leave.

The nurse read the names on the trays out. When the name "Bartholomew Banks" was called, Samantha rose from her chair. The nurse frowned at her. "I'm just collecting the tray for my friend here," she explained. "Bartholomew is new."

The nurse nodded grudgingly. "You better get over to Laurel, Samantha, or you'll miss your supper." she said. Samantha smiled and continued talking to Bartholomew, who looked politely confused. The nurse waved her hand. "Shoo, Samantha," she said. Samantha, head held high and dignified, rose once more from her seat. The nurse bent toward her. "You can't come back here tonight, okay?" Everyone was too absorbed in their sweet and sour meatballs and rice to notice. Besides they all knew Samantha wasn't allowed on the unit when Tony came on shift.

Samantha stood in the middle of the kitchen like a mountain peak. Adriana was afraid she might overturn a table. Instead she smiled graciously at Bartholomew and, clutching her purse in front of her, glided toward the door. Adriana thought she looked quite regal and wondered if Bartholomew thought the same. His eyes still glowed with a strange light but he was clearly absorbed in his meal, methodically spooning meatballs and rice into his mouth.

Adriana watched him as she ate. When he finished the meal, he got up and made himself a cup of tea. Gradually the kitchen cleared as patients took their trays to the counter and shuffled off to smoke or watch TV. Banks didn't move again, but remained at the kitchen table until everyone but

Adriana had gone.

She cleared her throat. "Bartholomew Banks." She said and stood up. He looked at her but it was as if he looked through her to something beyond her. Adriana shivered, but screwed up her courage. "You told me there was a wraith following me, a wraith that said I have everything I need." Banks's forehead wrinkled, as if he were trying to place her. "Remember? At the Westin?" Bartholomew Banks smiled politely and nodded to her.

A door slammed. Adriana jumped, as Melvin kept going, his eyes darkened by sun glasses. "What did you mean?" Adriana pressed him. "What did you see?"

Bartholomew Banks shook his head and looked down at his tray. He was an old man, Adriana realized. This likely wasn't his first time in the hospital. He raised his hand and let it fall to his side. "I'm afraid I don't remember," he said, in that mild, gravelly voice. "I've seen many things for many people." Adriana trembled. Banks peered at her, until a sudden look of recognition overcame him . "You came with a friend, didn't you?" Adriana nodded. It was typical that Jazz was more memorable than she was.

Banks nodded slowly. "I remember," he said as though something were slowly dawning on him. He frowned. "There was a man hanging," he said, and covered his eyes with his hands. Adriana stared, disbelieving. "You had a woman in white following you." Adriana nodded. "Her hair... she was bald." Yes, Adriana thought. Her mother was likely bald because the last she saw her, lying peacefully in her coffin, she was wearing a wig that was long and curly like her mother's own, but with more red in it than she remembered.

Bartholomew Banks squinted at Adriana, as though

the light was in his eyes. Adriana almost felt like she was melting, fading, blending into the background. He looked through and beyond her, as though she were transparent. Bartholomew nodded to someone, but Adriana looked and there was no one behind her. "You're almost done here," Bartholomew said, "Aren't you? You're almost ready to go home?" His voice was kind and slightly apologetic. Adriana nodded, a little shakily. Bartholomew Banks leaned his chin on his hand. "This place... can only take you so far," he said sadly. "You have to go home to get better." Adriana thought about it. She knew he was right, anticlimactic though it was.

Adriana got up to leave. Bartholomew nodded at her by way of goodbye, but she had a surge of courage. "What's wrong with you?" she asked, and the words seemed to her razor sharp. Bartholomew nodded again, to himself this time. "I hear voices," he said. "I don't think of it as a problem, but my children do." Bartholomew smiled. "The medication quiets them down, but I don't like to be alone in my head so I usually stop taking it." He shook his head slowly and sighed. "On the pills, it's like not being able to tune into my favourite radio station."

Adriana thought about it for a while. She understood Bartholomew Banks, because she was lonely too, without her mother gazing at her from the afterworld. These days, her mother looked like a faded facsimile of herself. She had not lived long enough to grow old, but was nevertheless disappearing before Adriana's eyes, for the second time in her life.

Bartholomew shaded his eyes, as though from a bright light. Adriana lifted a hand in farewell as she left the kitchen but Bartholomew Banks was absorbed by something going on inside himself. It was as if he were listening to a heated

conversation, one which required his patience and attention. Adriana saw him lift his hand but she could see it was
not a gesture meant for her.

She made her way down into the hallway, which was
like stepping into an ever-changing stream. People passed
her but she didn't recognize anyone. Then Melvin went by,
closing again the few doors that had been opened after his
first pass down the hallway. He grinned at her, but there was
something awful about it, as though he was in great pain.

Adriana felt sick. The woman with the wispy hair, whose
name she had never found out, wept silently as she passed
her. Adriana stopped and looked at her as she went by, and
the woman turned slightly toward her, with a cringing smile
under her tears. She wanted to connect, but it was as if she
didn't know how to do anything but cry. Adriana raised her
hand in greeting, but didn't try to talk. It was more than
she could bear at that moment, to reach beyond herself to
touch someone else's hurt.

CHAPTER 34

The next morning, Adriana called Jazz from the kitchen phone, but it was too early. She wasn't awake yet, Mrs. O'Connell said. She was doing well though, glad to be home. Adriana was about to hang up when Mrs. O'Connell asked, "But how are you doing, Addy?" Adriana wasn't used to Jazz's mum being interested in how her life was going. She thought about what she might say, but couldn't think of anything. After a few moments, Mrs. O'Connell asked, in a small voice, "Are you okay, Addy?" She was, she realized.

"Yes, thanks. Um, could you tell Jazz I called?" Adriana asked, as casually as if she were phoning from her own home, as she lay on the living room couch with a mug of coffee in her hand.

Adriana heard the phone click off. Poor Mrs. O'Connell, she thought. Jazz's mum had a decent job, a house and a beautiful, charismatic daughter, but she was the most uptight and unhappy person Adriana had ever met. She dialed her father's house. There was no answer, but the voicemail came on after four rings. Her father's voice, enthusiastic and cheerful, said "You have reached the Song family home." Beth's voice, a little wavery, chimed in "David, Adriana and

Beth are not in right now, so please leave a message." Her Dad ended with a cheery, "Have a nice day!" And the sound of the Chinese gong in the kitchen to end things off.

Adriana felt her chest tighten "It's Adriana," she said. "Just wanted to wish you a happy birthday, Dad." He would be 50, she realized, stunned. He had always said Beth was his best birthday present and that Adriana was his favourite Christmas gift, because she was born on December 24. She wondered what she could give him. The only thing she had was the olive green scarf she'd knit on short stay. Knowing her dad, if she gave it to him he'd start wearing it right away.

Adriana was walking away from the kitchen when she realized, with a jolt, that she was feeling okay, kind of normal. How had that happened? She wondered. Could the medication really be working?

She had a feeling of strength, that she hadn't had for a long time, along with a healthy seed of impatience, a desire for forward motion. It was as though she was ready for something and her body was resting, just waiting along with her for whatever came next. But Adriana knew she would have to wait. This hospital was an imperfect place, that did not operate in rhythm to the healing of its patients. It did not expel them at the first signs of health. She'd seen other patients reach this stage, more quickly than she had, and be held for days and sometimes weeks while the hospital took its time. Adriana knew that she had to depend on herself if she was to get out of hospital and back to the land of the living.

She plopped herself down onto a sofa in the common room. Melvin was sitting in the rocker, rocking steadily. He grinned at her from behind his sunglasses—that pained smile that he'd had since the hurricane. Adriana nodded to him. She had never really had a conversation with him, but she figured it wasn't too late. "Hey Melvin," she said quietly. He kept rocking, but turned his head toward her. "How are you today?" It was lame, she knew, but she had never been a master of conversation.

Melvin stopped rocking, and Adriana felt a jitter of nerves. In a calm voice, Melvin said, "Everything's cool," and started rocking again, no longer grinning. Adriana nodded, and sat back on the sofa.

A familiar voice called "Medications!" It was Elspeth. Adriana didn't take morning meds but got in line anyway. When she got to the counter, Elspeth smiled and gave her a little cup of juice. "Hello, sunshine," she said.

As glad as she was to see Elspeth, Adriana was filled with trepidation about what she had to ask. "How's Jeff?"

Elspeth smiled. "You'll have to ask him yourself. He's back on the unit this morning."

Grateful for a rush of relief, Adriana stepped aside to let Melvin receive his pills. Elspeth smiled at him and said something that made him throw back his head and laugh silently. Adriana felt a pang of jealousy, but she knew how it was. What Elspeth offered as a nurse was for everyone, not just her.

Adriana, relieved and thankful, decided to take a walk around the grounds. She hadn't been out much since she was admitted, although her privileges had been restored. Outside seemed like an unknown quantity. Adriana put on a sweatshirt and wrapped the olive green scarf she'd knit for her father around her neck. She doubted it was cold, but the scarf offered more than warmth—it was protective gear.

There were still branches and leaves strewn all over the ground, like an obstacle course. Adriana stepped over them, her sneakers quickly starting to feel damp. There were some big old elm trees with branches down at the north end of the property. It felt like something terrible had happened, like a glacier had just passed through or a club-wielding giant. But Adriana kept walking to the perimeter of the grounds, and stopped at the edge of the gravel track that led to the main road. She had no desire to leave the grounds today, now that she knew Jazz and Jeff were safe, and now that she technically had permission to walk the grounds freely. She mulled over the attempts she'd made to "escape" the hospital. She was more determined than ever to leave, but it no longer felt like an urgent necessity.

Adriana rounded the edge of the hospital property and turned back, past the brick laundry with its comforting smell, and the newer Mount Hope building where people lived for years and sometimes longer, if no spots were available in group homes. Adriana had not visited those units but she thought they must be something like a warehouse for human beings who were not able to take care of themselves. She felt grateful that would not be her fate.

Adriana considered the possibilities. She could go home—there were a lot of people she knew in hospital who didn't have a home to go to like she did. But it seemed to her that her father's house was no longer *her* home—it was the home of her sister and before that, of her depression. Adriana's face reddened. She knew she should appreciate it more, but something was pushing her away from the idea of returning to her father's house and toward her own survival.

Could she and Jazz find a place together? They'd talked about it in the past. Adriana thought she could get a part-time job as a cashier or something, and Jazz could get a student loan and continue going to school. Maybe she'd take a course herself. Just one. She could handle one. And she'd start thinking about the path she wanted to take, whatever that was.

Adriana felt relieved. She had a plan, and it made her feel like she had a future.

Adriana stopped at the common room when she got back to the unit. Surprisingly it was quite full. Jeff and Melvin sat together on one of the sofas and spoke in low voices. Jeff still had bandages over his neck and Melvin, in sympathy or comradeship, wore a white towel around his own neck. Jeff looked up at Adriana briefly and nodded. She felt herself crumbling, but with all the willpower she could muster, she sat down on the couch where Marlene dozed in her parka.

Adriana caught a smattering of Jeff's conversation with Melvin. "It was a strange time," he said.

Melvin nodded and said in a his clear, bell-like voice, "Things were weird here too." Melvin took off his sunglasses and rubbed his eyes. It was the first time Adriana noticed them and to her surprise, they were green.

"I like it better back here," Jeff said, stretching his legs out in front of him and putting his hands behind his head.

Melvin stretched out too. "Glad you're back, buddy," he said. Jeff nodded sagely. "Yes I think I'll hang out here for awhile," he said. Melvin threw back his head in silent laughter, and Jeff grinned.

Adriana cleared her throat. "Jeff," she said. Her voice sounded hoarse and strange. Jeff looked up.

"Hey Adriana," he said.

"Jeff I'm sorry," Adriana blurted and the rest came out of her in a river. "I'm sorry I gave you that jar. I'm so sorry that you hurt yourself. I feel terrible about it. I hope you'll forgive me. Please forgive me." Adriana stood trembling. Jeff looked up at her, confused. Adriana pointed to his neck. "You cut yourself. It's my fault." she said, hysteria rising in her throat.

Jeff shook his head. "Don't worry about it," he said mildly. "It happened and I'm glad. Relieved." He said. Now Adriana looked confused. "I mean when you have a hurricane to deal with, you do what you have to," he said. She felt stricken. Did Jeff think he could stop the hurricane by hurting himself?

"Hey!" he said brightly, pointing at her father's scarf. "Do you think, you could make me one like that? It would be nice to have something to cover my neck. I get cold sometimes." Adriana nodded. He wanted a scarf to cover his battle scars, and who could blame him? She felt relief rising in her like a loaf of bread. So there was something she could do, after all.

Adriana went to her room. She looked for signs that Samantha, or anyone else had visited, but her things were just as she's left them. She opened her locker and dug around in a bag of yarn for the knitting needles. They were long and lethal looking.

All she had were scraps of yarn, and one almost-full ball of the olive green she'd used for her father's scarf. Adriana decided that would make the main body of the scarf and the ends would be multi-coloured—blue and rust. It might be funny looking, she fretted, but it would have to do. She got to work, the rhythmic clicking of needles like an incantation.

Samantha knocked on the bedroom door, and her massive head appeared around the corner. "Hey there, girl," she said, "I brought you something." Adriana, startled, looked up. Samantha stepped into the room with a plastic bag and handed it to Adriana. Inside was a fuzzy lavender coloured wool sweater. "It's from the apparel shop," she said proudly. Adriana knew the apparel shop was a room in the Mount Hope building where patients could go to choose free clothing. Adriana thought the sweater was a beautiful colour, but she felt queasy when she heard where it was from. She'd never taken charity in her life. Samantha sat on the edge of her bed. "What are you making?" she asked.

Adriana had an idea. "It's a scarf for Jeff. To cover his..." She put her hand to her neck. Samantha nodded. Adriana fingered the sweater. "Would you mind if I took this sweater apart and used the wool for the scarf?"

Samantha laughed and clapped her hands. "What a wonderful idea!" she gushed, to Adriana's considerable relief.

"Will you make one for me?" Samantha asked excitedly. "I have an old wool sweater, my favourite from when I was..." Samantha gestured at the lower part of her torso with a sweep of her hand, "a man, and I keep it to remind me of the past but I would love it if you could make a scarf out of it." Adriana nodded, trembling. She felt too light suddenly. It was almost like happiness but with a tinge of anxiety.

Samantha stood up, and stretched her arms over her head, then bent toward Adriana. "I came to visit Bartholomew," she said in a confidential tone. She grimaced. "Tony has been off on stress leave, so I am allowed on Mayflower any old time. She grimaced. "I think it's over between Tony and me," she sighed regretfully. Her face brightened. "But I am very glad to have met Bartholomew. He is a fascinating, intelligent man." She fanned her face with her hand. "He told me I have a rare spirit," she said, her voice full of wonder. "Do you think he's right?" she asked Adriana, hands clasped ecstatically. "No one has ever said such a thing to me before."

Adriana rolled her head, in a gesture between a shake and

a nod. Samantha was a rare spirit, but Adriana wondered whether she was reading too much into what Bartholomew Banks had said, or rather, inferring too much. She hated the idea of Samantha being hurt again. She knew what heart break was like, and how it felt to slip down the whorl of a shell into a bottomless darkness. Maybe Samantha was not like her though. Maybe her heart was better protected, more shell than the soft creature inside. But Adriana knew this was not the case. It was just that Samantha was more buoyant, that she didn't hang on to the hurts as though they were precious objects, but let them pass through her like breath.

Samantha wiped some hair out of Adriana's eyes, which made her jump. "You look so sad," Samantha said, and her eyes were sad too. Adriana tried to smile. Samantha straightened. "You never told me about him," she said, kindly. Adriana shook her head and let her hair hang over her face.

The last time she saw Peter, he was walking with the girl with the auburn hair. Adriana couldn't shake the thought that she was replaceable, forgettable even. That there was someone else filling that place in Peter's heart, pushing her out. It was as though she were homeless now. And Adriana realized with a twinge of sadness, that she'd been holding on to the idea that his heart was a safe place, a home she could live in, against all evidence. Really, Peter offered her nothing beyond a friendly smile and a casual desire which was gone like a puff of smoke. She had tried to make-believe he was something else, and that had brought her reams of grief.

Samantha squeezed her hand and smiled. She left without saying a word, but turned at the door and waved at Adriana over her shoulder, her face full of sympathy. But she stepped as lightly as a schoolgirl, and Adriana knew she was happy.

Adriana was wide awake but didn't want to leave the room. Marlene would be going to bed soon and Adriana wanted to sit with her thoughts for a moment before she appeared. She sat up and picked up the sweater that Samantha had left for her. Where to begin, when unravelling something that was made not to unravel? Adriana thought she would start somewhere at the bottom. She took a knitting needle and poked around at the hem of the sweater. She soon realized she'd need scissors, and she'd have to ask for them at the nurses' station. It could wait until tomorrow, until she had the will to present herself to the world again. She lay the sweater out on her bed, arms extended. It made her think of someone lost at sea, floating face down in the water, arms outspread.

CHAPTER 35

The next morning, Dr. Burke wanted to see Adriana right away. He smiled at her with all his teeth—she hadn't seen him do that before. "Adriana," he said, "You seem to be doing better." She thought about that. Did she feel better? She felt normal. That was better, she supposed. "You were able to visit your friend in the hospital and come back on time. And you are eating regular food again." The doctor was clearly pleased. "I'm making you a voluntary patient. We'd like to allow you a weekend pass to your father's house, to see how you do. Does that sound good? And if that goes well we'll start working on discharge." Adriana tingled around the edges. She was getting out—it was hard to believe.

She took a lot of things out of her locker and put them on her bed. She needed her knitting and a change of clothes. An origami crane fluttered to the ground. She picked it up and examined the crisp creases. Would Marlene like such a thing? Adriana placed it on Marlene's bedside table which was covered with Styrofoam cups and candy wrappers. The crane sat among the debris as though in a cozy nest.

Adriana stood in the hallway, trying to think what to do. Her meds for the weekend would take a while to come up from the dispensary. She had to call her father to come get her at lunch time. Beth was probably at school. At least, where else would a Grade 6 student be? Beth had started school just before the hurricane, her father had told her, almost as an afterthought during their last conversation. Adriana was glad for Beth, and she hoped she'd have the house to herself for the afternoon.

When Mr. Song answered the phone, breathlessly, Adriana wondered whether it was always like that for her father now. Was he always worrying he'd get a call that something had happened to her or to Beth?

"Hi, Dad," she said in the calmest and cheeriest voice she could muster. It took more energy than she had.

"Adriana! How are you?" he cried. Adriana kept her breath even and told him she had a weekend pass.

"Could you come to get me at lunch?" she asked. She heard her father hold his breath, shocked.

"Of course," he said, "of course."

Adriana wasn't sure she was ready to face her father's excessive emotionalism and Beth's gloom. But she knew she had to, in order to reclaim her life. She ate her breakfast slowly, taking a long time to peel the hardboiled egg. It wasn't that she didn't want to go home, to her father's home, she just wasn't sure what it meant. Would things go back to the way they were, and if they didn't, what would have changed?

Jeff came into the kitchen with Melvin stuck to his side like glue. What did they get from each other, Adriana wondered. They made themselves a couple of Styrofoam cups of instant decaf and sat at the table farthest from her, talking quietly to one another.

"I'm going on pass," Adriana blurted. They looked at her, as though they hadn't noticed her before.

Jeff nodded. "That's good," he said solemnly. Melvin's smile flashed across his face. Jeff looked down for a moment then said, "I'm sorry I thought you were a spy. I know you're just sick like me." He looked slightly let down.

Adriana stared. Was she really just like Jeff? It felt like someone had cuffed the back of her head.

Melvin rocked in his seat. Adriana wasn't sure if he was upset or feeling good. Jeff spoke to him quietly, and he calmed down. "Let's go for a walk," Jeff said, hooking his arm through Melvin's. They stood up together, making Adriana think of Siamese twins. They really did seem to have some kind of connection that went beyond friendship or even brotherhood. Despite their different skin colour, they could be one flesh.

Adriana sat with her coffee and watched the sun pour through the kitchen windows. It was October, and the sky was a soaring blue, the geranium's petals glowing red against it. Adriana looked out on the world and felt, for the first time in a long time, that she was a part of it, but that she was looking out at it from the container of herself, a living and breathing creature who could distinguish her mind from the world outside it.

Someone sat down at the end of the table. It was Bartholomew Banks. He looked more ordinary to Adriana today, his eyes no longer burning coals. Perhaps he was tired, or maybe the meds were knocking him out. He ran his hand through his hair, which needed a wash. He looked troubled.

"Your friend," he said. "Samantha? We had a bit of a fight today." He was clearly upset. "I think she might have got the wrong idea about me... my intentions," he said. Adriana felt the pain in Samantha's heart. "She seems to think of me as more than a friend," he said, shaking his head wearily. "She's a nice lady and all, but this is no place to start a romance," he said.

Adriana took a sip of coffee. Bartholomew Banks looked like a man defeated, and Adriana felt a little surge of sympathy and generosity toward him. She shook her head. "Samantha is prone to falling in love," she said, almost apologetically. "She really is fond of you. And she admires you."

With his elbow on the table, the spiritualist stroked his chin. Adriana, startled, realized that he reminded her of her father. "Can you... will you tell her..." Bartholomew gave up. "Well, I should tell her myself," he decided. Adriana could see he felt resigned to a terrible fate, and it was impossible to tell how it would all end.

Adriana tapped the table in front of her with her fingertips, as though she were asking for more tea at a Chinese restaurant, a soundless gesture of politeness. "If you write a note, I can give it to her," she said. Adriana felt surprised that she had said such a thing. Normally she hated being a go-between. In high school, Jazz used to ask her to ferry notes between herself and whatever boy occupied her thoughts, and Adriana felt awkward and miserable in this position. Jazz finally caught on, and her romances became a secret even from Adriana, who wished now that Jazz had told her about her secret boyfriend and the pregnancy. She felt cut out of an important part of Jazz's life.

Lunch came and went and although Adriana waited, Samantha did not appear. Mr. Song arrived, breathless and happy, to take Adriana home. She collected her clothes for the weekend, a brown paper bag with her meds for the next two days, and hoped to say goodbye to Marlene but she was fast asleep, the white hospital issue blanket covering her like a snow bank.

On the drive home, Adriana kept her eyes on the scenery while her father talked a stream of news about how Beth was doing well in school, how Madeleine's car had been crushed by a tree during the hurricane and how happy she was with her new vehicle, which had GPS. His voice was soft, almost melodious, and he kept glancing at Adriana for a response but she was quiet and seemingly mesmerized by the passing houses, telephone poles and sidewalks. Beneath the balloon of happiness that floated above him, Mr. Song felt a residual sadness, and wondered whether it was inside Adriana too.

The house looked the same to Adriana, an old bungalow painted a faded grey, with black shutters. It was unremarkable, except for the leaves and branches that still lay in the front yard since the hurricane. Adriana had expected to feel something when she saw it, but in fact, it was almost as if the month in the hospital had never happened. She felt like she was coming home after a morning class, except that there was something funereal about the place, and even her return could not change its air of mourning. It was almost like a smell, and Adriana wondered whether it had always been there, and she was noticing it for the first time.

Inside the house everything was as she remembered it, except for a few objects she could not place—a pink Barbie tent perched on the arm of the sofa, and Barbie sitting half naked in front of it with a fishing rod. Adriana hadn't even know there was such a thing as a Barbie tent.

Mr. Song closed his eyes and took a couple deep breaths. "Home," he said. Adriana nodded and made an effort to smile. Her father squeezed her shoulders. "Do you want tea?" he asked.

Adriana nodded. "I'll put my stuff in my room." Mr. Song froze. He had forgotten to tell her that Beth had been sleeping in her room. But Adriana was halfway down the hall. She passed the study with its desk full of folders and paper, which her father was trying to sort out before making it into a bedroom for Beth. When she opened the door to her own room, it dawned on Adriana that things were not as she'd left them. The bed had different sheets and was a rumpled mess, and the books on her desk were being used by a couple Barbie dolls as a lawn to sun bathe on—or were they supposed to be dead? Adriana noticed a cut-out paper tombstone with the letters *R.I.P.* propped up against the spine of a psychology text.

Adriana stood in the doorway, stunned. Behind her, Mr. Song said, "I'm sorry Adriana, but it's only for a little while." Adriana looked out the window over the desk. Even the view had changed. The dead maple had blown down in the hurricane and where it once stood, there was a mess of branches. Firewood, Adriana thought. A nice big pile of firewood, that a person could make a bonfire with.

Mr. Song went to the desk and fingered the green construction paper that had been placed over the thick textbooks. It was covered with lines by a green marker pen, indicating grass. He didn't seem to notice the tombstone, but smiled at the two Barbie dolls, one of which was wrapped up like a mummy in toilet paper. "She's still a little girl, Adriana, isn't she? Still playing with dolls."

Adriana didn't feel the need to respond. She stood in the doorway, making no move to enter. It was occupied territory now, this space which had once been as close to her as her own heart. She barely recognized it. But it was okay. She had a sick feeling but it was actually fine. With a small smile, she said "I'll sleep in the study"

The study was clearly a male's room. It was plain and painted white, except for the wooden baseboards and trim, and much lighter at this time of day than Adriana's bedroom on the east side of the house. The desk was piled high with folders and papers, and a single white cot, which reminded Adriana of something from the hospital, lay against the opposite wall. Adriana put her bags of stuff at the foot of the cot and sat down on the edge of it, looking around her. Just like the room at the hospital, there was nothing here that spoke to her of herself.

Mr. Song stood in the doorway. "I've been going through some papers," he said "and photos." He looked shy. "I wanted to put something together for you and Beth about your mother." Adriana looked up at him. There were no photos of her mother, she thought to herself. Her father pushed a box in her direction, and Adriana saw on the very top of the pile a yellowing snapshot of a young woman, holding a baby swaddled in white. Her mother looked young, almost as young as Adriana was herself. She squinted at the camera, unsmiling. Adriana wondered whether the baby was crying, whether her mother looked so grim because she hadn't slept the night before, and whether she could remember that feeling of being in her mother's arms. It seemed to Adriana that her body remembered something about this moment, although her mind was blank.

Mr. Song smiled sadly. "Your mother hated having her picture taken. She said the camera made her look like an old frump." Adriana thought about it for a moment. Her mother hadn't been far off the mark.

Mr. Song shuffled a few of the photos around till he

found what he was looking for. "This is from before I knew your mother," he said. There was a yellowed colour photo of a girl who reminded Adriana of Beth, except that she was coquettish in a way that Beth was not, and might never be. She was sitting on a beach towel, among the tanned arms and legs of other teenagers, her head tipped sideways, her long curls swinging forward. Adriana saw that there was no bitter twist to her mouth, no veiled anger in her eyes. This was a girl she'd never known.

She thought it was likely her dad could tell the difference, between this girl and the one he was married to. Did it hurt him, she wondered? She looked up at him, his gaze shining. She knew her father's eyes were coloured by love, and he could only see what his heart, blind as a newborn kitten, could see.

"I'll make tea," Mr. Song said, and wiped the hair from Adriana's eyes. She blinked. Her father had always been mystified by her haircuts. Who wanted crooked bangs, he asked, shaking his head. What purpose did they serve? But today he simply smiled and said, "I'm glad you're home."

Adriana looked around. This room was not home to her. But she nodded and bounced a little on the cot to indicate her enthusiasm.

CHAPTER 36

Adriana slumped forward. This was not what she'd expected it would be like coming home. Everything felt unsettled, as though the hurricane had struck not only outside, but at the heart of her family. Adriana felt she had no control over anything, including her own life. She reached for her knitting needles, yarn and Samantha's sweater from the bag she'd brought from the hospital. At least there was knitting.

There was a sizzle of the frying pan in the kitchen. Her father had said he was making tea, but it sounded like he was getting ready to fry something. Adriana got up off the cot and avoided looking into her old bedroom door, taking her knitting with her as she made her way to the kitchen.

Mr. Song was frying dumplings and Adriana's stomach rumbled at the sound and smell. It felt like a long time since she'd eaten anything. Her father was wearing the same old apron. Didn't he have to get back to work?

"I took the afternoon off," he said, without turning around. "I thought I deserved it," he said, smiling over his shoulder. Adriana sat at the kitchen table. She hadn't had dumplings in years.

"Do you want to go for a drive when Beth gets home? To

see what the hurricane did?" Mr. Song asked eagerly. Adriana wasn't sure how to tell him, but she'd seen more of the hurricane than she cared to remember. Her father peered at her, disappointed that he wasn't able to interest her in something. 'No thanks dad," she said, to make up for it. "I'd rather stay home."

Her father put a plate of dumplings in front of her. "Chinese hotdogs," they used to call them. "You look hungry," he said. She knew he meant she'd lost too much weight, that he was worried.

She smiled and shrugged, while spearing a dumpling with her fork. "Hospital food. Leaves something to be desired," she said, with her mouth full. She was surprised at how good it tasted, how very early memories of her tiny grandmother, fingers dusty with rice flour in a dark Toronto kitchen, came coursing into her mind as though her sinus passages had just been cleared by wasabi.

Mr. Song watched happily. "Beth and I made them," he said. Adriana looked up. Her father hadn't made dumplings with her since her grandmother died. "She wanted to make something special for you to come home to," he said. His eyes were half sad. "We froze them... a bit of an experiment." Adriana imagined him chopping the pork, water chestnuts, green onion, ginger and garlic with his cleaver while Beth, eyes wide as if spellbound, shaped the little rounds of rice flour dough as efficiently and mindlessly as a machine. She'd probably been doing it since she was a preschooler at Aunt Penny's elbow.

"Beth likes to cook," Mr. Song said, almost to himself. "She'd like to be a chef when she grows up." He shook his head. "I never expected. I always thought she'd be more like your mother than me." Adriana felt her cheeks flush. It was *she* who was more like her mother, Adriana realized. She didn't cook, had no interest, and she could read for hours in bed, like her mother had, mooning and melancholic. It was easy for her to wander around the house in a dressing gown, without noticing the passage of time or accomplishing anything in particular, just as her mother, with a cigarette between her fingers, had done. Adriana was grateful she didn't have her mother's wicked temper, but maybe it was buried in there somewhere, trying to gnaw its way out.

Adriana was eating the final dumpling, already filled with regret for the meal's end, when the screen door slammed and she looked up, startled. Beth stood motionless, staring at her. She looked healthy Adriana thought, with rosy spots on her cheeks. "Hey Beth," Adriana said, raising her hand weakly in greeting. She felt wobbly, as though she were a newborn colt. "Thanks for the dumplings. They were delicious."

Mr. Song gave Beth a hug. "Adriana's home for the weekend," he said. "Isn't that..." he squeezed Beth's shoulders. "I'm just so happy!"

Beth said nothing but sat down at the table, on the other end of the seat to Adriana. She took her homework out and bent her head over it, pressing hard with the pencil as though she were trying to carve with it. Every so often she'd glance up as though to see if Adriana was still there.

Adriana wasn't sure but she thought Beth might want to be alone. "I'm going out into the yard," she said. As an afterthought she said, "I'm going to take some knitting." Mr. Song squinted at her, surprised. Adriana "I want to take a look at the dead tree," she said by way of explanation. He nodded eagerly. "The hurricane took it down for me," he said, beaming at both of them. "Good old *Juan*."

Adriana let the screen door bang shut behind her, and felt

her father's eyes follow her across the yard from the kitchen window. The air was still the endless gold of the September just past, but the shadows were a deepening blue in the late afternoon. Adriana rounded the pile of wood that came from the old maple tree and sat on a stump, out of sight of her father. She missed the smell of the fires her parents used to make to burn piles of leaves and weeds, and the potatoes they buried in the ashes to bake, that came out charred or glowing like coals.

Adriana took out Samantha's sweater. She was surprised how quickly and easily it came apart in her hands, the blonde wool full of kinks and curls, like her mother's hair. She cast some stitches on to her needle and knit, her mind wandering like wood smoke, her hands working as though under a spell.

Darkness was pushing into the sky when Adriana finished the scarf. She wrapped it around her own neck and made her way toward the light from the kitchen window. She could see her father moving back and forth from the stove to the counter and table, as he cooked. When she opened the screen door she saw Beth sitting at the kitchen table, head bent over a drawing she was making, her ringlets gently swaying above the table. She didn't look up when Adriana sat beside her, but her eyes shifted to a spot beyond the paper, in front of her. Adriana glanced down at the drawing. It was a picture that seemed to have been drawn by a much younger child, of herself and Beth and their father. Mr. Song stood with long arms outspread over both of them, like a scarecrow, with a shock of black hair. Adriana had a slim but curvy figure in a brown dress with pearls (it must have been something Aunt Penny wore at some point, Adriana thought, but she recognized herself because of the lopsided haircut). Beth had drawn herself squatting and hunched over something—a doll? An animal? It was hard to say because it was covered in a nest of scribbles.

She put an arm around Beth's shoulders. Beth stopped drawing but didn't look up. Adriana thought she felt a jolt, like metal in the sudden presence of a magnet—as though Beth were clinging to her, even though her arms remained by her sides.

Mr. Song dished up some rice and beef stir fry and set a plate in front of each of them. He was beaming, tenderly, Adriana thought. Both his girls sitting together at the table, his family together at last. Adriana half-smiled at him but she was concerned about Beth, who seemed exhausted. Defeated.

Even though she was half full of dumplings, Adriana picked up a fork and ate. She was tempted to feed Beth, pushing a fork into her mouth but thought better of it. She squeezed Beth's shoulders and smiled, squinting at father, who chewed happily, his eyes shifting back and forth between them.

"I got word today that I can retire, next month," he said, cheerfully. Adriana stared at him. Beth looked up, blearily. "Early retirement," he said. "They're downsizing and offered me a package." It was hard to believe he was so cheerful. Adriana knew her father loved his job. "I'll be able to spend more time with you guys. Travelling and such." He said.

Mr. Song talked about the way it had happened. He had been sitting in his office, working on a problem and had to go to the bathroom. As he stood at the urinal, his boss casually parked himself two urinals over. Mr. Song was nervous because usually he didn't cross paths with anyone in the bathroom, particularly his boss, who maintained a deliberate, almost exaggerated, friendly but formal distance from his employees.

"You know, David," Mr. Bridges, said, as if confiding a secret. Mr. Song stiffened. His boss cleared his throat. "Our company has been going through some changes, as you know. We're restructuring. And rethinking our priorities. And your life has changed too...it would seem you might like to spend more time at home." Adriana could see Mr. Bridge's face. Smarmy, tender-eyed. Hard as iron.

Mr. Song felt shocked. He stood at the washroom mirror after his boss had left. It dawned on him that what Bridges had said was true. He did need to spend some time with Beth and Adriana. That's what was missing, what they were all missing.

"And so I decided to come home," he said to Beth, who stared at the table and Adriana whose eyes darted around, avoiding his.

Adriana knew then that she would call Jazz that very night, and that with or without Jazz, she'd move out, the same week if she could. Before her father's change of life, and before she was sealed in the tomb of her childhood once and for all. It was different for Beth. She still needed to be a kid, but Adriana's problem had always been that she needed to grow up. After supper, Beth went to bed in Adriana's room, without brushing her teeth or washing her face. Maybe Adriana's sudden homecoming, along with their father's big news, was too much for Beth to absorb—but she knew her sister was making an effort because Beth had thrust the picture she'd drawn across the supper table to her. Adriana smiled and waved her goodnight as though she might never see her again.

Adriana sat at the kitchen table, only half listening to her father's cheerful chatter, and knit a second scarf, this time for Jeff. Around 9 p.m., she called Jazz at home from the spare room. "Hello?" came a sleepy voice on the other end of the line. There was something fatalistic sounding about it.

Adriana rubbed her cheek. "Hi Jazz," she said, sounding as upbeat as possible. Jazz perked up.

"Where are you calling from?"

"My dad's," Adriana said. "I'm on a pass."

Jazz was silent. Adriana hurried on. "Jazz, I had an idea. What if we got an apartment together, you and me?" She had to get it out of her mouth, to make it real. "I could get a job, and you could get a student loan, and we'd be roommates." They'd rent a modest place, in a shabby old house somewhere in the north end of Halifax. They'd shop for some second hand furniture, eat like students, and start to make a grown up life for themselves.

Jazz still said nothing. "Jazz, are you there?" Adriana asked, anxiously.

After a pause, during which Adriana's heart tumbled into her stomach, Jazz said, in a hopeless monotone, "Okay."

It was Adriana's turn to go silent. She had hoped Jazz would be enthusiastic. "Well," she said finally, "Do you want to... wait until you're feeling better to decide?" She could hear Jazz shrug, hugging her elbows with the phone tucked under her chin.

"No," said Jazz, "It doesn't matter. Let's do it." Adriana didn't know how to respond. "Okay," she said. Jazz put the receiver down without saying goodbye.

Adriana stood there for a few seconds, with the phone in her hand. This was Jazz, who taught her to blow smoke into a bottle of beer and drink it; Adriana's comfort and protection in high school when her friends froze her out. Jazz, who volunteered to babysit for a girl who'd got pregnant in Grade 10 and dropped out, and who wheeled the baby in the stroller to school and up and down the halls, smiling and waving like the Queen. Jazz, who after talking to the school psychologist over several months about her father's death, decided to become a bereavement counsellor, if she could dress up like Pippi Longstocking and make balloon animals for the kids. She was told that perhaps she could not, so Jazz decided she'd be a doctor instead.

Adriana realized that, weak and fragile as she felt, it was her turn to be the strong one, the cheerleader and coach, the surrogate parent. It would be Adriana getting Jazz out of bed in the morning, making sure she got out the door to class, cooking their supper when Jazz came home. Adriana knew it and she was willing. Her father would be fine, and her sister, well, Beth could come over on the weekend, and Adriana would talk to her about Viera. She would tell Beth a different story about their mother than the one she had told to herself. The Viera she shared with Beth would be gentler—less hurricane, more wounded—a woman far from her home, whose eyes crinkled with tenderness over the swirl of her child's hair. That was how Beth would come to know her.

CHAPTER 37

Adriana returned to the hospital on Sunday evening, just before 9 p.m. with the scarves she'd knit for Samantha and Jeff in her backpack. She looked in the kitchen and common room for Samantha, but she wasn't there. Elspeth greeted Adriana at the nursing station with a smile. "You're back!" she said. "Right on time."

"I'm not staying, Elspeth," Adriana said. "I just came to say goodbye to you and Samantha." Elspeth's forehead wrinkled. "I can't blame you for wanting to leave," she said quietly. "But would you consider waiting till the morning for discharge? To see the doctor one last time and get your meds and prescriptions?" Adriana shook her head firmly. "Dr. Burke can let my GP know what to prescribe me," she said. Elspeth's face relaxed. "Well you know what you want. I knew you had that in you."

Adriana felt shy suddenly. Elspeth had paid her a compliment that was worth receiving. "Is Samantha here?" she asked, glancing up the hallway. Elspeth's mouth was firm. "She's been discharged Adriana. That's about all I can tell you." Adriana felt stunned. "But where did she go?" Adriana asked, in a small voice.

Elspeth didn't answer, but her eyes shifted to someone coming down the hall behind Adriana. It was Marlene, in her red parka and fur hat, humming "We Shall Overcome" in a tremulous falsetto. She wore sunglasses, But Adriana could see a blue and brown bruise the size of an orange around her left eye, and a cut to the right corner of her mouth, which dragged it down in a lopsided frown.

Adriana stared in horror, as Marlene ambled up to her. "Marlene, what happened?" she asked. Marlene came too close to her and poked her in the breastbone. "Your friend," she said ominously. Adriana looked confused and took a step back. "Your friend, that overgrown cow," Marlene continued, her voice rising. Elspeth, her back to a post, arms crossed, simply said, "Marlene," and Marlene whirled around and screeched, waving her arms in the air. "I don't want her near me," she yelled. 'Don't come near me!" Her angry sobs echoed down the hall till she slammed the door to her bedroom behind her.

Adriana's stomach ached "Samantha didn't..." she began, but the look on Elspeth's face stopped her. "You know I can't tell you anything, Adriana," she said regretfully. Adriana knew. She held out her hand to Elspeth. "Good bye," Adriana said, squeezing Elsepth's fingers. "And thank you." Elspeth nodded. "You'll do just fine," she said quietly, and disappeared into the office.

Adriana, went out to wait at the bus stop. Jeff and Melvin were standing at the gates with a few other patients, who were having their final smoke of the evening last. It was dark but Adriana could see they were sharing a cigar between them, the glowing end leaving a trail like a fire fly behind it as Jeff waved it in the air. "And when Bartholomew told her he had no love to give her, she lost it. She turned over a table like this,"and he swept his arms forward as though shooing away an animal. "And then Marlene started ranting, and Samantha lost it again, and then they got into it." Jeff tipped back his head as though contemplating the stars, and blew a column of smoke above his head. "They both gave each other shiners. I don't know who got the worst of it. Samantha was stronger, but after the first punch she just let Marlene beat her like an egg."

Adriana stood beside them, not knowing what to say. She took the scarf she'd made for Jeff from her backpack and handed it to him silently. "Adriana!" he said, " Wow isn't that perfect!" He seemed overcome, and unsure of what to do. "Thank you," he said humbly, fingering the olive-coloured wool, fringed in blue and rust and lavender.

Adriana crossed the street to the bus stop. From there she could see Jeff drape one end of the scarf around his bandaged neck, passing the other end to Melvin, who wrapped in over his own shoulder. The two of them swayed like drunken men and pretended to dance the cancan, while Jeff held the cigar high in his right hand. Melvin's laughter, clear and bright, pealed into the night sky like a trumpet.

EPILOGUE

One Sunday morning, a couple weeks after Adriana and Jazz moved out to a basement apartment in the north end, Mr. Song called to invite them both to dim sum, to celebrate Adriana landing a job as a cashier, and his own retirement. When he and Beth drove in the laneway to pick them up the car made a noise like a passenger plane. The muffler had fallen off, but her father insisted they go to the restaurant all the way downtown anyway. When they pulled up in front of it, the three girls had their hands over their ears, Adriana bundling the ends of Samantha's scarf into ear muffs. She wore it every day in memory of her friend, hoping against hope that she wouldn't find an obit in the Herald or a news story about a murdered transgendered hitchhiker. Samantha had simply disappeared.

Adriana followed her father into the restaurant. Jazz and Beth brought up the rear, looking pale and gaunt, Beth with a runny nose from a cold she'd contracted at school. She was doing very well in her class, better than Mr. Song had hoped, even, but she seemed as prone to infection as a preschooler. Adriana worried that it was due to post traumatic stress's effect on the immune system. She'd told her father this and he'd mentioned her concern to his GP, who rolled his eyes and said Adriana better go to medical school before making diagnoses like that.

Adriana thought seriously about that. She wondered what her chances would be like of getting into med school, and figured if they knew about her mental illness, they'd be slim to none. Doctors were the very last people to admit to having a psychiatric illness, Jazz had told her. Apparently it was okay to be a crazy person working as a drug store cashier or on social assistance, but not a doctor or a nurse. She figured the only place her experience in the mental hospital would be seen as an asset and not a liability might be if she became a peer support worker, or maybe a writer.

Mr. Song was chattering away in Chinese to the waitress, a petite, middle-aged Asian woman with a pony tail, whose smile brought out the lines around her mouth and eyes. When she walked away with his order, his eyes followed the slapping of her sandals against her heels.

Beth and Jazz were playing "Rock paper scissors" below the table top. Beth giggled in a slightly off-kilter fashion, her eyes wide in her long face. Adriana gazed at the walls, with their giant paper fan decorations against a velvety dark pink wallpaper. The local CBC station was playing on the radio, and as the noon gun on Citadel Hill sounded, the hourly news came on. Out of a habitual obedience, she listened, catching the newsman's tone lighten as he announced, "Transgendered woman Samantha Johns placed third in the over sixty women's speed walking competition in Victoria, British Columbia." He went on to say that she had been a speed walking champion earlier in her life as a man, and that her participation in the recent competition had been marked with controversy. Then a sound bite from

Samantha herself, in her cheery, Julia Childs voice: "Oh I have been through many worse storms than this. Love and hurricanes and all that, you know? After many years I'm taking up walking again and I adore it." Then with a characteristic Samantha dramatic flourish: "No one can stop me. They don't have to give me any prizes, but I will walk until the day I die."

Adriana felt the corners of her mouth rise and lift, and her face begin to glow, from a warmth that came from deep in her stomach. She laughed out loud and clapped her hand over her mouth when the Chinese family the next table over turned and peered curiously at her. Jazz raised her eyebrows and Beth gazed at Adriana as though at some mysterious mountain peak, and Mr. Song, sitting back in his chair, beamed at them all. "Dim sum is a Cantonese tradition. From my part of China," he said proudly, tapping at his chest. "And Chinese food," he said to no one, and to everyone, "is the best in the world."

ACKNOWLEDGMENTS

I would like to thank the Canada Council for the Arts for the travel grant that got me to the Czech Republic for a one month residency at Milkwood International in 2011, where I worked on the first draft of this novel; the Mental Health Foundation of Nova Scotia, which gave me a grant to cover the cost of the residency; Arts Nova Scotia, for a Creation grant in 2013 that funded me to finish *Low* in my new home of Antigonish; and the Writer's Federation of Nova Scotia, for reviewing my contract with Invisible Publishing.

Speaking of Invisible, I cannot thank them enough for agreeing to publish my second novel. To all the folks there, especially Robbie MacGregor, I say a thousand thank yous for all your hard work and support. And to my editor Michelle MacAleese, a special thanks for your pruning and shaping of my manuscript and many suggestions that have undeniably improved it.

I owe many thanks to a number of mental health organizations that have supported me and my work over the years. They include the Canadian Mental Health

Association Halifax-Dartmouth Branch, the Empowerment Connection, and the Healthy Minds Cooperative. They are good folk and dear friends at all of those places, and I hope they will like this book.

A special thanks to Dr. Nancy Robertson at the Nova Scotia Early Psychosis Program, who, for a good chunk of my recent past, was my encourager in health, writing and life.

And to all my friends and family, who have shown me love and support throughout my life, in sickness and in health, I especially thank you. If not for you, I wouldn't be here. I wouldn't have a reason to.

INVISIBLE PUBLISHING is a not-for-profit publishing company that produces contemporary works of fiction, creative non-fiction, and poetry. We publish material that's engaging, literary, current, and uniquely Canadian. We're small in scale, but we take our work, and our mission, seriously. We produce culturally relevant titles that are well written, beautifully designed, and affordable.

Invisible Publishing has been in operation for just over half a decade. Since releasing our first fiction titles in the spring of 2007, our catalogue has come to include works of graphic fiction and non-fiction, pop culture biographies, experimental poetry and prose.

Invisible Publishing continues to produce high quality literary works, we're also home to the Bibliophonic series and the Snare imprint.

If you'd like to know more please get in touch.
info@invisiblepublishing.com

Invisible Publishing
Halifax & Toronto